ALSO BY ERIKA J. KENDRICK

Confessions of a Rookie Cheerleader

Appetite

One World   Ballantine Books   New York

Erika J. Kendrick

Appetite

A NOVEL

A One World Books Trade
Paperback Original

Copyright © 2009 by Erika Kendrick

Published in the United States by One World Books,
an imprint of The Random House Publishing Group, a division
of Random House, Inc., New York.

ONE WORLD is a registered trademark and the One World colophon
is a trademark of Random House, Inc.

ISBN 978-0-345-49498-6

Printed in the United States of America

www.oneworldbooks.net

2 4 6 8 9 7 5 3 1

Book design by Laurie Jewell

*To the closet superstar in each
of us with the guts to polish her shine;
pull up a chair and get to know her . . .
maybe dinner or drinks, or just
a quiet lunch sometime.*

Appetite

Chapter 1

My right nipple stands at attention. In my stupor I feel myself trace my fingers over my barely-there breast, stopping just shy of my left nipple, now erect and saluting me. I hack through cobwebbed lungs. Cotton mouth. *Damn Capri ciggies.* I force my eyelids open; a thunderous Biz Markie bass line pounding between my ears had been holding my thoughts captive. I squint through the blurs in the distance. Dangling from the edge of the leather lounger across the room, the middle hook on a lace bra catches a ray from the sunlight pouring through, drowning out the bay window. It flickers. Slowly I reach beneath the damp sheet and touch my bare breast again, confirming that it is, indeed, *my* bra. Shit!

Realizing that the jigsaw puzzle that is last night is missing a few key pieces, I whip my achy nakedness around to the crescendo of a bellowing snore. Yikes! A strange man is stretched out on the floor beside me entwined in half my sheet—clearly one of the puzzle pieces misplaced somewhere between the first Bacardi Mojito and last call's obligatory double shot of Patrón. Triple shit!

Immediately, I snatch the other half of the sheet away from him to shield myself (from what, exactly, I dunno). I am totally stuck as I watch him roll a tumble and a half toward me—naked and tanned—very *nicely* tanned! He slowly shifts his body, his muscles flex, and I feel my mouth drop as he adjusts himself. It is beyond evident that at least one part of his randy body is already wide awake. *Wow.* I sigh.

My thoughts begin to race. I try to rewind my mind while blinking away the foggy film on my contacts. With each clarifying blink, Stranger clears into focus and before I can catch myself I reach toward his thick blond hair and nudge it away from his temples. He stops in mid-snore. I'm staring under his arched man-brows, willing his eyes to stay shut, when I sneak a peek at his round ass and strong long defined legs. Six foot three, I guesstimate, and I finally remember to breathe.

The last thing I can recall is toasting with my girls at Marquee and my BFF Hannah ordering me to "throw it back," and right along with my head went the evil that was my fourth Patrón shot. Now I'm in hangover hell without the slightest idea of who this wildly arousing hottie is stretched out on my parquet floor. I can't seem to help myself so, while clutching the sheet to my neck as if it were Grandma's heirloom pearls, I lightly touch his shoulder and decide that he is, in fact, real. I touch him again and images flicker before me and I'm breathlessly, carelessly being carried to my couch between sloppy, deeply sensual, kisses. I blink hard. A moan slips from between my lips and the back of my neck stings from a power surge of sexy.

"Hey there," Stranger mumbles raspily through a sly smile. He reaches out to comfortably settle his hand on my inner thigh and squeeze softly. "Coffee?" he casually inquires as he blinks his way into morning.

Dumbfounded, I scoot away, sliding on the floor and riding the sheet, continuing to shake my head in disbelief. *Who are you? How did you get here?* I practice asking, still unable to spit the questions out. Another image flickers before me: *my legs stretched over his shoulders . . . deep penetration . . . moments of ecstasy accentuated by heavy breathing and textured moans.* This time the power surge extends up my neck and straight down to my uterus. I shake it off just as Stranger is beginning a far too indulgent stretch. Immediately, I toss the sheet at him. It flies from my body onto his. With the realization that I'm now the one on the floor vulnerable and exposed, I jump up and run to my room to grab something— ANYTHING!

"I'm sorry, I—I didn't get your name," I hear myself uncomfortably scream from my bedroom as I get granny-pantied and double-knot my robe.

"No need to yell; it's far too early for that," Stranger's scratchy morning voice offers in close proximity.

I'm rubber-banding my long bushy hair when I look up to see him moving toward me in the bedroom, apparently unaware that he's been abandoned by the sheet somewhere between right here and OVER THERE!

"Uh, the sheet. What happened to the sheet?" I anxiously inquire, looking over him and next to him—anything but *at* him.

"Want me to make the joe?" he smoothly continues, as he looks down at his bare body with a shrug, completely indifferent that the sheet has, indeed, moved on without him. I freeze as I watch him wet his lips and take hold of my shoulders. He inches toward me and, in one swift beat, Stranger is gently kissing my neck and cheek. I shake in anticipation as he begins to caress my earlobe with his tongue. I desperately try to keep the secret that I am now wickedly weak.

"Morning, Kennedy. I hope you enjoyed your private birthday party last night," he whispers seductively into my ear. "I know I did." Pulling me firmly into his morning wood he continues, "You know the celebration doesn't have to end yet. Today is your official birthday and since you're already in your birthday suit, how about I take you for a swim?" Stranger suggests, as his tongue greets my inner ear. *Helll-lllo!* My legs go limp. He takes my arm with his left hand and wraps it around his waist. I am under his spell. With his other hand he frees me from my robe and any and all resistance, and within seconds we are on my bed misusing the satin and abusing the silk, satisfying leftover PM cravings and indulging ripe AM appetites.

Chapter 2

"No, Bug, I can't find it," I whisper frantically into the telly to Hannah Marie Love, my absolute bestie since somewhere around age ten. Now a cutthroat music exec, she was sitting soo-per pretty as third in command at Tru Records, the hippest urban-chic label on the landscape. And it was no secret in elite hip-hop circles that she was being groomed to take over.

"What do you mean you can't find it?! Every man carries his wallet in his pocket," she said reassuringly, as I fumble through Stranger's denim, searching relentlessly for any piece of identification—an electric bill, voter registration, library card—while his shower sounds off on full blast. "Keep looking; maybe he tossed it into his shoes, or maybe it's in one of his socks," she suggests.

"I hate that I can't remember," I admit. "I feel so vulnerable and embarrassed."

"Nothing to be embarrassed about, seeing that you two just went at it again for forty-five minutes," she corrects, musing mischievously.

I plop down on the damp sheets. "It's like I was in a trance, a total sex trance," I mumble, staring at the floor, shaking my heavy head. "I can't believe I've been celibate for almost five years and just like that, in a night of drunken birthday debauchery, I extinguished my burning flame of discipline."

"Seriously?! You really don't remember gyrating on the bar in your lace bra to J.T.'s 'SexyBack'?" Hannah's giggle has now escalated to serious LOLs. "You were down to your thong by the end of Vanity's 'Nasty Girl.' " She can barely catch her breath now. "Max had to sling you over his shoulder and fight you off the bar when Marvin Gaye's 'Sexual Healing' hit liftoff," she spouts between snorts. "You were feelin' no pain by the end of the night and after drowning your face in that final swig of amnesia-in-a-shotglass, the Brats took charge of getting your overly stimulated vulva home safely," Hannah informs between bellows. "But I honestly have NO idea who he or how he—"

"Shhh, I don't hear the shower anymore." I look over my shoulder. "And I still don't know who the hell he is!"

"So what! It's called a one-night stand—and you were long overdue. Just think of it as a birthday present sent to you from *The Vagina Monologues* with a greeting card that reads: Welcome to the world of the grown and fucking."

I run my fingers through my damp, mussed hair that reeks of anonymous sex. "I feel so dirty."

"Ahhh, good times!" Hannah chimes. "I remember the first time Max tossed me into the air—and not for a stunt jump, just to be clear."

Usually I go gaga whenever my BFF talks of her moonlighting days as a professional cheerleader for the Chicago Diamonds when she high-kicked herself into love—and apparently acrobatic sex—with the star player and most eligible bachelor in the NBA, Max Knight. And yes, it was beyond brillz when he popped the Q on the JumboTron and in front of tens of thousands, but right now just isn't the time; I am dangerously hyperventilating over here.

"No! There was absolutely no stunt jumping last night—I don't *think*." I am sinking in amnesia. "But I'm definitely super sore."

"What do you mean you're sore?" she questions. "Ohhh, you're *sore*?"

"Muscles I didn't even know I had." I flinch in pain.

"You mean you didn't *remember* you had."

"No, I'm pretty sure most of these muscles have NEVER been used before." A snapshot of Stranger bending me into a sexual pretzel makes a mental cameo. "EVER!"

She laughs even harder. "Sounds like Blond Boy did his thing and officially turned you out! Let's just hope he's not a pro . . ." She pauses way too long for my taste. "But come to think of it—"

"A pro? You mean—" I gasp. "Like he's expecting some sort of, of—"

"Com-pen-sa-tion," she enunciates, for the sake of clarity.

The horror! My heart races as I open my junk drawer and rifle through the pencil case where I keep tip money for late-night deliveries. I glance at my haggard, albeit dewy, reflection in the mirror. *This would definitely qualify as a delivery.*

"And if he is a pro—"

"Gentleman of the night—"

"MAN-WHORE!"

Ew!

"It sounds like he was worth every penny. So, fuck it, two points for team Brad Pitt."

On second thought . . . I slam the drawer and go for my wallet instead, pulling out a crisp fifty.

"And Team David Beckham."

I grab another twenty.

"And Team Josh Duhamel!" Max yells into the phone when Hannah laughs so hard, she can no longer hold the telly.

"Stop it! This isn't funny!" I yell, then fade to a whisper, fetching another five, feeling my vaginal walls throbbing inside. "Is there a cream for this? Like a vaginal Ben-Gay?"

"No, Sweets," she rejoins the line, "you're on your own with this one; Summer's Eve can't help you now. It's called getting off the wagon, taking off the training wheels, riding with no hands, and—"

"But I can barely walk." I massage my inner thighs.

"That's cuz you been poppin' wheelies for the past twelve hours." She breaks into a roar. "I gotta go ring Britt and—"

"Uh-huh, laugh all you want but I gotta get him outta here; I can't be late for my first day on set and—"

"His job is done. Just pay him and tell him to leave. Or get out. Or kick rocks. Or—"

"But, Bug, it was really good, tantric even."

"We've been telling you that the ridiculous degree of celibacy you had going on was absolutely counterproductive to everything, and that, well, once you let the snake out of the bag—" she muses, hanging up the phone mid–punch line, raging at her dead joke.

I sigh as I *triple*-knot my robe this time, completely intoxicated by the impromptu encounter and honestly hungry for more.

Chapter 3

"You didn't want to join me in there?" Stranger asks, his ripped body emerging from the thick steam like a retro Fabio book cover. "I was hoping you would have stepped into heaven with me again."

The phone falls to the floor and I swallow hard, staring at the towel in his hand that could've just as easily been wrapped around his waist. Instead he rakes it across his golden blond stubble then through his wet hair.

"So, about that coffee?" he coolly asks, glancing at the wad of money I've since crumbled between my moist fingers. He throws a smooth smile over his shoulder as he brazenly walks toward my kitchen.

"Listen, uh, uhm . . . You. This is really kinda so far past embarrassing for me at this point—believe it or not." I look down at the floor and shake my head. Fidgeting with my fingers, I'm now delirious for a ciggie. "So before we settle up, uhm." I grip the bills tighter. "Would it be too much trouble for you to tell me your name? I mean, really, you clearly have all the balls here and far more info than I have about, well, everything." I pause, feigning diplomacy. "And it appears to me that you are well aware of this little discrepancy." I follow him into the kitchen. "Truth: I have no idea who you are or how you got here. I was twisted last night. Twisssted!" I stare at the floor. "I mean I was really gettin' it in." I shake my head again at this revelation before finally peeking up at Stranger and inhaling the thick misty air that seems to be following him. I struggle to find my lost focus. "But I digress. Yesterday was a big day for me with celebrations all around, and well, I hit my wall at some point and woke up to you and—"

"Great sex!" he finishes, still smiling as he rummages through the cupboards searching for filters.

Assisting him in his search, I hand over the box from behind the coffee grinder and set the bag of Turkish coffee on the granite countertop. "I'm quite serious here."

"So am I." He smirks, eyeing the triple knot around my waist. "When was the last time you had great sex?" Casually, Stranger moistens his lips and preps the coffee to brew. "Or better yet, when was the last time you had sex—any kind of sex: good sex, average sex, bad sex?"

I swallow hard. My eyes avert to the floor, darting past his nakedness. "Would you care for another towel or your boxers or maybe your jeans—or *anything*?!"

"No, I'm good," he says, leaning against the sink and crossing his arms over his hard chest. "What about disastrous sex?"

Anxiously, I fiddle with the lonely ciggie in my robe pocket, my eyes averting his man-scaped dick. "So I take it you're not dropping any hints about last night's forgotten sequence of events, are you?" I press, ignoring his series of frank and incredibly intimidating questions. Frustrated beyond belief, I slap the money down on the countertop and push it toward him. "Here."

He eyes me closely before pouring his coffee into my Berkeley Alumni mug. He holds it up for inspection. "You?" he asks, nodding at the cup.

"Uh-huh." I close my eyes and rub my brows.

"Humph." And without a word he takes the crumbled money and gulps down three piping hot swigs of joe. "Ahhh, now that's good coffee." He steps into my personal space a few inches from my lips and eyes me intently. The corners of his model mouth turn up into an easy grin. "It's getting late; gotta run," he says abruptly, heading for his denim and his pristine suede purple-on-purple Pumas next to my couch. "You should let go a little more often. You've got real potential—and potential is very sexy."

My mouth drops and a gust of hot air escapes.

Stranger is dressed and at the front door faster than I can gather my thoughts about all that he's just implied. *Potential!*

"What do you mean, *potential*?" I challenge, tightening my robe until I can barely breathe.

"Happy Birthday, Sexy," he whispers into my ear for the second time this morning and that same set of chills revisits the race through my body. "I hope I was able to jump start your thirtieth year and set you down a more fulfilling path," he says, reaching for the front door. "You definitely deserve it." His azure blue eyes look straight through me. "And thanks again for the joe."

As Stranger bends down to kiss my forehead he changes direction and gently bites my earlobe just before turning to head out. "*Real* potential," he restates with emphasis, finding comfort in his subtle swagger down the hall.

"Uh, you, uh, you have a good day, too," I utter clumsily when I hear the doorknob across the hall rattle open. "Yep, we'll talk later," I improvise, bending down to pick up the *New York Post* and dodge my nosy neighbor.

"You little slut!" she hisses.

No such luck.

Chapter 4

"Cut the shit, Annie; I was scoping through the peephole," Brittany Alexis Lee, my fraternal twin sister and self-proclaimed independent whore, implores, as she swings open her apartment door. "Besides, Hannah called me twenty minutes ago to dish the detes," she admits, clutching her coffee thermos and the morning paper on her way out to work. "A Blond Boy, huh?" She pauses briefly, conjuring up memories. "Well, he's definitely a hot piece of cock," she admits, admiring Stranger as he saunters away. "How much did that set you back?" She laughs. "And was gratuity included?"

"Not today, Brittany! Please!" I beg, unsure if the selective amnesia and I are equipped to handle her early morning ridicule. She is the quintessential bitch. "Par for the course," she always said. "I'm an animal—a tycoon!" My sister, a cutthroat real estate mini-mogul, has her sights set on becoming the top bitch in the Northeast. "I've got Donald Trump on speed dial, Annie." And she did. Having already conquered Chicago and most of the Midwest, she'd moved to New York to put her Louboutins down, her fashionable footprint in the Hamptons' sand. My sister was direct, thorough, and ambitious—a bitch, by most men's standards. Vicious, lethal, and scary by mine.

"Don't be such a crybaby."

I lean against my apartment door and stare at the carpeted floor, fidgeting with my lonely cig. "I'm not going to hurt you—not today, not on our birthday."

My eyes pop open when I hear a smoldering accented voice emerge from behind my evil twin's head.

"Gracias, Mami," a Puerto Rican bombshell who resembles this year's international pageant winner slinks into Britt's personal space. She tosses her thick lustrous hair over her shoulder and tucks her silk blouse into her red pencil skirt. "Have a good birthday, Baby; I'll call you later," she oozes, seductively kissing Britt with her pouty lips, her tongue lingering there for a fiery bit.

"Don't make me wait too long, Jesabelle."

Too easy.

"You know how impatient I can get."

"No, Mami, never that, not on your birrrthday," Puerto Rican Pageant Queen purrs, as she slides her fingertips across Britt's tits. *"Buenos diás,"* she casually greets, when she finishes molesting my sister and glances at me.

"M-m-morning," I stammer, and nod my head instinctively, my lowered eyes darting down the hall, pretending not to see. I clear my throat while Britt taunts me with her beguiling smile.

"Now what was I saying?" Britt refocuses, wiping away leftover Latina lipstick stain.

"And who—what—who was—"

"I'm an equal opportunity provider," she explains. "It is what it is, Annie."

"Don't call me that!" I fluster. "I'm not anorexic!"

"Humph," she quips, eyeing her exotic conquest as she slithers down the hall. "It may be *our* birthday today, but that, well, that was my present to me." She was a predatory lover of everything rich: food, shoes, and decadent lovers! "And why not? She was *très* hot!" Britt runs her tongue across her teeth salaciously and looks down at her bodacious breasts. "And have you *seen* me?!"

I shudder. "Ugh!"

"Take notes, grasshopper." She shuts her door and double-checks the lock. "But from the looks of it someone's already been paying attention—and lucky you! Coochie cobwebs are never cute."

"UNBELIEVABLE!" I turn to walk back inside.

"Not so fast, Chickie." She clears her throat and switches toward me. I listen to her Spanx rustling against her size fourteen thighs and prep myself for her double dose of routinely mean sibling rivalry.

"A word: Is it true that you really have no idea how he ended up in your bed?" she rhetorically quizzes, placing her hand on her heavy hip as she shifts to shuffle the *Post* at me. "Well I hope the fuck-me-and-forget-me was worth it, neophyte, cuz amnesia and a yeast infection aren't the only problems you're waking up to this morning."

"Yeast infection?"

"Give it twelve hours," she advises. "Here." She shakes the newspaper at me. "Seems like you're going to make a name for yourself in this town, after all. Take my *Post;* it's already open to your debut exposé."

"My what?" I snatch the paper from her and read the minuscule font in the bottom right-hand corner of Page 6.

PAGE 6!!! I flip the page in search of page five and page seven. "Is this real? I made Page SIX?!"

"And look, there's a picture of our newly crowned resident whore." Britt points to the small shot of Max holding ME in his arms. This can't be good.

I read aloud.

SPOTTED: NBA megastar Max Knight escorting former model and New York's Newest "IT" Girl, Kennedy Lee, out of MAR-

QUEE late last night (and without his fiancée in tow) after
Lee's belligerent striptease on the bar of the exclusive night-
spot. Scoop: The exotic "actress" was recently dropped from *All
My Children* and is now set to star on the sizzling daytime soap,
America's Next Sweetheart.

"But that's *Max.* Hannah—Hannah was right behind us. Why
would they make it sound so creepy?"

"How would you know where she was; thought you didn't remember?"

"Well she was . . . wasn't she?"

"Keep reading, Annie. It gets greater later."

"Haters! Who wrote this?"

"Top secret CIA spies! Who the fuck do you think wrote it?"

But stumbling and half-naked with her designer shirt tousled
and unbuttoned, Lee looked more like America's Next Lush on
Max Knight's arm. Rehab anyone? Good luck with that beautiful disaster, ANS!

"OMG!"

"Well, I'm off." Britt smiles.

"Wait! Oh God, Britt, wh-wh-what am I going to do?" I survey
the striped hallway wallpaper for answers. "I have to go to work
today. It's my first day and like, all of America reads the *Post*!"

"Britain, too."

I look down at the picture of Max's arms wrapped around my
waist as he hopelessly tries to steady me out of the fancy
schmancy nightclub.

"Hot hair, though."

I slink against the wall. "Who am I?" Terrified and shaking in
my fuzzy bunny slippers I inspect my hands, awaiting an answer.

"Wait! I'm—I'm—YOU! I've fucking turned into you!" I wince at the promiscuous thought of it. "What'm I going to do?" I freak, massaging my temples, feeling a wave of heat beneath the Brinks Security System that is my robe.

"Ticktock, Sweets," Britt taunts, tapping her French mani over the glass of her diamond-studded timepiece. "Try getting your inebriated ass to work on time. And for God's sake, Annie—a dab of perfume! You stink!"

In the middle of her catwalk down the hall she double-backs and settles into a smile, "Oh yeah, and happy birthday, Baby Sis!"

Chapter 5

In a matter of milliseconds, I slam the door and press my entire body against it, desperately trying to steady my world. I grip the newspaper in my sticky palms. The words are on repeat in my mind: "stumbling and half-naked . . . America's Next Lush . . . beautiful disaster . . ." and the now-battered cig is perched firmly between my lips. Anxiety is erupting and with no time to scramble for matches, I spin down the foyer and around the corner to the stove. As the Capri catches the blue-tinged flames in midair, I drag sooo hard that the tobacco buzz snatches me up. My brain scrambles as I . . . sway. *Shit! I'm still drunk,* I think, when the room begins to spin and takes me away. How did this happen? I slide down the wall onto the floor and remember how everything was so simple six months ago when we all moved here, destined to follow "The Fabulous" (read: our careers and our men!). But unlike Hannah, who had a delicious fiancé, and Brittany, who entertained an assortment of mouth-watering boys and the occa-

sional irresistible girl, several years ago I'd started a monoga-
mous relationship with Vick, my vibrating dick. And I'd never
been one to cheat; it was against my True Religion.

I open my eyes to the time on the digital stovetop blinking in
my periphery. It snatches me out of my daze. I jump up and top off
Stranger's lukewarm coffee to the realization that I am, indeed,
late for my first day on set and I'm still unbelievably twisted! I
really didn't fancy getting canned from my gig before I was even
issued a building security badge.

I flick the lit ciggie into the stainless steel sink and struggle to
untie my robe, wrestling with each captain's knot and swallowing
the puke that is fighting its way up.

Halfway through the second knot and the third swallow, I make
a fast break for the loo to upchuck my lost last-night memories,
sure to bring me much ridicule. But I'm paralyzed by the scribble
atop the mirror penned in my recently purchased M.A.C. Russian
Red lipstick:

POTENTIAL CAN BE SEXY. SEE YOU AROUND, SEXY!

—J.J.

Chapter 6

"Look, lady, either get out or sit here, whatever you want, but I'm
not stopping my meter. YOU! PAY! EITHER! WAY!" the fidgety
Iranian cab driver insists as we sit at the intersection of 64th and
West End.

I glance up at the jumbo network letters bolted to the building
then at the meter again and then at my watch. *SERIOUSLY?!* I'm al-

ready twenty minutes late. I scratch at my throat and Cabbie snatches the money from my hands without proffering the three dollars in change owed me in return. *Asshole!*

This was my first big break. I'd never seen the show before, but after a very brief telephone conversation with the head writer I was expected to just jump right in with my bloodshot eyes, ruined reputation, and a fistful of cardinal sins! But then again, I think to myself, there was always the possibility that no one has seen the tiny font in the bottom right-hand corner of Page fucking 6-6-6. *Right?* I zip my studded motorcycle jacket, cross my fingers anyway, and yank at the studio doors.

"Uhm, hi, I'm Kennedy Lee," I say, shoving my aviator sunglasses into my hair, channeling the winner within. "It's my first day here and, well, I'm an actress on *America's Next Sweetheart* and . . ." I inform the security guard/doorman who looks like his name should be Bert.

"I'm Ernie," he says dryly, with a nod. "ID?"

Ernie glances at his clipboard hidden beneath a McDonald's breakfast sandwich wrapper. "We've been expecting you." Ernie points to his newspaper that's been strewn across his desk beneath a long row of monitors. "You!" he says sternly, pointing to my picture. He shakes his head in disapproval and hands me a security pass. "Go straight through those doors to your right, around the corner to your left . . ."

The Infamous Side-Eye.

". . . up the elevator to the second floor . . ."

And from the Security Guy!

". . . and Bert will take it from there," he directs.

The elevator doors close and God speaks to me. "Kennedy Lee, to hair and makeup! Kennedy Lee, to hair and makeup!"

Now, because I am the only one in the lift I don't bother to look around in search of God, but because He was speaking to me, I figured (given the sticky circumstances and all) I'd better speak back.

"Are you there, God? It's me, Kennedy."

No answer? I must be officially on timeout.

The bland industrial carpet and pasty yellow walls remind me of a county hospital in Anywhere, USA, until a glam-tastic, albeit anorexic, woman darts right past me with enormously big hair and even bigger cartoonish balloonish boobs. Choking a bronze statue of an oversized piece of soap in her hands, she's spewing venom, cursing everything in her path. As she revs right past me, I whip my neck around to eat her dust when a veiny brown hand yanks me into the third room on the left—just off the hall.

"Kennedy Lee?! In here!" The freakishly long fingers point toward a cushy salon chair. "Sit down, Newspaper Girl, and don't mind Bitch—I mean Bliss."

Newspaper Girl?

"Uh-huh, that's right," Freaky Fingers says, nodding at her *Post* sticking out from under her Chinatown faux Fendi special.

I sink into the chair.

"I'm Kennedy."

"You're *hungover,* Newspaper Girl."

I sink lower. "Uh—"

"Trinity."

Really?!

After an emphatic sigh, Trinity rolls her eyes around in her head and points to the door. "Now what you just witnessed out there was the routine wrath of Bliss. It's her character's name but good luck getting her to answer to anything other than Bliss, just Bliss; you know like Cher, just Cher. We've yet to uncover her 'government' but beware; the bony bitch is *always* around, needing something and wanting everything . . ."

She doesn't take a breath.

I take one for her.

Trinity is a pint-size woman, who looks to be no older than nineteen, who even with a short spiky maroon faux-hawk, and in her streetwalker-chic four-inch disco heels, stops just short of my modest chest. The bossy dynamo dons an industrial tool belt crammed with goo gobs of makeup.

"This sunken red puffiness on your pale skin underneath these Oriental eyes . . ."

"Korean."

"Isn't that what I said?! Eyes that hot need to be catered to, not abused. Here, hold your head back," the midget commands, as she grabs my neck and pours a bottle of Visine over my eyeballs. "That should get you through your first few scenes." She palms the back of my head and presses a rotation of brushes over my face with speedy precision and, by her watch, in exactly fourteen minutes and twenty-five seconds, my face is FEE-yarce—and award-winning daytime drama ready. "Now *that's* some sun-kissed skin with a hot honey glow. And not to blow my own horn, but TOOT TOOT, cuz you look better than you did on those reality shows *The Intern* and that other one, you know the one, uh, uh—"

"*The Second Assistant.*"

"That's what I said!" she snaps, as she assesses her work of genius in the mirror. "Bless you, Baby! Those cheekbones are fiyah and that luscious hair would turn Goldilocks into a hater." Trinity flips me out of her chair down the assembly line to "Hair" and straight into a diatribe about the CHI flatiron, the "hottest ceramic to ever hit a head!"

I'm mid-snooze when I feel Trinity poke me. "Wake up, Newspaper Girl; your layered curls are now official! Better hurry and see Marge so she can throw your tiny tail into *Sweetheart* garb. That rocker-chic vibe of yours needs a complete one-eighty."

"Marge?"

"Wardrobe stylist—best in the biz," Trinity says, already

power-powdering one of the extras for a street scene. She twirls her brush between her fingers and points to my face and hair. "FEE-yarce!"

"Kennedy Lee to Stage twenty-six. Kennedy Lee—Stage twenty-six."

Oh Lord, it was "God" calling and everybody in the manger knew I wasn't ready.

"Marge?" I panic, clutching my Michael Kors tote and script to my chest.

"Two doors down the hall to your left."

"Kennedy Lee—Stage twenty-six."

"To my left, right?"

"Right!"

I shoot a pleading look over my shoulder to Trinity and head two doors down the hall to my right. Light-headed, I fumble to open the jammed door, feeling my insides gargle my morning. In slow motion the door swings open as my stomach finally explodes—all over the back of a cream-colored cashmere blend shirt, onto both sides of a dark denim jacket, and all over pristine purple Pumas. I DIE when I look up to lock eyes with J.J., who is hemmed up against the wall with his face buried right between Bliss's big balloon tits!

Chapter 7

DING! Round 2.

I wipe away the slime from the side of my mouth, but playing nice is the last thing my stomach is intent on doing. J.J. and his plush purple Pumas rush past me, trying to dodge my last and final round of chunks flying through the air.

If this is how I'm going to die, at least I've discovered that I, too, am part of an elite sisterhood that is multiorgasmic, I think as I start to lose focus in a random bathroom stall. A faint smile embraces my lips. The room fades to black, and suddenly I'm on an acid trip standing on my middle-school tip toes outside my emaciated mother's bedroom door peeking through the tiny hole. I watch her eyes roll around in her head as she naughtily nods off into oblivion with her bottle of happy pills and Russian vodka by her side. I feel my father scoop me high into the air and carry me away in his arms for a routine distraction to McDonald's for steaming hot french fries, Burger King for char-grilled patties, and Wendy's for brain-freeze Frostys. My heart is skipping beats from the Cadillac's backseat as I watch Brittany curled up next to Papa, hoarding all the goodies on the way to the neighboring park. She stuffs the steaming fries five at a time into her chubby cheeks. I watch her and Papa enjoy the tempting treats, thinking that I am strong and she is weak. *I won't eat any and they can't make me. No one will ever make me weak! I am strong. I am STRONG. . . . I AM NOT MY MOTHER!*

"Are you all right, dear? Kennedy, dear, are you okay?"

"I'm okay, I'm okay," I finally hear myself say to a notably round woman who resembles Mrs. Claus. She bends over and her ravishing long locks look like special care was taken to spin each shiny white strand individually.

"Sit up slowly, dear. It looks like you've banged your head pretty hard here. Are you dizzy at all?"

"No," I lie, peering around the men's (I realize now) bathroom. I lift my head and unable to find equilibrium, quickly place it back down against the cold tile. *Très sexy!* I close my eyes, in total disbelief that this is my life on the first day of the biggest job I've ever booked. Silently I say a prayer that J.J. doesn't saunter in to pee and witness my grand display of unprofessionalism. *Amen.*

"I've been a very bad girl," I whisper to Mrs. Claus.

"We all have our days, dear."

"Danced naked on the bar."

"Shh, just rest for a while."

"Had strange sex with him."

"I see, dear."

"And the paper—Newspaper Girl . . . Lush Girl . . . all ME."

"Just relax. This should cool you down," Mrs. Claus says, gently dabbing my forehead and neck with cold compresses.

Feels. Good. Cool. Sleep. Now.

"No, no, dear." I feel a gentle shake and spy her tangerine-orange Crocs resting against me. "You mustn't fall asleep on the floor. I'll call someone."

"No!" I gasp, and jerk my head up, despite the dizzy. "Really, I'm okay," I lie, finally forcing myself to sit, then stand. I exit with a bundle of wet tissue pressed against my forehead, Trinity's record-breaking face-beatdown all but ruined. "I need a refresher," I mumble, glancing in the mirror at the clumpy, runny mascara that's boycotting soap star glamour. "And a shower."

"Right this way."

"But first . . . I'm supposed to be looking for Marge," I mutter to Mrs. Claus, who hasn't left my side.

"You're lookin' at her, dear."

After a quick wash-'n'-go, I emerge from the shower feeling somewhat refreshed. Marge is waiting patiently with a smile and a robe. "Hi, I'm Newspa—Kennedy," I say, officially, extending my hand. "And I'm totally embarrassed."

"No need." Marge grins as we move quickly to the wardrobe room. "I saw you really give it to Jesse James."

Jesse James? . . . J.J.!

She motions for me to disrobe. "He's our resident bad boy. Calvin Klein model. Fan favorite."

OUTLAW!

Marge purses her lips and takes my measurements. "You be careful with that one." I tense through her cautionary words, but feel myself begin to calm only after she hands me a romantic sundress with fantastic girly frills around the plunging neckline and soft ruffles swirling the hem. "Take these, too." She hands off a gorge pair of Dushi Trade silver-and-amethyst hoop earrings with cascading feathers. "Just try everything on for now and let's see how it all fits." I remove my smelly clothes. "I'll have more choices ready when you return from lunch for the afternoon shooting." She takes my leopard-print red-and-black skinny jeans and wifebeater from me. "I'll take these and have them cleaned. They'll be good as new when you're done today," she whispers before stepping back and admiring me in the dress. "Now, that's perfect. And the earrings are the perfect accent. You're tall and beautiful, just like they said you were. And your eyes are exquisite."

"Thanks, Marge," I say, and glance in the mirror at the wan girl. In my rearview, an erratic uptight boy with buzzed brownish hair and singed tips of overdone Honeywheat Blonde #139 bolts into the room. He's wearing a headset and tightly clenching a clipboard—*among other things.*

"Kennedy Lee, they're waiting for you! They've *been* waiting for you!" he snaps as he rolls his eyes at me, tapping his manicured nails on the clipboard. "Marge, why isn't she ready?! Don't you have today's call sheet?!" He slinks inches away from Marge's face. "AS IF!"

Frightened and shaky, I remove the couture dress and tie the robe around my still gurgling waist. Marge smiles disingenuously at Headset before ushering me out the door, but not before wrapping my hand around a stick of Doublemint, encouraging me with a wink.

"Seriously, Marge!" Headset yells one final time as he grabs my elbow and leads me down the stark hallway and through the thick steel doors marked STUDIO 26.

"Sorry about being late. It's totally my fault," I confess to Headset and pop the stick of gum into my mouth. "Marge really had nothing to do with it," I plead with him but he ignores me and panics into his mini-microphone, shaking his head as if he can't believe the switch-hitting world has just run out of Honeywheat Blonde #139.

"Listen, Girlie, I don't give two shits about you or your hangover-havin', passin'-out-in-the-boys'-room ass! Page Six or not, time is money, honey, and you're costing me. Now get your fat ass in there."

FAT?! I suck in my stomach until breathing is no longer on the menu. "*MOOOO!*" Skinny Cow taunts from inside my mind, urging me to the little girls' room this time.

"And in the event that you don't literally become America's Next Sweetheart I'll be beyond happy to kick your flabby ass out the front door and watch you crawl right back to wherever the hell it is you came from. You can hop your inner skankiness right back on top of last night's bar for all I care!" Headset pops his hip out and stares me down. "You weren't my first choice anyway."

I hear my voice quiver before I even speak. "I, uh, I don't know what to—"

"Say? Page Six said it all." He flips today's call sheet over on his clipboard and yanks the *Post* from underneath. "Let's see, 'shirt unbuttoned, America's Next Lush, REEE-HAB anyone?' . . ."

I stare at the seam that seems to be coming undone on my vintage cowgirl boots.

"Now that we're on the same page, Ms. America, let me be absolutely clear: *Your* job is to look hot and make steamy kissypoo, *your* job is to con all of America *and* your scene partner into falling madly in love with you." Headset points across the huge lofty soundstage at my love interest. "*Your* job is to learn your blocking and focus on him!" he fumes, stomping the sole of his shiny black shoe into the concrete floor while pointing toward the backside of a tall blond boy. "Now beat it! Jesse James is waiting!"

Chapter 8

Whispers move quickly through the large crowd of crew and talent and, for a nanosec, I think I even hear a boom mic and camera snicker at me from the sidelines as I make my way over to Jesse James, standing seductively beside Bliss. I eye them as they giggle to each other and I wonder if this day can get any worse.

Bliss smells of superiority. She taunts me like a predator, smirking through her glossy lips and Chiclet veneers. Slightly taller than me with layers of blond hair that I'm positive has been enhanced with gallons of Jessica Simpson Weave, Bliss bats her lengthy lady lashes and denies me even the smallest courtesy of an introductory nod. She grips her script in one bony hand and with the other engulfs her entire emaciated waist, challenging me to a subliminal waist-off. I suck in my gut until it touches the back of my ribcage and coolly await my blocking direction, growing maddeningly lightheaded. I exhale. She nods her head in victory. *Maybe skinny bitches really are evil!*

Jesse James sneaks in close and slides his hand down my back. I shiver. "Did you get it all out?" he whispers.

Mortified, I glance up at him, wanting so desperately to hate him, this freakishly hot man who was sleeping on my hardwood, beckoning me with his very own hard wood. *What is he doing here—in my world?* I scratch at my throat and pitifully simulate inhaling the tar from a cigarette toke.

"Sorry," is all I can muster into his hard pecs, defining themselves against his crisp white cotton shirt. *He could be a supermodel. I wonder if he's seen today's paper. I wonder how he got into my apartment. I wonder how he got into my PANTIES!* I feel my knees knock and weaken when I involuntarily recall the force behind his manly thrusts in a brief doggie-style memory. I take a deep breath, the Doublemint cool rescuing me from myself.

"No problem; nothing Wardrobe and a quick shower couldn't cure," he says, smelling like a fresh summer day and Binaca combo. "This is Bliss," he says, finally offering the introductory nod toward her. She glances up from her script at me, without even a hello. "Don't worry about it; she just has to warm up to you."

"Seriously?! Why are you talking to her? Do you actually *know* her?" Bliss's sultry voice challenges him.

He flashes an insanely perfect grin at me. "We just met."

"Ew!" Bliss goes back to her lines for a few more beats before throwing her script at a shy girl with a big floppy pigtail dressed in a crapload of black. On cue, the girl ducks then retrieves the script from the floor.

Since Jesse James avoided any acknowledgment of our completely sexed-out morning together, I decide that I have no other choice but to play along. It's ridiculous that I'm not able to scream that just one and a half hours ago his head was buried between my legs, spelling out my name with his tongue as I crescendoed into my own multiorgasmic BLISS. And now, he has the nerve to be starring as my love interest on the television show that's supposed to catapult *me* into superstardom. Yes, apparently my day could get worse—much worse.

Chapter 9

When blocking rehearsal (read: worst morning E-VA!) finally ended, I had enough time to get lunch; the afternoon would be spent finally shooting those arduous scenes. I grab my motorcycle jacket—thankful it hadn't gotten caught up in the morning's hurling—hiccup, and bundle up before bolting across the street to the Starbucks knockoff for a salad and nonfat latte. *I deserve an extra shot today,* I think, before toying with the idea of drizzling dressing on my mixed greens. Hell, maybe I'd even go wild and top it off with a quarter-cup of croutons.

Delicious thoughts of dried bread whirl around in my head and I enter the café and momentarily forget about Jesse James and Bliss the Bitch. As the barista grabs my majorly boring salad and latte, I stare at the dark chocolate cupcake with the buttercream frosting and strawberry sprinkles in the display case. The mean, menacing, anorexic cow in my head utters, *"Moo."* I ignore her. *"MOOOOOO!"* Skinny Cow taunts louder, jarring me from my high-calorie cupcake reverie.

"I got her, Roy," I hear the familiar seductive voice offer. "Put her, uh, whatever, on my tab."

Flushed, I refuse to look back at Jesse James but have to speak up. "Uh, by my calculations you already owe me seventy-five bucks; I, uh, want my money back and we can just call it even."

"Don't be like that." I can feel him breathing down the nape of my neck as he eases my lunch money out of my hand.

I turn around to snatch at the twenty-dollar bill, but he shoves his hand behind his back.

"Watch it! That's a quarter-of-a-million-dollar ass right there and right now it belongs to a dude named Calvin."

It belonged to me a few hours ago.

"But you and me here together—working together and now playing together, well now, that's very sexy." Jesse James leans in and nuzzles the skin against my neck. For one quick sec I close my eyes and succumb to his spell. He reaches around me and hands Roy my twenty-dollar bill.

"Seventy-five bucks!" I stare past his chiseled cheeks into his gripping blue eyes and concentrate on remaining in control.

"But I earned every bit of that. I was under the impression that it was payment for a job well done—and so were you. Besides"—he frowns—"*seventy-five?* That's just insulting!"

Okay, so maybe that registers as Discount Dick. How was I supposed to know? I fidget with the zippers on the sleeve of my jacket and study him before blurting out, "You knew I'd be starting today, didn't you?"

Nothing.

"You knew I'd be playing your character's, Blake's, new love interest on the show, didn't you?"

Still . . . nothing.

"Did I happen to mention any of that last night—that this . . . this role of a lifetime, was one of the reasons for my drunken balls-to-the-wall celebration?"

I don't blink.

Neither does he.

"J.J.!" I huff, flashbacking to the M.A.C. Russian Red still smeared across my mirror. "Answer me!"

His blond brows furrow and the hint of a smile escapes his lips. Finally breaking my glare to stare down at his brand-new vomit-free black-on-black Pumas, Jesse James shoves his hands into his pants. I feel a series of stings simmer behind my eyes just as

Roy calls out my order. I snatch it from him and storm out of the café, not caring that Jesse James still has my haggard reputation, my seventy-five bucks, and my leftover change from my reduced-calorie coffee/salad combo wrapped tightly in his hands.

Chapter 10

"Kennedy, dear, are those your spiked cowboy boots I see sticking out from behind that rack of clothes? I think I'd recognize those glorious legs anywhere."

"No, Marge, it isn't me," I say as her Crocs shuffle my way.

She pulls at the movable rack and looks down at me picking at my dry lettuce and guzzling my overpriced lukewarm coffee. "What are you doing in here, dear? And why are you on the floor?" She sighs. "Nice corner office you found for yourself there. But you know you do have a dressing room."

"Not that I know of."

Marge grabs her two-way walkie from the cluttered shelf of Essentials. "Izzie should've shown you everything, including your dressing room. That's not like her," she says, putting her hand on her round hip while she pages Isabella. "She's the senior production assistant and is usually on top of it." She turns toward me and places her soft hand on my shoulder. "Of course you have a dressing room, dear."

"Yes, Margie?" The girl with the fuzzy ponytail pokes her bifocaled face into the doorway before I'm barely off the floor.

"Izzie, why hasn't Kennedy been shown to her dressing room? She's been here almost half the day."

"I'm so sorry; I'll tour you right away." She turns back to Marge. "It's just that Bliss had me walking her dogs for the last two hours and they wouldn't go poo," her voice trails off into a whisper. "She said I absolutely couldn't bring 'the bitches back till they shat'— all four of them!"

. . .

Following Izzie around the maze of hallways and through the cafeteria was particularly painful. Everyone huddled together in their respective cliques, buzzing about the day's events. Today's paper was being passed around and one by one they each made a point to stop what they were doing and snark at me. I just try to keep up with Izzie, who is moving at a furious pace.

"The grubby guys at the tables in the far back, way off to the side, are the lighting guys," Izzie offers, pointing to the table of randomly bearded burly men who were gobbling up big plates of fried food. "They stick to themselves, but they're usually pretty cool— for union guys, I suppose." She shrugs indifferently. "The cameramen camp out at the table next to them," she says, and nods to a handful of thirtysomething men who appear oblivious to anyone else in the room except each other. "The younger skinny boys at the middle round table with their coveted headsets are PAs. They always dress in your basic black and because they'd just die if they ever missed anything, they religiously stalk from that same table in the center of it all—'cept for me; I'm like the only girl and I hardly ever get to eat lunch." She shoves her thick glasses back up the sloped bridge of her button nose, then looks back down at the floor. She's barreling her way through the lunchroom lanes like a champion sprinter, forcing me to resort to a quick skip.

"The two tables next to the soda machines are usually where the extras hang and eat, but that's only when a big scene is being shot. You know with our tight schedule and even tighter budget . . ."

I watch her as she rattles off the lunchroom hierarchy and think that buried behind all the distracting accessories, Izzie is probably a completely cute girl.

"Then the three tables by the door are where all the talent eats, except for the stars, of course."

"Of course," I agree, unsure of whether that would be my requisite spot or not.

"You'll sit there."

I watch as the table of superskinny, all-girl talent move tiny portions of food around their plates, being careful never to actually put anything into their mouths. The Herculean crew adjacent to the gaggle of slinky girls looks like an Abercrombie ad, and though Jesse James could've been a poster child for the rambunctious frat, I knew he was probably over it all, having already been there and already done that.

"The executive producer and the director always order in so you'll hardly ever see them in here unless they pop in for something special—but then again, usually I'll go for whatever it is they need myself. I mean, that's why they call me the gofer." Izzie raises her head and looks at me for the first time with what appears to be resolute pride.

"Even though I've been a PA longer than anyone else here . . ." She rolls her eyes at the carbon-copied crew of production assistants who sit uniformly cross-legged with identical dressing-free salad/Fiji water combos and fitted black cotton girly-man tees.

"Thanks," I say, smiling, as we continue through the cafeteria chronicles. She stops momentarily and inspects me. I squirm.

"You're welcome." She smiles, before bolting behind the narrow corridor of stage sets, around the props, and finally up the steel stairs and down the yellow-brick hall filled with coveted dressing rooms.

"Here we are. This one's yours." Izzie nods toward the door that has a bedazzled B on it. She digs into her shirt pocket. "And here's your key."

Squeezing the key tightly in my hands, I click my heels three times and my pulse quickens with excitement. I stare at the door and turn back toward Izzie, who is gone, rounding the corner of the hallway with haste.

"Thanks, Izzie," I call out.

I plug the key into the door yearning for a few stolen moments of solitude in a safe secure space where I won't be taunted or teased. I'm thinking that I'll put my bag down, freshen up a bit, and then slip out a freight door I'd spied earlier on my haunted house tour for a quick smoke break. Rainbows and Capri ciggies are dancing in my mind when the door flies open without provocation of any kind.

"Can I help you with something?" Bliss, the Wicked Bitch, roars from the other side.

"Uh, hi, Bliss. I'm just—"

"WHAT?!" She swipes at the white dust loitering around her nose repeatedly, and flips her beautifully streaked blond horse mane over her bony shoulder.

I look down at the key in my hand. "I, uh, was just coming to get settled in my dressing room." I am finally able to force the words out when the key slips through my dripping-scared fingers to the floor.

I freeze.

Bliss swoops down to scoop it up before my knees can knock. "Sorry, sweetie, this is *my* dressing room. You must be mistaken." She stands over me in stilted heels and her big dilated eyes roll into the back of her head. "The extras hang downstairs, next to the soda machines," she hisses. I promptly feel a windstorm, the door slamming in my face.

Jesse James rounds the corner at the bottom of the staircase and takes them two at a time. "What's the deal, Sexy? You okay?" He gently tugs at my chin until I'm looking into his dusty blond lashes. "C'mon." He grabs my hand, easing me down the yellow-brick hall.

"What's up with the crocodiles?" I watch him cautiously as he hands me a bottled water from the mini-fridge in his room. "You're the birthday girl," he says, pacing around me, before moving in closer to wipe away a few tears. "It's illegal in, like, all fifty states to cry on your birthday."

I back away from him. "What's the deal around here? You can't all be freaks?! Can you?"

"Hey, wait a minute. I can explain."

"I doubt it."

"Let me at least try to explain my side of the story."

"You had your chance to do that this morning over your seventy-five-dollar cup of joe, *J.J.*" I'm infuriated again, watching the corners of his mouth turn up into a slick grin.

"Really, I meant to. I had every intention of explaining what went down last night as soon as I realized you really didn't remember. You know how you girls play the selective-memory-morning-after card."

"Yeah . . . NO!"

His polished swagger is impressive but his FedEx delivery of bullshit isn't. I fist-fight to find my courage. "Really, J.J., give it a rest; this morning, your face buried between Bliss's breasts?!"

"What are you talking about?"

"When I hurled all over you this morning—in the closet—you had your face nuzzled between her nipples."

"I did not; maybe Blake did, but J.J. didn't."

"Okay, that's it!" I shake my head in disbelief. "I'm outta here! You're officially—" I pull away from him.

"C'mon, Sexy, we were rehearsing a scene." Then Jesse James did that thing again where he lifts my chin into his stare and I momentarily forget my name. "Sometimes we practice in the closet. No one can find us when we're in there."

I break his spell and head for the door. "Whatever, J.J.—or

whoever you are!" I say into the air and escape down the brick hall with my tote, my script, and my warm bottle of H₂O—still with nowhere for any of us to go!

Chapter 11

The cool November breeze escorts me through the double doors and outside into the freight alleyway. I lean against the building and flip the collar of my jacket up to my earlobes. I inhale the first drag of my Capri ciggie like my life depends on it, desperately confused about how I ended up here! Just twenty-four hours ago I was twenty-nine years old, safely saddled in my four and a half years of celibacy, and in complete control of every stitch of my devoutly disciplined life. Scoring the role of Lacey Madison on *America's Next Sweetheart* was the next logical and biggest step on my journey to über-stardom. It was scripted perfectly: Lacey Madison, an exotically beautiful PR Princess, recklessly indulges in a clandestine love affair with her superstar client, Blake Blass (oh BE-HAVE!). But unbeknownst to her, Blake is also secretly involved with her tragic boss, the notoriously lethal and the most hated MAY-JAH bitch in town, Bliss—just Bliss—who is later revealed to be Lacey Madison's, dunh, dunh, dunh . . . MOTHER! (GASP!)

Lacey Madison was slated to be the next soap sweetheart and everyone around town was buzzing about the budding supermodel who was cast in the coveted role, the industry's new "IT" girl. But I was anything but "IT"; as a matter of fact, in the last twenty-four hours, I'd become more like "NOT"!

Now, hiding behind the Dumpster outside the studio's freight door, I'm dragging out all the leftover nicotine in my filtered butt, holding back tears. I pull at the shrinking ciggie and close my eyes, relishing the thought of meeting up with the Brats later at Marquee, the exclusive hotspot that was quickly becoming our Regal Beagle—only to be interrupted by my shrilling cell.

"O.M.FUCKING G.! I'm so stoked you called, Bug. You're soooo not gonna believe the day I'm having! I was totally late this morning and can I just say that I'm still D-R-U-N-K! And second, my scene partners are complete and total douches—wait! Aren't you supposed to be at the *Vogue* shoot with Rain?" I wasn't about to let my dramz overshadow one of the biggest opps for Hannah and her rockstar sex kitten. "You worked your heinie off for that shoot. You're a total demigod!" And not just cuz she made history restructuring the most lucrative deal in the music game for Rain earlier this year—although it *was* scandalicious! But she'd managed to score Rain the cover of Anna Wintour's firstborn—right behind Bey and First Lady O! Hannah was beyond brillz; diversifying Rain's career, positioning her to do blockbuster films, a colossal clothing line, and summer on Broadway.

"It's nuts over here, bananas—BA-NA-NUTZ!" she says, unfazed that she's holding the entertainment world in her Hermès pocket. "But I still had to take a sec and check in on my Sweets; it's your thirtieth and the first day of your new career!"

I ignite another Capri.

"Now start from the beginning—abbreviated version—don't shoot me, only have a min."

I exhale the disappointing deets of my day right along with my secondhand smoke. "Well, let's see, my scene partners are legendary and I think I actually hate them both. HATE! And yes, I know Nana wouldn't approve of such language, but I'll do the five f'ing Hail Marys for this one. There are just no other words." I take another loooNNNGGG drag. "I don't have a dressing room, well not exactly, but sort of. I'm sharing it with Dr. Jekyll and her cokehead Hyde—total psycho bitch! Plus I kinda barfed every-where, the cast and crew think I'm a joke, the blocking is mega hard and, well, IT'S MY FUCKING BIRTHDAY!!!!"

I rush through my morning before I reveal the coronary, the massive Dish-of-the-Day. "And Bug, even though this hangover is kicking my ass, that's hardly the killer!" I whisper into the receiver. "I totally know the secret identity of my creeper."

"Man-whore?" She gasps.

I take one last pull on the ciggie. "A total OUTLAW!" I fume, throwing the cigarette over my shoulder with force.

"OWWW!!!" A deep husky voice rages from behind me.

"OHMYGOD!"

A tall, subtly sexy man is hunched over, smashing his fingers against his eye. "Shit!"

"Are you okay? I'm so sorry," I say when I see my half-lit ciggie slowly losing life on top of his Prada loafer. "Gotta go, Bug, I think I just got myself fired!"

Chapter 12

"Mr. Cohen, are you okay? Are you okay, sir? Please say some-thing," I beg of the f'ing executive producer of *America's Next Sweetheart*. "I'm so sorry; I didn't know you were standing there. I didn't know anyone was standing there."

"I guess I should have said something," Mr. Cohen manages through clenched teeth.

"Can you see, sir? Did my Capri burn you in the eye?" When he doesn't respond I bend over toward him and soften my voice. "Did I kill *your eye*?"

Sam Cohen stands up and after putting himself through a series of blinking and eye-batting trials, he says, "I'm good, you just killed my cigarette." He looks around the ground and into the Dumpster. "And maybe my lighter." He pulls out another cig and tilts his head to the side, eyeing the fag. "I wish I knew how to quit you." He chuckles to himself, and I spy a noticeable sparkle hiding behind his thick lashes. "I swear I'm really going to quit one of these days," he says into the air, before shaking himself from his Marlboro moment. He looks into the Dumpster again then at me. "Collateral damage."

"Wait, sir, I know I may have killed your fire and I'm so sorry about that, really," I ramble, rummaging through my cluttered tote. "But I think I've got something in here somewhere that you can have."

"Must be a sign that I should quit sooner rather than later," he says, digging into his jeans and pulling out a book of matches. "Don't sweat it."

His thick hair is dark and wavy, and as I'm quietly admiring it I notice a hint of gray around the left temple of one of the most powerful men in Daytime. He follows my gaze and reaches up to touch it then lets his fingers find their way through his waves to the nape of his neck. I'm thinking he could easily have been cast as the hot hair guy in a vintage Head & Shoulders ad. I relax into a vision of Hot Hair Guy lathering up in the shower pimping a bottle of dandruff detox in his soapy hand . . . but press pause when I realize he's smiling down at me mischievously—as if he knows I'm standing right here, right now, wishing him naked. Now majorly uncomfortable, I shove a handful of curls behind my ear, tighten my grip on my tote, and begin my maneuver toward the freight door to try to reclaim my delinquent day.

"I'm Lacey Madison, sir," I say, stopping in my tracks to mind my manners. I turn around to extend my hand toward him. "I mean that's who you hired me to play. I'm Kennedy Lee—in real life. Or Sweets, my friends call me Sweets, but then I guess Kennedy would be more—so yeah, I'm just Kennedy."

"Of course you are," he says, smiling down at me, flashing an insanely perfect set of teeth. After a few seconds he obliges, reaching out to shake my hand. "Sam. And it's nice to formally meet you."

"Thank you, sir."

"Not 'sir.' Sam."

"Sure." I shrink away nervously at The Big Boss.

Sam pulls his handkerchief from his back pocket and dabs at his eye. "So I hear you've had a bit of a rough day."

"Excuse me, sir?"

"Sam."

I scratch at my throat and fish lightly. "You heard what exactly, now?"

"On your cell phone . . . to your girlfriend—or boyfriend."

"Nooooo! I mean yes . . . that was my girlfriend—*BFF* girlfriend. Best Friends For—"

He crosses his terrifically toned arms over his chest and lowers his thick brows into his deeply set eyes. He smiles at me again. "Cute."

Sheepishly, I smile back.

Casually, Hot Hair Guy leans against the wall and before I can give it much thought I'm mirroring his stance, leaning against the bricks and mortar with him. A chill creeps under my jacket and over my cleavage.

"It's nothing, sir—uh, Sam. Just first-day stuff."

"Sounded like some pretty shitty first-day stuff to me."

"Sir?"

"Sam."

"Uh, how long were you standing there?"

He chuckles, then drags on his Marlboro. "Long enough to

strongly suggest moving our 'welcome to the ANS family' chat up a few days." He scratches his cheek beneath his stubble. "I usually let the talent get settled in before I roll out the welcome wagon, complete with ANS rules, regulations, and other discretionary bullshit."

"I see."

"But"—he pauses—"how about instead of talking in my cold, uninviting office we grab a bite tonight—after you're done shooting your last scene."

"A bite?"

"Just the diner across the street. Nothing too—"

"Uh, well—"

"You've gotta eat. And well"—he crushes his Marlboro under his loafer—"we really do need to talk—sooner rather than later. Besides, I know how it can be in the beginning, especially around here. People aren't the most accommodating."

"Yeah, I kinda noticed that."

"The key is to just get through that dreaded first day. Once the big bad first day is over, the hard part is done. It's mostly the fear of the unknown that gets to a person, but if you can get past that, all you've gotta do is just keep coming back. Part of my job is to make sure that happens. And at the rate you're going—" He smiles then looks down at the gravel, over the tips of his scuffed loafers.

"Dinner, uh—"

"Sam. You might wanna work on that."

Right.

He turns his body directly toward mine. "Nice to meet you, Sweets." Something warms our awkward moment as we stand still, taking each other in, until a loud, long, red truck pulls up, interrupting our silence.

Chapter 13

I look around the set at all the frenzied action, take a few deep breaths, and try to center myself. "Focus, dear; the time is now to have everything you've ever dreamed!" Marge said after fitting me in her Zac Posen creation and twirling me around for inspection. I adored the pleated gray organdy blouse with its jeweled bow, and the navy duchess-satin skirt with its matching jeweled belt was to die for. I haven't felt this epic since traffic court. My knees slightly wobble when I wonder if Sam is watching me right now, enjoying my display of high-powered pretty. I'm ready to prove that I can be Best in Show and not just another desperately tragic bitch.

Instead, Jesse James catches my eye and suddenly I can't remember my first line. I bow my head and promise God that I'll never have sex again—if He'll just get me through this scene—this one last time. Pinky swear. *Amen.*

EPISODE 69: HOMECOMING

In today's scene, Lacey Madison has just arrived back home in Destiny after graduating summa cum laude from business school. She is promptly thrown into the ranks at work to begin fulfilling her legacy: taking over the family business, Sweethearts, Inc.

I smack my lips together to secure the shiny gloss in place. *I am Lacey Madison. I am Lacey Madison. I AM Lacey Madison. . . . I need a cigarette.*

The blocking races through my mind. A bearded man behind Camera 1 watches as I nervously take my mark on the elaborate stage that's been prepped for afternoon scenes at Sweethearts, Inc. Jesse James and Bliss are already running lines onstage when Smith the Director coolly intercepts my approach.

"You look beautiful, kiddo," he says matter-of-factly, in his Aussie accent, conjuring the voice of the late great crocodile connoisseur. I comfortably decide that Smith the Director could've been a California Dreamer in his day and the remaining blond hair on his head that he's trying so desperately to hold on to probably blew in the wind somewhere between a surfboard in Sydney and some beach's blue sky in Malibu.

"Now do you remember what we went over this morning?" He digs his fingers into my shoulders and steadies me.

"Uh, I, uh, think so," I shamefully answer, hoping the blank I'm suddenly drawing is temporary.

Smith the Director eyes me carefully then speaks slowly as if he is fully aware that today I'm riding the Short Bus. "Hey kiddo, you really do look beautiful and, honestly, that's half the battle in soap-land." He takes a deep breath, spreads his legs, and centers himself. "Now I know it's your first day, but try to relax. We've got a lot to get done and we're already behind." He takes one of his hands from his corduroy slacks and flips the pages of his script. "We'll run the blocking one last time for you. Then I need you to just jump right in."

Bliss slithers into my periphery and scopes me silently. I dig my fingernails into the cover page of my script.

"Kennedy, dahhhling," she rasps. "I'm just so thrilled to be working with you today. We're gonna have tons of fun."

I look around. I point to myself. *Me?*

"Yes, I've heard so many amAAAzing things about you and your work and your powerful presence on camera," she gushes. "I just know we're gonna get along like the best of friends." *You and ME?*

She loops her skeletal arm through mine and inches toward me, rubbing her index finger across my collarbone. "Your skin is soooo beautiful. You exotics have all the luck. I so wish I was born a biracial exotic, but such wasn't my dessstiny," she dramatizes, turning her full lips up into a pout. As I look closely I'm convinced I can actually see the needle marks from her last series of injectibles. "Now, dah-hhling, let's make magic." She blows a kiss into the wind, and after an abbreviated pregnant pause she swoops down from the stage.

Does this mean I get my dressing room back?

I turn toward Jesse James, who's now discussing blocking with the assistant director, completely oblivious to this sudden shift in Bliss's mood-i-tude. But when Izzie comes bolting through the door, I grab her by the elbow before she can fly away.

"What's the deal with her?" I question into Izzie's ear.

"Who, Bliss?"

"Yes! Who am I working with here? What *is* she?"

Izzie shrugs. "You never know from minute to minute. Just fasten your seat belt and hold on tight," she advises in a whisper, and runs hastily toward Headset who is yelling off a myriad of things for her to do.

I take a step back and nervously survey the landscape. Makeup and Hair are diligently dabbing and spritzing, while Wardrobe pins and pokes. Tons of crew are gathered around the soundstage, either checking equipment or fidgeting with ladders and lights. Three cameras stationed evenly around the stage are staring through me. Nervously, I stare back. The multicolored lights hanging from the lofted ceilings and stationary stadium bulbs situated on either side of our set don't do much to ease my internal thermometer, already surging. I fan the script at my underarms and catch the bearded Camera Man on my left slide his head from behind his lens. He smiles. I frown!

"Okay, people, from the top," Smith calls out, as Trinity rushes over to powder me down one last time. "Let's walk it quickly for posterity then get this baby in the can. I don't wanna be here all night. The wife is home sick and the baby doesn't realize she's one wail away from being tossed out the window. On your mark. Get set . . ." He claps his hands and Headset mimics him into the beginning of my first scene.

"Quiet on the set . . ."

Chapter 14

New York's November winds warn me about ever calling the Windy City, well, *windy* again. I shiver through the thin leather of my jacket and struggle to light my cancer-rette as I stand on the corner of 64th and Worst-Birthday-Ever, waiting for Sam.

"Let me get that for you," his deep voice rasps, as he jogs down the block to join me on the corner.

I spin around and immediately laugh at the blazing torch my cigarette soul mate is calling a lighter. He lights my cig and slips his heavy jacket around my shoulders.

"Thank you." I snuggle into the leather bomber and take a long drag, a welcome relief from an even longer afternoon-turned-evening of "Take two" and "Again from the top" and far too much "Perfect job, Bliss. . . . Now Kennedy, if you could just nail that blocking, kiddo! We all wanna get outta here!"

"Had to wrap up some last minute stuff; thanks for waiting," Sam says, nodding across the street to the diner. "It's nothing fancy, but I think you'll like it."

I look past Sam and observe Headset switch by, shouldering his LV girly satchel. "Good night, Mr. Cohen." Headset smiles brilliantly at Sam and pushes his shoulders back.

"Night, Jack."

"See you tomorrow, Mr. Cohen," Jack pipes, poking his chest out as far as his very fitted tweed coat will allow.

"Yes, tomorrow, Jack," he agrees, before blowing into his palms, intensely seeking warmth.

"Maybe this isn't such a good idea; maybe I should just go," I say impulsively, feeling Headset's eyes boring through me. I look around the corner and consider a taxi home. I still hadn't managed to accept the much cheaper friendship the New York subway proffered.

"Not an option; we need to talk," he says sternly, as he grabs my hand and leads me through traffic. "Besides, I don't like to eat alone and from the looks of it, it's you or him," Sam says, laughing, as he nods across the street at Jack. I eye Headset anxiously, wondering what he's thinking as he hops into the only cab I'd seen all night.

Chapter 15

The petite woman behind the register smiles at Sam and me and peels two menus from the stack. She seats us in a cozy, secluded corner near a window toward the back. The air is thick and the smell of grilled eats and freshly squeezed orange juice makes my stomach churn. Sam casually flips through the menu, but I people-watch, deliberately trying to avoid watching him. A young girl with pink choppy hair and a ring wrapped through her bottom lip passes our table. We lock eyes. One of hers is lazy. I look away and listen to the eclectic buzz of everyone and randomly wonder where each of them is from.

"So what's your pleasure, Kennedy Lee?" Sam finally looks up from examining his menu.

"I'm not really that hungry. Maybe a cup of coffee—decaf," I answer meekly.

I study the Postimpressionist paintings on the walls and the chatter in the room dulls down a decibel.

"Not your typical diner, I know."

"Yeah, I was just thinking that." I ponder what, if anything, Sam knows about my anonymous sex with Jesse James or the Snitch Column in the Pain-In-My-Ass *Post*.

"Hey, it's okay if you look at me, you know. I won't bite you."

This time I look directly into him. "Yeah, but are you gonna fire me?"

Sam sets his menu down. He is clearly taken aback. "You mean that?"

"Uh-huh, just tell me now cuz I don't have any other options lined up and if I need to start looking for another temp job, I really need to know—like yesterday. That last one—just the thought of it makes me break out in a rash. It was far less than ideal, let me tell ya, even for a temp job is all I'm saying." I throw my hands in the air and decide to stop talking.

"What would make you think I'd fire you?"

"Because of everything you heard me say earlier—on my cell. Because I was so—"

"Honest?" He looks down at my fidgeting fingers and reaches out for them. I pull back and put both hands under the table.

"Sure that works."

"Listen, there's nothing wrong with you being honest about the day you had. You wouldn't believe some of the days I've had. I mean, there have been some days." He stares past me and fixates on the Seurat painting hanging on the wall above the buzzing water fountain. "Boy, have I had some days," he whispers and fades into thought.

"Besides everything else I've already told you there's something else, uh, Sam." I look for the words to ease him into the reality that I've been crowned the official ANS soundstage slut. "See, the thing is that I made a really big mistake and it could possibly, maybe, affect my performance on set. And since you're gonna find out anyway I guess I should be the one to—so, yeah, what I'm trying to say is that I, I kind of may have—"

I attempt to thwart thoughts of Jesse James nuzzling my right ear while my left leg was stretched somewhere over his strong shoulder.

"Okay, that's it! Just stop it! You're killing me here and I honestly can't take any more!" He shakes his head and covers his ears. I don't want to laugh, but I can't help it. "Seriously, Kennedy, now listen to me. It's all about the work. The work, Kennedy. And I saw your work today and I didn't see anything wrong besides normal first-day jitters," Sam says soothingly. "Your work was solid. Now try and let some of this stuff go, start putting it behind you. Please, I'm begging you. It serves no purpose. And besides that, you're giving me a headache."

"Okay." I relax. "So, you're not gonna fire me, regardless of everything—I mean, I really put it out there."

"Man, you're relentless, aren't you?"

"Well, don't you have the power to fire me?"

He looks down at his menu again. "Let's be clear here—I'm sure you already know that being late for work is just dumb, no matter what kind of morning you've had. People end up standing around waiting on you and then, you know, there's that whole professionalism thing I like my team to try and abide by. I'm sure you can understand that." Slowly, he grins through the reprimand. "But back to your question . . . Am I going to fire you? No, your job is safe." Sam takes in a deep breath. "And that's a promise under one condition." His face is suddenly resolute.

I surrender. "I knew it. I shouldn't have said—"

"That you order something to eat." My boss stares across the table at me and the edges of his mouth turn up. "It's okay, I won't tell."

"Okay, so what's good here?" I unzip my motorcycle jacket.

"The steak. The steak is pretty good here."

"At a diner?" I wince at the pitch in my voice.

"What's wrong with a diner?" he whispers, still grinning.

"I just wouldn't have figured a guy like you for picking out the Angus at a diner—that's all I'm saying."

"What's that supposed to mean—'a guy like me'?"

I look around the room then lean into the table. "I'm just saying that I figured you more for Morton's or The Palms or—"

"I'm insulted—again." He slides his menu away and folds his hands over it.

"It wasn't meant to be an insult, just a speculation, at best."

"An assumption—and a very bad one. I would've expected you to be more open, especially considering the day you just had."

"Are you saying that I'm tragic?" I fold my hands and rest them on the table, listening intently to one of the most authentically handsome men I've seen in a long time.

"No, not at all, but you have to admit, the day you had kind of was."

Well, that's true.

"So tell me why you think I'd only be ordering my prime rib at a fancy restaurant and not at the neighborhood diner?"

"Well, obviously I was wrong, so I'll keep this cowgirl boot out of my mouth, thank you very much. It's clear I don't know very much about you besides . . . well, besides your name."

"You know more than that."

I shake my head. "If you say so, Sam."

"Sam says so."

"So what else does Sam say?" I stare at his lips.

He lowers his voice. "What would you like to hear him say?"

I think about the delicious directions this conversation could go. Sam is watching me closely, stroking his stubble. I picture his hands stroking my breasts and reach for my water.

He grabs my wrist gently. "I'm listening."

I let go of the water. "So, uh, Sam . . ."

"Yes?" He lets go of my wrist.

"Why *do* you like ordering your steak from here? I'm sure there's a reason you're here and not at The Palms."

"Of course I've got a reason." He brushes his finger against mine. "Because this is where you agreed to eat with me."

The waiter joins our table and lights the two candles between us. *Relief.* He pulls out his pad and awaits our order.

"I'll have the steak, medium rare, and a Coke, please."

"And I'll have the arugula salad."

Sam raises his brows.

"With a cup of vegetable soup."

Approving my addition, he takes my menu and hands it off and then twists my stare in his. My pulse skyrockets. I look away and glance at my watch. "It's getting late; I really shouldn't have ordered. I need to get back so I can memorize my lines and be ready for tomorrow."

"I've got a better idea. How about we run lines now?"

"What?" I look at him again and admit to myself that I really enjoy looking at him, maybe a little too much.

"Come on, pull out your script. Let's run lines. I can feed you and prep you at the same time. I'm a multitasker by nature; it's one of my things."

"What are some of your other things?"

His laugh dissolves into a seductive stare. I wonder if it is deliberate. "Don't change the subject. Pull out your script. I can give you good backstory, we can work on character development, and still get some housekeeping out of the way."

"Housekeeping?" I study him.

"We can make this our first business dinner."

Business dinner. Something about that is disappointing. I tug at the script in my tote and spot my cell hidden underneath it. "I should really call my friends. I know they're expecting me—with it being my big birthday and all." I pretend to sulk.

Sam slides his tall athletic frame out of the booth. "Go ahead, I'll be right back."

Awestruck, I watch him walk away and with each swagger I slink slowly underneath the table, wondering how often he works out. Every day and twice on Wednesday, I decide.

Chapter 16

"But it's your birthday, Sweets! Where've you been? We've been tryna reach you for the past few hours. So you didn't get fired, I take it?"

"No, thank God; can't go into it now, but let's just say I've been more or less preoccupied."

"Who am I talking to? Where's my Sweets? You're sounding super-cryptic, just like Britt."

I can't bear to tell Hannah that I'm now out having dinner with my Big Boss, the EP of the goddamn show.

"THE EXECUTIVE PRODUCER OF THE GODDAMN SHOW?!" she shrills.

"It's a *business* dinner."

"My ass!" Hannah scoffs. "I'm telling Brittany."

"Please don't; I'm begging you. She'll haunt me about it. She's already saying that I've flipped and turned into, into . . . her!" I quiver at the thought. "She said that's what the Great White Dick did to me."

"Well . . ."

"Yeah, well, speaking of Blond Boy . . ."

"WHAT?!"

"I couldn't believe it either. He was right there in the utility closet nipping at her tits."

"Kennedy, come home right this second! I'm not playing with you. You've lost your celibacy and now you've completely lost your mind—way too much Caucasian cock for one day!"

Sam rounds the corner and I whisper into the receiver. "His lips are sooo-per kissable and I honestly don't know what's gotten into me but I just wanna—"

"You absolutely CANNOT fuck two men in one day!" she gasps. "Now you listen to me, Kennedy Sun Lee! Promise me you won't fuck two men in one day! Kennedy?! . . ."

Chapter 17

"So, did you check in?" Sam asks, this time sliding into the booth beside me.

I toss the phone back into the tote and scooch over, getting a whiff of the residual cologne buried in the microfibers of his shirt.

"Let's get you ready."

I feel my Kegel muscles involuntarily contract.

"So what page do you come in?" Sam cues me and I go through my scenes several times, taking them line by line, incorporating all his insights into my delivery.

"You're really good at this, Sam."

"Yeah, but I'm not the gorgeous one."

"Gorgeous?" I whisper to myself.

Sam moves a thick curl of hair from my eyes. "Yes, you are insanely gorgeous!" he whispers back matter-of-factly. "I love watching you work."

I reach for the first response I can find. "So, is that why you hired me, cuz you think I'm *gorgeous*?"

His face is blank. He doesn't flinch. "Listen, Kennedy, I need to just say this now." He steadies himself and peers at me. "You're the real deal. I knew it the minute I saw you on that show, *The Intern.*"

My mouth drops.

"And you wouldn't let me forget you when you popped up on that other reality rip-off, you know the one."

My eyeballs nod.

"I had to have you. I've been paying close attention to the moves you've made and I know you're ready." He clears his throat. "The truth is I made them find you."

"You—"

"I always know what's hot and I've developed a solid reputation in this business for discovering the next big thing. And I think you're it. You've got great timing, your look is universally appealing, and you're a fast learner. I know today wasn't the best you've got, but I saw real raw potential on that soundstage. You commanded the stage, even while you fumbled through your blocking. The camera loves you and the bottom line is that you're good—I mean really good. You've got to believe that for this to work. I just need you to keep showing up—sober and on time would be nice."

Shamefacedly, I look away just as our food whizzes through the air. Sam nudges at me when his plate is placed in front of him. "Now, Gorgeous"—he sighs—"I need some elbow room to tear into this diner Angus." He jabs his forearm into my side.

I still don't move: In my mind, I elongate every syllable in the word he's just used to describe me. *GORRR—JUSSS!*

"Move!"

I slide over.

"Now, eat. That was part of our deal, remember?"

I nod my head and pick up my spoon and watch as he cuts a piece of his steak and holds it up to my mouth.

"Try it. It's not Morton's, but it's pretty damn good."

"I don't eat meat."

"That's too bad," he whispers into my ear, laughing to himself. "You're full of surprises."

If he only knew; the cat has been let out of the bag and now she won't stop purring. *Somebody make this thing stop!*

"So, Sam," I digress. "Why exactly are you so hell bent on me eating all of this?" I ask between gulps of the sodium-saturated soup.

"Honestly? Because I've been on the scene long enough to know that you all go to ridiculous extremes to stay thin. You don't get to be at the top of this game where I am and not see it. Impossible."

I don't dare say a word. I can feel the soup at the gateway to my stomach and all I want to do is make a run for the border to the ladies' loo. "*Mooooo,*" Skinny Cow challenges, like she does every time I consume calories after 7:00 PM. I shove the soup bowl away.

". . . And I don't want you to starve yourself." He glances at my bowl. "You can stay thin and be marketable and still be healthy." There is depth in his eyes. "You've got a long future ahead of you, Gorgeous. Believe me, I know."

"Really?" I mutter, surprised at his unabashed flattery.

"Yes. Really." Slowly he reaches out to wipe the corner of my mouth with his finger. I close my eyes without thinking and take a deep breath. When I open them, he brushes the back of his hand against my cheek before pulling away.

"Listen, uh, I just want you to know that I'm not a—a—cliché. And I don't think you are either. So, I'm thinking we should just—"

"We should just eat, right? That's what you were going to say . . . right?"

He smiles appreciatively before turning toward me again.

"It's fine, Sam, really. I kind of appreciate you even more for that. So, no worries; we're both on the same page. Besides, I work for you. You're my boss." I knock elbows with him and watch him slip into a smile as his shoulders relax into comfort again. "It really would be impossible for me if people thought we were, well, you know being—"

"Cliché?"

"Yeah, that."

"I'd still like to check in on you, if that's okay."

"I don't know about that, either. I'm not much of a teacher's pet kind of girl and I don't want to give them one more reason to hate me."

"No one hates you; they don't even know you. It would be ridiculous for someone to get to know you and not like everything about you."

"Well, you didn't have the day I had with them."

"That's right, I forgot, it was quite tragic." He reaches out and squeezes my shoulder. "How about tomorrow at eleven hundred hours we meet at our secret spot and you tell me how your day is going. I'll be ready to hear how much better it is the second time around. And of course, if you need any encouraging words of wisdom as you navigate your way through Day Two in Destiny, well then, I'm your man!"

"Ooh, secret meetings with synchronized watches in alleyways behind Dumpsters. So James Bond, Sam." I rub my hands together at the thought of it. "It'll be our own little taste of espionage."

"And speaking of tastes," he changes the subject, motioning toward my salad. "This eating thing I see is going to be my personal challenge with you. I'm not so worried about you getting to work on time, and sober isn't on my list of concerns either." He coughs into his fist. "But not eating, that must be one of *your* things."

"What would make you say that? I eat."

"Looks more like you just push your food around like most of the other actresses I know."

"I bet you've known a lot of actresses," I blurt.

"I've known some."

"Oh. I see."

"But don't try to change the subject and corner me," he evades coolly. "This isn't about me."

"Fair enough." I wipe my hands on my napkin and straighten up. "Okay, well if we're being serious, I don't think you could ever really know how hard it is for us. We're trying to stay competitive and get noticed out of hundreds, sometimes thousands, of other talented attractive women."

"Look, I know the pressure is crazy, believe me, I do." His eyes soften with a sincerity that makes me feel silly, and when he puts a forkful of salad up to my mouth, I swallow it. My stomach boils over and I immediately feel sick.

"It's not a big deal," I lie.

"Good." He leans over and wipes my mouth with his napkin. "So tell me"—he juggles the energy around again, finishing the last bite of his steak—"why exactly don't you have a dressing room?"

I swig down three big gulps of water and order my esophagus to swallow. "I don't really know."

"Cuz, you know, I got that loud and clear . . . that you don't have a dressing room, but you kind of have one—but not really." He laughs.

"It's really not funny."

"Yeah it is; you're hiding out in the wardrobe room. That's classic." He leans back and runs his hand through his hair. "Okay, I'm listening. Really, what's the deal with that?"

"Izzie showed it to me. She even gave me the key."

"So, what's the problem, Gorgeous? The key didn't work? Was the door jammed? Help me out here." He crosses his arms.

"No, someone else was using it."

"Who?"

The mention of Wonderboobs wouldn't be good for my extracurricular efforts to keep my food down.

"I'm serious, Kennedy. Who? All the principals have been assigned a room so this really shouldn't be a big deal at all." He scoops up another forkful of the wilting warm lettuce and puts it up to my mouth. I feel myself being pushed over the culinary edge. *"Moooooo!"*

"Shut up!" I sternly warn Skinny Cow under my breath.

"Okay, okay, I get it; you've had enough." He laughs lightly.

I roll my eyes at the intrusive lettuce, angry for ever inviting it to our business dinner.

Sam touches my hand gently.

"Sorry, I just can't eat any more of that."

"Hey, it's cool." He reaches out to me and I scoot a few inches into him. "I've been down this road before." He whispers into my ear matter-of-factly. "I'd never claim to understand what you guys go through. I wish I could change it for you." Sam takes my chin and forces me to look into him. "I'm really sorry, Gorgeous."

"For what?"

He squeezes my shoulder and continues. "Cuz now I know you're gonna hate your surprise."

"My what?"

The entourage of servers rush our table and burst into song. "HAPPY BIRTHDAY TO YOU, HAPPY BIRTHDAY TO YOU . . ."

The waiter places a blazing oversized carrot cupcake with white chocolate cream cheese icing in front of me. "I've been having a secret love affair with cupcakes most of my adult life." The decadent dessert has a miniature yellow-and-white number 3 candle next to a pink-and-white 0 with rainbow sprinkles all over.

"HAPPY BIRTHDAY, TO KENNEDY . . ."

"The sprinkles are my favorite part."

I sniff the sweet icing and I swear I can taste the sugar as it flies up my nose. Sam leans back into the booth, watching me light up and turn thirteen right before his eyes. The choir claps and whistles and after the incredibly shitty day I've had, I indulge myself and join in with them. I shut my eyes tight but before I make a wish, I open one and peek over at Sam. He rubs my back with his strong hand.

"It's your wish; whatever you want."

I think carefully and glance at my script, at my leftover food on the table, then over at Sam again. When I blow out the candles the room is still.

"So, you gonna tell me what you wished for?"

"I can't . . . then it won't ever come true."

"If you say so, Gorgeous."

"I say so."

Sam situates his arm around the back of the booth behind me and I sneak a few more inches closer to him. He brushes my cheek with his lips then whispers into my ear. "Hasn't anybody told you?"

I close my eyes and sigh into silence.

"I'm the Dreamweaver . . . I make dreams come true."

Chapter 18

Sam and I make a mad dash from the diner doors into the frigid air. We aren't standing on the corner longer than a few nanoseconds when a shiny black Mercedes E-Class stretch turns down the street and stops directly in front of us. The driver hastens from the car and tips his hat.

"Evening, Mr. Cohen, sorry to keep you waiting."

"It's fine, Winston, we just walked out."

"Good thing, sir," he replies, opening the door for Sam.

Sam steps aside, nodding for me to get in. "Perks of the job," he says when I don't move. "Come on, Gorgeous, you've got on my coat; I'm freezing my ass off over here."

I slip onto the supple ivory leather and Sam slides in beside me. "Buckle up; I can't let anything happen to you."

"Where to, Mr. Cohen?" Winston asks, as he lowers the dividing window.

Sam looks at me. "Well, Ms. Lee, where to?"

"Home."

"I can't say that I committed that stat to memory."

"Right. Uh, downtown—West Broadway and Prince, please."

"Right away." Winston nods and raises the divider.

"Great address," Sam says approvingly. "SoHo's one of my favorite parts of town."

"My sister's the mini-mogul; real estate's her thing. She's got all the 'ins' and I get to mooch."

"That's right, I remember now. From your show; you talked about her a lot. Your twin sister, right? Her name is—"

"Brittany."

"Right, Brittany." He nods his head and bites down on his bottom lip. "I told you I watched you." He studies me, watching me blush. "That was an awful show, by the way."

I turn away and look out the window at the reflection of the city lights twinkling against the Hudson River as we fly by Trump's complex just off the West Side Highway.

Sam reaches out and touches my shoulder. "But you were beautiful. I mean, you made the whole thing work."

"Thanks . . . I think," I say into the windowpane.

There is a seductive tension in the air as we quietly ride along the edge of the city. The turn of events has been a welcome piggyback to my dogged day but I am acutely aware that tomorrow will be weird to walk back onto Sam's stage.

"So, what about you? Where do you live?" I ask, attempting ordinary small talk now that we are ages away from the buzz of the diner, in the backseat of luxury—completely alone.

Sam relaxes into himself. "Hmmm, let's see. Well, right now I'm in between two primary places—the Village and the Upper East Side."

"I thought that part of town was zoned for rich old ladies and trust-fund babies," I tease.

Sam shoots me a disturbing glare.

"Do tell, Mr. Cohen."

"Will you respect me in the morning?" He chuckles.

"That depends on how the night ends," I spit out before I can shut myself up.

"Well"—he pauses, a few shades redder—"My father was in the business and his father was in the business and his father—so, yeah, I had the requisite trust fund. But fuck the money, I just wanted to be part of the business—to work hard, Gorgeous." He eyes the console between us and then looks up to study me, unassuming. "It was important to me to make my own name."

"Well you definitely did that—and you're still a baby—I mean you're so young. Still."

"Thirty-nine isn't *that* young." He laughs. "I mean, maybe I'm young for soaps, but not compared to some of my friends I went to film school with. They're already doing it big."

"And you don't think being the executive producer of a hit soap is big? That's huge!"

"No, it's great, don't get me wrong. Since I've been on board ratings are up, we dominate in our time slot, and now we've officially got the hottest talent." He winks at me. "But I just think I'm—" He glances over to the mahogany minibar for the second time then pours himself a glass of cognac.

"What?" I ask when his face turns slightly sour. "Marge told me today that *America's Next Sweetheart* won more Emmys this year than any other serial. So obviously, you're one of the best in the business."

"Yeah, I'm *the* best, but—" He quiets.

"Some of the all-time greats got their start doing soaps—Meg Ryan, Brad Pitt, Demi Moore, Buffy the Vampire Slayer . . ."

Sam takes a long drink from his glass then knocks the ice around. "Then they moved on."

"So where would you like to move on to? After producing?"

"*Executive* producing."

"Of course, that's totally what I meant," I correct, posturing myself. "So, Mr. Cohen, what is it that you really want to do? What moves you? I mean, what are you really passionate about in life?"

Sam drums his fingers against the console between us and closes his eyes. I take my cue from him and stop talking. When his fingers finally quiet against the soft leather, I rest my hand beside his. It is easy between us. Smooth. We ride without interruption across Christopher Street, making our way through the alternative hipster's West Village.

"You know, nobody ever asks me that question."

Deafening silence.

"Thanks for that."

You're welcome.

"They just expect me to keep doing what I'm doing now, only better."

"Yeah, like me in med school when they were all like—" I catch myself this time. "But if you don't mind me saying so—"

"I have a feeling you're gonna say it anyway."

"It just sounds to me like you've already been asking yourself that question, you know, about your purpose, your passion—"

"You're pretty intense, you know that?" He opens his eyes to look at me, then studies me conspicuously.

"Maybe a little cerebral." I look out the window and murmur under my breath, "I just wanted to know what you'd be doing right now if you could have your way and . . ."

Another slick smile surfaces across Sam's face when I turn to engage him. Instead we lock eyes and my throat dries.

"Water?"

"Please."

He palms one of the chilled bottles and hands it to me. And when I reach out to take it from him, he wraps his fingers around mine. We linger. I flip the top and take a swig.

After devouring me with silent thoughts, Sam knocks on the divider and Winston reappears.

"Yes, Mr. Cohen?"

"Take a left at the light and slow down when you get to the end of the block."

"What's this?" I ask when the car purrs into park at MacDougal Street.

Sam eyes the red-brick building on the corner. "That's Minetta Tavern."

"Never been there before."

He rubs his chin and watches as a young couple huddle together, exiting the restaurant. "It's where they filmed *Mickey Blue Eyes*," he explains, and taps the window a few times, signaling to Winston again.

"I didn't know that."

"Did you see it?"

"Yeah, with Hugh Grant and James Caan."

"No, with James Caan and Hugh Grant . . . gotta give the veteran top billing."

"Not in Hollywood. Youth rules, you know that."

"Yet another problem with this twisted business."

As the car turns the corner and picks up speed, Sam glances back one more time. "Used to be a speakeasy in the twenties. Interesting building; *Reader's Digest* started in the basement."

"Never knew that."

He leans back into his comfort and grins. "Most people don't."

"So . . . you want to open a speakeasy?"

Sam reaches across the seat, pushes my hair over my shoulder, then raps on the window again. We ride around and eventually turn onto Fifth Avenue.

"Where are we now?" I ask, when the car silences.

"This is Cru," he says, after taking a deep breath. "Filmed *As Good As It Gets* here—you know with Jack Nicholson and—"

"Helen Hunt," I finish. "Love that movie. But I love anything Jack Nicholson does."

"He's a true legend." Sam's eyes are heated, burning a hole through the front of the building. "But in the movie it was the Rose Café and Bar."

"So let me get this straight, either you wanna make movies or you have a serious obsession with restaurants that have *been* in movies."

"Oh, jokes from the gorgeous peanut gallery?"

"Nope, just trying to understand why the mini-tour of the Manhattan movie scene." I wink across the seat at him. "And you still haven't answered my question."

Sam looks out the window one last time before signaling to Winston, who promptly pulls away, heading downtown. He takes a big sip from his glass then rests it in its holder beside the champagne bucket. I fold my hands on my lap and watch the shiny happy people who are crowding the downtown streets without a care that tomorrow is a workday or a concern that the evening's chill has hit a record low. The dawn of the holiday season seems to have swept up the island and resounded throughout the town. But inside the car we sit motionless, quietly making our way home.

Sam bites down on his lip and stares out the window as we pass the Minetta Lane Theatre.

"It's the *only* thing I want to do."

Chapter 19

Winston quiets the car when we arrive in front of my building, jumping out when a uniformed doorman rushes out to greet us. Both men reach for my door handle and fume in a muted face-off over it. Sam lowers his window and his breath frosts into the air at the two of them. "Gentlemen, please. I'll get the door." He peers at Winston.

"Of course, sir." Winston rushes back to the car and gets in.

Sam eyes me. "So."

I eye him back. "So."

"I hope you enjoyed your birthday. I know it wasn't sipping Magnum at Marquee with your friends but—"

"No, it was much better." I blush. "My day aside . . . the night was pretty fantastic!"

"Fantastic? Must've been the cupcake that sealed the deal." He leans forward in his seat and presses his fingers together. The car is still and the air thick. "Listen, Kennedy, I know you had a rough first day. All I wanted to do was raise the bar tonight; we're not all bad at ANS."

"I know." I look down at the floor. "And I certainly wasn't at my best today. I made my share of mistakes way before I ever walked through the front door," I struggle to admit.

"After all, tomorrow is another day." He reaches over and moves the frizzy hair away from my eyes, awaiting a reply. I stare back at him blankly.

"*Gone With the Wind*. Scarlett . . ." Sam leans back in his seat. "I just want you to be happy working with us. I know it's not *All My Children*, but I think we're a far better fit anyway. They just got to you before I could. I think it worked out perfectly."

I pinch my eyebrows to my lids, envisioning Sam reading the *Post*'s snitch piece. "How did you know about *All My Children*?"

"It's my job to know what's going on with everyone I'm interested in."

"But I didn't get that job," I answer, sort of sheepishly. "So how did you know about it?" I fish, crossing my fingers that he doesn't make mention of the tabloid tattletale.

"Sure you did; you got the job. They just changed their minds at the eleventh hour and decided to go in a different direction."

Anger and resentment begin to simmer inside me as I recall the day after I was dropped from *All My Children*. I trudged helplessly into the temp gig and shamefully put up with Mr. Stuttering Insurance Man calling me "B-b-babe" and renaming me "H-h-hon." Then at quitting time I relentlessly beat the pavement auditioning for the street hookers, the strung-out baseheads, and the single mothers on welfare. My heart swells at the agony of the hustle. But I was convinced that this was altogether different. I steady my voice. "The truth is I was a little *too* black, too ethnic for them."

Sam laughs.

I don't.

He stops and clears his throat. "Is that what they told you?"

"Yes," I lie. "Well, no, but that's what happened."

"Where'd you get that? Did Casting or somebody at the studio call you to say you weren't being contracted because you're black—

well, actually you're half black, which puts you in a different cast-ing category altogether."

Why is he taking their side?

"Kennedy, they could have changed the storyline, they could have scratched the storyline altogether, or maybe they decided that you just weren't a good fit with whatever it was they had com-ing down the pipeline."

Pipeline? I reach for my tote and re-knot my scarf. *Wasn't he the one who said I have what it takes to make it, that I'm so goddamn gor-geous, that I'm the Next Big Thing?*

"Sometimes when we're juggling so many characters and story-lines we realize that the pieces don't fit together the way we thought they would. And the puzzle pieces don't have color."

"Everything has color, Sam." I look away, realizing I'm fighting the urge to unleash the little Negro finger and her second cousin, the Infamous Neck Roll. So I shoulder my tote, swing my door open, and hustle out of the car. Winston's door flies open, and as he's prepping to step onto the sidewalk, Sam beats him there.

"Where're you going?" Sam says, grabbing my arm.

"Home! I don't want to overstay my welcome." I look up into his glassy eyes. "Thanks for dinner—and for the ride."

"You're just gonna end the evening this way?"

"I'm not ending anything. It just ended itself!"

"This is silly, Kennedy. We had a good time tonight."

Silly?! MY TRUTH ISN'T SILLY! "It was fine," I say, acknowledg-ing the residents entering the building behind me with a forced smile.

"A minute ago it was fantastic; now it's just fine?" Sam's face is rigid and I can't recall any of its familiar warmth. "Look, get in the car and let's discuss whatever this is that's got you so upset. I know it can't be because *All My Children* didn't hire you."

"That has nothing to do with it."

The music video director's words slice my soul as he tells me to "shake 'em harder, ma. Make it bounce, ma—jiggle on the beat, ma." I feel the wetness lodged in the corner of my eyelid. I swipe at it. I'm quite sure they never told Sam to "Make it clap!"

I step into the distance between us anyway. *This isn't how this is supposed to go.* Attempting to slow everything down and explain my position with what little dignity I have left, I profess, "You could never understand how devastating it was for me to get the call that I'd been dropped. It was really hard."

But Sam just stares down at me, opting to not say a word this time.

Say something! But the seconds drag on. "I think I'd better go."

He looks past me. "Yeah, I think that's a good idea." He turns around and walks toward the car.

"Well, good night, Mr. Cohen," I call out to him.

"Ms. Lee," he replies without affect and slides into the car. Winston preps to shut his door.

"Sam!"

The door slams.

Sam.

He doesn't look back.

Chapter 20

Just ten more seconds. Nine. Eight. My heart is racing, my palms clammy. I fumble with my door key. *What does he know? Seven. Six. He can't possibly understand what it's like to be on The Negro Grind.* Slamming my front door, I fly through my hallway overcome with angst. In my haste I manage to put the chain on—just in case. *Five. Four. Three.* I whip around the corner to the half bath. *Two.* Without bothering to close or lock the door, I flip the seat up and bow down to the toilet bowl, jabbing my finger past my tonsils. *He doesn't even know what The Chitlin Circuit is.* My eyes glaze over when rumblings of soup and roughage rush toward my tongue. With each gag my guts splash into the toilet water. *You don't know my truth.* With each heave the bowl fills with my subconscious diet. *You're never going to be good enough. You're never going to be thin enough. You're never going to be . . . ENOUGH!* I thrust my fingers down my throat again and only stop when I feel endorphins kick in and a flash of euphoria surge through me. I buckle to my knees. *I am not my mother.*

Chapter 21

My apartment door rattles. "Sweets, can we come in?" I hear Hannah yell from the front door. I yank the air freshener from behind the hamper and spray. "Sweets!!"

The icy water feels good against my sticky face. "Coming!" I yell back, flushing the toilet. The girl in the mirror stares back at me with sad eyes. *It's okay; it was a rough day.* She deserves forgiveness.

I tighten the Scope and dab my face dry before running to unleash the door.

"Happy birthday to you, Happy birthday to you, Happy birth—" Hannah stops singing and cups my face in her hands. "What's wrong? Are you okay? You look like you've been crying." Her hands slide down my arms.

"No, I'm fine," I only partially lie, finally starting to feel settled inside. Balanced. Normal.

"Well, rumor has it that you've been porking our birthday

away," Brittany muses with an open bottle of champagne in her hand and a diamond tiara on her head. "Start dishing, and it better be good, cuz you already stood us up for sushi at Nobu and you know Mama loves her some yellowtail sashimi with jalapeño and squid pasta with garlic sauce and . . ."

My twisted insides attempt to tune her out.

"Yeah, Sweets, and I missed my rock shrimp tempura and black cod with miso," Hannah cosigns, oblivious to my PTPD (post traumatic *purge* disorder).

I snatch the glass of warm water sitting on the countertop and guzzle. "I'm sorry, really I am. But trust me it wasn't all ecstasy and orgasms on this side either."

"Well, what exactly have you been doing since I talked to you a few hours ago?" Bug asks, glancing at the bathroom door.

I sideswipe her and pull it shut as soon as they begin to buzz about my apartment, fiddling through music and torching assorted soy candles.

"And why are there hints of Febreze and Hugo Boss running through your place?" Britt asks, both hands on her heavyweight waist.

Hannah shoots her an "off-limits" glare and Britt turns up her head, swigging her Veuve instead.

"I told you that dick would send her over! She should've eased into the booty-clappin' cuz now her whole hormonal balance is fucked," she whispers loudly to Bug. "Seriously, you shouldn't screw with the Pussy pH." She rifles through my cabinets until she finds two more champagne flutes.

I flop down on the couch. "I think I may have gotten myself blackballed from the entire soap opera industry," I finally confess, and take the rest of Britt's glass of bubbly to the head.

"Just tell me one thing," Hannah demands gently as she nestles in to coddle me on the cushy couch. "Did. You. Fuck. Him . . . *too*?"

I slam the empty glass onto the coffee table.

"Oh, God! YOU DID!" Hannah shrieks, jumping up from the couch as I nosedive into the sofa cushion. "Holy Dicks, Batman!" She begins pacing around my living room. "Okay, okay, just breathe." She zens herself a deep breath. "Now there's gotta be a way we can fix this," she laments, throwing her arms into the air. "CAN YOU HEAR ME?!"

Brittany noshes on a handful of snap peas. "I'm pretty sure our Bridge and Tunnel neighbors heard you."

I begin laughing uncontrollably. Hannah rushes the couch.

"What's funny?" She winces. "Is this part of the breakdown?"

I grab her by her shirtsleeve. "No, no, Bug, I didn't have sex with Sam." I pull her into me and wipe my runny eyes with her cuff.

"You really didn't, or you more like Clinton/Lewinsky didn't?"

"No! I, Kennedy Sun Lee, didn't!"

"Oh. Well, okeydokey then." She recovers, kneeling on the patchwork throw rug beside me. "Then that means whatever it is, it can be fixed."

"I don't think so."

"Please start from the beginning and clue me in cuz where I left off you were the *Post*'s answer to rehab and you'd totally hurled all over Blond Boy, who you'd coincidentally caught nippling Cher—*just Cher*." She stops to take a long gulp from her glass. "Things get a little hazy for me after that: dinner with your boss, his kissable lips, and now him blackballing you?" She props me up beside her and attempts to hide her grimace.

We talked through another bottle of birthday Veuve and by the time Britt popped the third, she was belting out Katy Perry's "I Kissed a Girl" from my fifth-floor living-room window. And I still had no new insight into anything at all.

"But you can't really think he's a racist, Sweets, can you?" Hannah asks seriously.

"No, I don't think he's an outright racist, but some sensitivity training—"

"Let's keep it one hundred!" Britt barks. "Who fucking cares what he said or what he meant. You need to just focus on your money cuz you're one short phone call away from being called a video ho—again," Britt says, trying to console me. "Video *vixen* my ass; Quincy could've kept that shit."

"He called me dumb," I interrupt, trying to reconnect with my anger.

"No, he didn't, Sweets." Hannah pats my knee like I'm a poodle. "He said you weren't making any sense."

"You really need to man-up, Annie, cuz if *his* truth makes your bony ass cry, you'll never survi—"

"I'm nowhere near skinny, not compared to those girls on set."

"Here you go! I really can't stomach this shit again about how it's professional suicide for you to eat a fucking french fry. And please don't start preaching to me about the camera adding ten goddamn pounds. I can't listen to that shit tonight and I shouldn't have to. It's my birthday, too, bitches!"

"I'm just saying, those girls aren't retro Mary Kate skinny," I try to clarify.

"Nicole Bitchy Richie skinny?" Hannah-Bug queries.

I nod vehemently.

"You mean pre-preggers?" Britt challenges. "Cuz chick been gettin' it in lately."

"I know, right," Hannah agrees. "A complete one eighty."

I clear my throat. "HELLLOOO?!"

"Oh, Sweets, but you're perfect," Hannah encourages. "I don't know how you deal with the pressure; I'd die without food."

"Dumb girls do every day—DIE, that is! Did you know they even have a full name for it—first, middle, and last?!" She eyes me bitterly and twists her neck into a slinky. "Introduciiinnnnggg . . . Miss Anorexia Bulimia Nervosa!"

"Kill it, Brittany!" Hannah commands. "I mean it!"

Britt pours herself another glass and refreshes mine. "Look, Annie, first of all you're not fat, hell, you're not even thick. Most of the time you look like a nine-year-old boy."

"Your point?!" Hannah scolds.

"Right." She recovers. "Now, I wouldn't go all out and say you're perfect, but maybe, sometimes, occasionally, you can be borderline fabulous," she says decidedly, gulping her drink. "But nothing said in this Kumbaya circle matters if you don't start believing it. Me and you—flesh of the same flesh, blood of the same blood, Baby Girl. We've been to hell and back, looked death in the face on more than one occasion. And laughed. But having you as my side-chick for the last dirty thirty—well, let's just say I could've done worse." She raises her glass to me but before I can clink drinks, hers is gone. "Ahhh." She releases a sigh, and then continues. "But you really need to decide how you wanna roll. YOU were the one who wanted to get off the bench and scrimmage with the Big Girls last night—you know, when you were dry humping the bar in your push-up bra."

Hannah glares at Britt.

"Well?!" She zips up her juicy Giuseppe Zanotti snakeskin boots. "I'm just sayin'."

Hannah rubs my thigh softly. "Marquee with us for birthday libations?"

I shake my head into an *I can't*. "I need to be ready for tomorrow. I still don't wanna disappoint him." I surrender for the first time all night. "Bug, he said he believes in me."

"He's not the only one."

"I bet he won't even meet up with me tomorrow. I mean, the way we left it I'm sure he doesn't want to have anything to do with—"

"If he knows what's good for him, he will. Just wait and see. I mean, really, has he *seen* you?!" Hannah says, lightening the mood, then pulls out an Around-the-World antique snap.

I exhale into her love.

"Now, who's the Prize?"

"I'm the Prize," I say dryly.

"Who in control?"

"We in control," I respond blandly.

"That was sad, just sad."

"Sorry." I drop my head into my hands. "I really shouldn't have implied that he couldn't relate."

"Honey, please, he probably *can't* relate; he's a rich white man running a super successful show who happens to be fucking hot!" Britt declares.

"You know what he looks like?!" Hannah and I both exclaim, turning toward Britt.

"Of course I do; he wins an Emmy almost every year. He's one of the sexiest men runnin' Daytime."

"You watch the Emmys?"

"There's still so much you bitches don't know about me."

Chapter 22

"Hel-lo!" I grog into the cordless telly that is halfway hidden beneath my pillow.

"Morning, Annie! This is your first and final wake-up call. Oh, and if you want a ride into work on this fantastically frigid morning I suggest you get your bony ass up and outta bed. My car will be here for pickup in exactly twenty."

My eyes fight to open. "Why are you just calling me now to tell me this?"

"Dunno." The line goes dead.

In overdrive, I jump into the shower while the coffee brews, quickly going over my lines in my head. There is barely enough time for me to cower in fear about the day that is ahead. I hear the telly shrill again. I shut my eyes tight and visualize a skinnier version of me answering it. I place my feet together and slide my hand between my thighs to ensure that there is still ample space between them. There is—even though they look like cellulite Snausages to me. On the pad in the medicine cabinet (beside the diet pills and next to the laxatives), I jot down 114.3 beside today's date and nervously compare it to yesterday's weight: 114.

MOOOO, Skinny Cow taunts. "Chop, chop! Three minutes!" Britt's pitch stings from the answering machine. I cover my ears with both hands.

"SHUT UP!" I scream into the mirror.

I pop two Zenadrine, throw a black cashmere Kangol on my damp bedhead, and slink into my Chip & Peppers and yesterday's wifebeater before I tiptoe to the fridge.

I crouch down to the veggie bin and feel around beneath the garlic and red peppers. My hand begins to shake as I dig my fingers deep inside. My eyes glass over when I pull my fingers from my lips. *Euphoria.* The red velvet cake is ecstasy, melting seductively in my mouth. As I lick the cream cheese frosting from my fingertips, I am alive for a few indulgent seconds—right before my arm begins to twitch from sudden guilt. Grossed out, I close the foil and hide the cake behind the cucumbers and asparagus tips.

I am strong. I am strong. I AM NOT—

I look at the pale five-foot-nine reflection of the beautiful disaster staring back at me in the mirror. With my tote in one hand and the steaming coffee mug in the other, I force a smile and fistfight another urge to purge my delicious morning mini-treat. *This time I win!* I think, as I hurriedly grab my motorcycle jacket and the double-layered woolly scarf on my way out the door. She smiles back. *YOU ARE THE PRIZE!*

"Why the rush?" Britt calls out to me as I clumsily round the corner to meet her at the elevator banks. "We've got plenty of time."

I ignore her morning attempt at sarcastic wit and try to collect myself. "Thanks for the ride." I can't help but notice how impeccably fab she looks in her Dior suit as I wipe away the sweat and hair-drip mixture that is inching its way down my face.

Chapter 23

"I can't find my badge anywhere, Ernie," I say to the security manager as I frantically search through my satchel of stuff, terrified that I'll be late plopping into Trinity's Chair for my AM face beatdown. I look up at him with pleading eyes thinking that, like everyone else at ANS, he'd be happy if I found employment doing my now infamous jig on somebody's bar.

"Oh, that's just fine, Ms. Kennedy. We've got you covered!"

"Me?" I ask, still rumbling through my tote.

"Of course, silly." He grins. "Now, I've called Bert down to personally escort you through," Ernie says, with a smile of shiny dentures that would make Polident proud.

"Right this way, Ms. Lee," Bert sings, shuffling as we make our way through the building maze, past a crowded talk show audience and onto the elevator.

I fumble to find my script, eerily aware that Bert hasn't stopped crooning at me.

"This weather sure is somethin', huh, Ms. Lee? Hope you stay bundled up good out there; wouldn't want you to catch a bug."

I fight my desire to inquire about this sudden shuck-and-jive show when yesterday he wouldn't even acknowledge me. "No, Bert, we wouldn't want that," I say, exiting the lift.

Surging down the corridor I notice everyone tossing glances at me. I quickly check to make sure I haven't been caught in an ill-timed nipple-slip. I round the corner to the dragon's lair and overhear, "All I know is that Trinity told me that Natalya told her that Bliss told her that Ed the Camera Man told her that Jesse James told him that Jack—" The room is silenced when they look up and see me trying to decode the gossip.

"Uh, hi Kennedy!" Natalya, a ravishing Russian principal, who's been playing Bliss's assistant and partner in crime for the last three years, interrupts. "You go ahead; I'll wait till you're done." She hustles to her feet and snatches off her makeup smock, clearly in the middle of her coveted beatdown.

"No, it's fine; you were here first. I can wait." I frown at Trinity, who purses her lips and looks the other way.

"No, I wouldn't hear of it. I aaabsssolutely insist," she urges, in far too energetic a tone for someone who sour-pussed me yesterday.

As Natalya moves in record speed to gather her script, Trinity rolls her eyes into her faux-hawk and baton twirls her foundation brush through her fingers with precision.

"I'll be in my dressing room, T. Just call for me when you're done, 'kay," she says, and rushes toward the door. "Ooh, and I love your belt," Natalya declares, pointing at my waist. "And those cowgirl boots are divine!"

"Uh—"

"And if you ever wanna grab lunch, I know a great Italian place that has the yummiest tiramisu."

As if she'd ever.

"We can totally dish about ANS stuff." She winks, then raises her left brow with immense interest before leaving me with a handful of finger tootles.

Trinity points the makeup brush at the chair. "Still damp," she says, running her veiny fingers through my hair. "I'll dry you out before I pat your face down," she says starkly.

I turn around to look at her. "Can I ask you something?"

She doesn't answer.

"What's going on with everyone today? I mean, first it was Bert and Ernie, then the Russian. Are they always like this? Was I just too out of it yesterday to notice?"

She plugs the Conair into the socket and blasts it into my earlobe without saying a word. I try to make eye contact with her through blades of flying hair, but she forcibly nudges my head into my chest.

"Thanks for the *Extreme* Makeover; I know I was far from my best this morning," I joke with her after our session and three sugary greetings from cast members later. "My sister woke me up late, offering me a ride in so I didn't really get to—"

"Yep, it's my job," she interrupts, turning her back to page Natalya. "Enjoy your new dressing room, especially the cushy casting couch," she quips, just as Izzie pokes her head into the tense space.

"All done in here, Kennedy?"

"Yeah, one sec, though, Izzie." I turn back toward Trinity. "What's that supposed to mean? What casting couch? And what dressing room? You know I don't even have a—"

"Actually," Izzie clarifies, "that's why I came—to show you to your new dressing room."

"When did that happen?" I look back and forth between Izzie and Trinity.

"Humph," Trinity jibes.

Izzie shrugs her shoulders. "All set?"

"I guess."

"Great! Right this way," she pipes and bolts from the room as quickly as she bounced in.

I turn back to check for Trinity again, but she is meticulously cleaning her station, deliberately denying me any leftover sista-girl love.

Chapter 24

"Well, here we are," Izzie announces, skipping past all the principal dressing rooms to a secluded suite in an adjoining wing at the corner end of the yellow-brick hall.

"What's this?" I ask, clenching my tote to my chest. "I thought everything was taken." Looking around I notice there are no other rooms on this wing besides the control suite that is connected directly to Sam's booth.

"It's your new dressing room. Duh!" Izzie answers, wryly, pointing to the plated sign on the oak door with my name etched into it.

"But where is everyone else? And why am I all the way over here in a completely separate country?"

"You must have done something right." She smirks into a giggle and turns the key to open the door. "Welcome to the A Suite, your new home away from home."

She opens the double doors and a golden glow envelops the room.

"I know, she's something else." Izzie sighs into the atmosphere, taking it in with adulation. "Used to belong to Annabelle T. Covington."

"Who?"

Izzie throws her head back in delight and shakes out her ponytail, letting out a rambunctious laugh—a total *Falcon Crest* moment. "She was the executive producer of one of the longest-running daytime soaps in television." She juts her chest out, overcome with pride. "Legend has it that she was also the daughter of the richest oil tycoon in Arizona." She shrugs. "Never knew they had oil in Arizona." Izzie steps back into the doorway. "And even though it's been updated, it never seems to lose the Annabelle touch—designed it herself." Izzie declares, settling into a satisfied smile. "She's all yours now," Izzie proclaims, handing me the key. "Enjoy!"

The old world Hollywood-esque dressing room is breathtakingly worthy of a vintage voiceover from Robin Leach. Luxuriously appointed with fabric-covered walls, a crystal chandelier, French-school paintings, and a marble fireplace whose mantel is topped with the most delicate flowers I've ever seen. The suite looks like something out of a magazine. Every piece of furniture is so fantastic, I can't fathom why it isn't all covered in plastic.

"An ornate gold mirror, two light bars, and a wall-length vanity? Izzie, seriously, who was this woman?" I ask as I fall into the plush sofa set in the center of it all.

"Like, television royalty." She sighs and plops down beside me. When I look over at her she immediately jumps up and re-ponys her tail. "Sorry."

"Is this the cushy couch Trinity was referring to?"

"Don't think so," Izzie continues, unfazed. "Now, you've got your fridge against the wall next to the flatscreen. It's already been outfitted with all the standard goodies. Then over there you've got your top of the line setup for Playstation, your TiVo and high-speed Internet access. And the room is completely soundproof, so no one will ever hear what's going on in here." She giggles, making me slightly uncomfortable.

"Izzie."

"Through that sliding door, there's a marble bathroom with a steam room and a sauna, if that's your thing," she finishes, and studies me quizzically before turning to leave.

"Izzie!" I yell through her ecstasy trip.

"Huh?"

"No way, José. This can't be *my* room!" I protest. "I thought I was gonna share space with Bliss, not that I actually thought she'd ever let that happen, but you know what I mean." I plead with her for an inch of understanding. "What's really going on?" I look around the room slowly then back at her.

"Look, I don't make the decisions. My job is to execute and my last directive was to get you situated in Annabelle's—I mean, the A Suite. So," she says, taking a deep breath and shoving her specs up her nose, "here you go!"

"Just let the cat outta the bag already; this *can't* all be for me. I'm Newspaper Girl!"

"I'm totally positive that it's all for you; there's been no mistake."

"Please, Izzie. *Pretty* please."

She looks at me with empathy, then down to the floor, then back up at me.

"With whipped cream and cherries on top," I beg.

"Okay, okay," she begins in a hushed tone. "Early this morning, I mean *early* this morning—like before the sun came up early—Jack blasted our BlackBerries, obsessively clear about every detail down to the number of bottled waters that were to be stocked in your bins."

"But—"

"I gotta go; I've already said too much."

"Izzie, why would—"

"Now, your shooting schedule and any script revisions will be left in your box outside your door," Izzie says hurriedly, "but Marge is waiting for you in Wardrobe and you'll need to be on set for blocking as soon as you're done." She opens the door to leave. "Oh, yeah, and one more thing—I've been instructed to tell you that your lunch will be brought in for you whenever you want so there'll be no need for you to have to go for it, which by default now makes me your very own gofer."

"But I thought you said only executive staff got that courtesy."

"Yeah, well, apparently things change fast around here," she says breathily, and promptly closes the door behind her.

"And you're sure you didn't fuck him?" Britt quizzes me, after her assistant patches me through.

"As if! I'm no mattress actress and Jack is sooo not fuckable."

"And you didn't slide him any monetary motivation?" She slurps in my ear, indifferent that I can hear her swallow.

"Of course not!"

"I'm just sayin', you seem to enjoy giving money away to the men over there in Destiny."

Why did I dial her? I knew better. When Hannah's cell went to voice mail I should've just journaled. It would've been far less a waste of time. "I told you I confronted him about my seventy-five bucks."

"Well, good luck with that, Annie."

"You're not helping. And I need help!"

"Yes, I know. But whining doesn't become you."

"Just tell me why on earth would Jack give me this suite? It's *Good Housekeeping* on steroids!"

"Keep your friends close and your enemies—"

"Maybe you're on to something; he totally HATES me and when I said—"

"Ooh, Annie, gotta go; Chuck Bass just walked in. XOXO."

Chapter 25

"But I don't understand, Marge. Please tell me what's going on around here."

Marge hands me a magnificent magenta Betsey Johnson silk

pleated minidress with a deep front V-neck and an open back. And I fall in love at first sight with the ruby-red sparkling pumps.

"So," I tread lightly, knowing she is my last hope. "I kind of need a few answers and I know that *everyone* knows that you know everything there is to know around here."

Marge eyes me delicately. "All righty, dear," Marge surrenders, as she softly shoves her banana-yellow Croc against the door. She whirls me around to zip Betsey. "Where'd you go when you left here last night?" she asks pointedly—no chaser.

Immediately I lose my air. I shut my eyes and see Sam on the corner comfortably puffing away on his Marlboro and Jack clutching both his LV girly pack and my reputation in his Nancy Drew hands. My head begins to spin and I hear that familiar bass line quietly revving up between my ears. Jack the Rat!

"This may be a big show, dear, but it's a small cast and an even tighter crew, and gossip around here is the preferred pastime."

"But Marge," I whisper nervously, "nothing happened. We just talked."

Marge motions for me to twirl around in the couture.

"But—but—what exactly is he telling people happened last night?" I murmur into her ear, terrified of *his* truth.

"All I know is that rumor has it that Jack saw you and Sam getting quite cozy on that corner. Then Jack, well, being Jack, paid his cabbie to keep the meter running and sat curbside while he watched you two get cuddly in the back booth of the Gotham Café. I believe you ordered an arugula salad and a cup of vegetable soup, all before you two hopped into Sam Cohen's limo—*together.*"

"Jack the Rat stalked us?"

EW!

Chapter 26

I light the Capri as fast as I can, not minding the brisk breeze that seems to tornado into high winds with each passing puff. I tighten my jacket around my wardrobe robe and choke my neck with my scarf. My head is pounding, my hands are trembling, and my ears are bruising red. Nevertheless, there's still absolutely nowhere else I'd rather be than sucking back tar and nicotine next to this neon orange industrial garbage can.

I pull on the ciggie again and think to myself that I may as well toss my reputation in said garbage can, since it *has* already been trashed. Jack the Rat and his rumor mill have seen to that! The cancer stick is almost burning my fingertips when I finally chuck it aside, along with any realistic thoughts of being able to withstand the next thirteen weeks of my stay at *America's Next Sweetheart*—more like America's Next Sour Tart!

My watch taunts me. 11:05. It screams even louder that SAM! ISN'T! COMING! *So much for our clandestine meeting, I think. He's still miffed at me for making assumptions about his success. But having the girl-nads to just say it to his face? What was I thinking; nobody talks to the Big Boss like that!*

I look at my watch again. Still 11:05. I pull out my lighter and dedicate this next cig to pushing Sam out of my mind completely.

"Isn't that supposed to be my job?"

When I look up from my Capri, Sam is standing beside the Dumpster in a Yankees cap and a Mets T-shirt that's halfway tucked into a pair of jeans that look like they were custom-fitted for his frame. I take a deep breath but don't say a word; instead, I watch him as he shifts from side to side. He follows my gaze and looks down at his shirt. "Yankees, Mets, I can never decide," he rambles, and zips his leather bomber.

"I—I thought you weren't coming," I stammer, looking past him to see if he'd been followed.

"Don't worry, I came alone," he whispers into a smile. "And I took the long way—the scenic route."

"Oh," I say, letting a small smile escape my mouth.

"It's nice to see that."

"What?"

"Your smile."

"Oh, this old thing; I've had it for years."

Sam lights his cigarette and grabs my hand. "Come on; follow me."

"Where are we going? I've gotta be on set for blocking in ten." I catch up to him as he slides through two big trucks in the driveway and onto the fire escape of the building next door. I watch him climb the stairs, taking two at a time, until he reaches the top. "Are you serious?" I call out to him, still in full pursuit in my distressed retro cowgirl boots.

"You're almost there," he says, reaching out to grab my hand and pull me onto the rooftop with him.

"What are you doing?" I look around the empty industrial deck.

"Giving us a little privacy; I remembered what you said about not wanting to be seen with me."

"I didn't put it like that, exactly," I say, still out of breath. "And why are we on somebody else's roof?"

"This way I can look over and see who's coming and going. I like to watch." He blushes two shades of mischievous red. "You'd be surprised at some of the stuff I see from up here."

"What about the people who own this building?" I ask haughtily, and peek over the edge of the two-story building.

"I think the guy is pretty cool."

"The last thing I need today is a trespassing violation."

"The owner would give you a pass; I have a feeling he'd be into you."

"Okay, so I'm obviously not so smooth on the uptake. This is you?" I connect, finally catching on.

"Yeah, well, I'm just one of the owners." He leans against the railing that encloses the deck. "It was on the market a while back so we bought it," he explains, glancing over the rail. "It was supposed to house my film company, but it's kind of just been sitting here," he says, sullenly.

"I see."

"So, uh, Kennedy, listen." He turns toward me with pensive eyes. "About last night . . . I just wanna say that I may have been out of line and well—"

"It's fine, really. I mean, you weren't alone out there; I was definitely an equal and willing participant in that." I look down at the specks of gray in the black tar. "I've been thinking a lot about it and I shouldn't have said, you know, what I said about you never having to work hard for anything and having everything handed to you."

"You never said that."

"Yeah, well . . ."

"I admit, I can never know what it's like being you, but when I look at you I just can't imagine it being so bad."

"My point exactly, Sam; you'll never know."

He takes a deep breath and adjusts the baseball cap on his head. "But there are some things that you don't understand either. Everything isn't always so black-and-white, Gorgeous."

"We come from different worlds and—"

"And I'd like to hear more about yours." He touches his fingertip to mine.

Oh.

"Would you be up for that?"

"I don't really know if that's such a good idea." I turn around to face him head on. "There's an entire cast and crew in there that think I got this job and that new dressing room because I've been, well, fucking for tracks."

"You've been—"

"Vernacular."

"Fucking for—?"

"Hooking up!" I explain. "Like the skanky singer who'll do anything to claw her way to the top, Jack told everyone that he saw us last night and that I'm fucking for—that we're *hooking up*," I stress, annoyed again.

"Because he saw us standing on the corner?"

"No, because he parked in his taxi and spied on us all night until we left with Winston."

Sam mushes his Marlboro into the tar.

"So everybody's tweaking out, not talking to me like normal. It's like they all caught the vapors."

"The vay—"

I look at him sideways. "Keep up, Sam."

"Trying." He rubs his hand against the back of his neck. "Are you sure you're not just being hypersensitive because of everything that happened yesterday?"

"Why do you think everything is always in my head?" I take a step back.

"You do make a lot of assumptions," he says mindfully.

"Sam, you sit in your booth on top of your world and you have no idea what it's like down here where I am." I feel my blood sizzle so I turn away from him. "I know what I feel and I know what I see. . . ."

"Hey—"

"But maybe you're already too removed to get that."

"Intense," he says, taking a step toward me, closing the gap. "But I'm here." He reaches out and squares my shoulders. "And

I'm listening." He slides his fingers down my arm and rests his hand next to mine.

"So what can I do to make it better?"

"Nothing; there's nothing you can do. And it's probably just better if we don't talk for a while—I mean like this," I say, looking around the remote rooftop.

"Is that what you really want?"

"Well, no, but they're all saying—"

"That you're fucking for tracks?" I watch him furrow his brows then slowly slip into a grin.

"I'm serious, Sam."

"Intense."

"You didn't want to be a cliché, remember?"

I stand in frigid silence and shiver. Without hesitation he slides out of his bomber and slips it around my shoulders. I snuggle into it.

"So I did notice that you got a new dressing room today; should've made you feel better," he whispers over my head, just above my ear.

"No, it didn't; that's actually what started it all," I fume. "I'm sure Jack thought that by giving me the keys to the Fantasy Suite that he'd either get on your good side, cuz he thinks I'm your Monica, or that he'd put me on blast and get everyone gossiping cuz, again, he thinks I'm your Monica."

Sam takes a step back and starts to furiously bite down on his bottom lip. His face is solemn. He rubs his fingers against his barely-there beard that appears to have been given extra attention today.

"My Monica?"

"As in—"

"I get that one." He looks distraught. "So you don't like the dressing room?"

"Are you kidding? It effing rocks! But there's just no way I can ever be taken seriously around here, especially by the cast cuz now everyone thinks I'm just your—"

"Monica." He removes his baseball cap and shoves it back on. "Oh boy!" Sam shakes his head in disbelief.

"What?"

"Well, if you didn't hate me after last night, you're definitely gonna hate me now."

"Uh-oh; my ears are itching. I don't like the way this sounds."

"Jack isn't the one responsible for assigning you Annabelle's suite."

"Sam, please tell me you didn't!"

"Well?"

"Sam?!"

"It's just that you were so upset about not having a dressing room yesterday—I mean you were *really* upset! So when I got home I called Jack and told him exactly what I wanted you to have—the Annabelle Suite with all the amenities." I look into his pleading stare. "I just wanted to make it better for you. And truthfully I thought it would do Bliss some good to see that she's not—"

"But you were so mad at me when you left last night."

"Yeah, well, let's just say that I calmed down somewhere between SoHo and the Upper East Side," he explains. "And I wasn't upset with you as much as I wasn't prepared for you."

A chill shoots up my spine. I swallow. "And now?"

"I'm here."

"I'm glad you didn't fire me," I admit meekly.

"What is it with you? Do you just choose not to listen to what I say? I thought I told you yesterday that I'm not going to fire you."

"You did but I just thought that after—"

"Fucking intense." He laughs. "This can't be good for our relationship."

"Employer—employ—"

"Shh," he quiets me, putting his finger to my shivering lip. "I can see you're going to be quite a challenge."

He slides his hand over mine and I feel my heart dance.

"So what do we do now?" I finally ask, as we straddle each other's personal space on the rooftop where Sam once planned to build his dreams.

He brushes my cheek with the back of his hand. "It's your call. And you have my word that I'll follow your lead."

"Somehow I find that impossible to believe."

Chapter 27

I pull at the steel doors and enter Studio 26 with renewed focus. The pep talk Sam delved into on our way down the fire escape was on repeat in my mind. "The camera loves you and soon all of America will, too."

When I realize Smith the Director and Jack haven't finished the blocking for a restaurant scene on one of the adjoining sets, I discreetly head over to the craft service table for a cup of coffee. My energy is waning and I know I'm long overdue for a workout. A fat dose of endorphins would serve me well.

Squeezing in a quick run at The Sports Club after taping today is what I'm thinking about when I spy Jesse James lurking on the other end of the smorgasbord. Fireflies swarm in my belly; I know he's already been put in rotation on the rumor mill.

"You don't waste any time, do you? I guess you figured that sleeping with the star of the show wasn't good enough, so you went straight to the top."

When I turn to walk away from him, he grabs me by the elbow with the force of a bitter man, digging his fingernails into my skin.

"OW!" I shriek under my breath.

"I'm more annoyed with myself though," he seethes into my ear. "I actually fell for all that sweet innocence—crying crocodile tears outside my dressing room because Big Bad Bliss hurt your feelings." He takes an intimidating step closer. "I guess you showed her; now you've got God on speed dial."

I snatch my elbow away from Jesse and spin around to face him, suddenly overcome with fear. "I don't know what you're talking about."

"Cut the shit, Sexy."

"Jesse—"

"Even the janitor knows you fucked Mr. Cohen last night. But I'm not mad at your plan; I'm just disappointed in myself for underestimating you. I can usually spot them before they ever see me coming."

"Like you did with me?" I lash back.

"You wanted it."

"You took advantage of the situation."

"That's not what you were saying when you were screaming out my name!"

"Are you high?"

Jesse scowls.

"For the record, nothing happened between me and Sam!"

"Oh, Sam, is it?" He reaches out and rolls the ends of my hair between his fingers. "I just wonder if you told him about *our* special time together. I think he should know that his newest starlet pulled a two-in-one, a doubleheader—giving me head in the morning and hitting him off later that same night."

"EW! And it didn't go down that way. Nothing happened—

really," I force the words out of my mouth, through infuriation, scanning for gawkers.

"Right, and that's how you got the A Suite that hasn't been used since Donatella Versace made a guest appearance on the show last year," he challenges smugly. "You must've given him some powerful brain, because like I said before, all I got was potential." I shudder. "Now, Sexy, what are we going to do about our little situation? Looks like we're gonna have to put our heads together and come up with a plan that works for both of us, unless of course, you've already told Mr. Cohen that you stepped out of bed with me and into his with him."

"D-did you tell anyone that?"

"You mean did I tell anyone that after your striptease on the bar you told me to meet you at your place thirty minutes later after your friends left? Is that what you're talking about? Or are you referring to the naked lap dance on your couch? Or after that, when you did things to me that I've only seen done in some of my favorite amateur porn?" Jesse James takes a step back. "Or did you mean the part about conveniently forgetting it all, including my name, after five sweaty hours of manic, tantric sex?"

"Jesse, please," I beg, feeling my bones rattle.

"You were quite good at begging that night, too, now that I think about it."

"Don't. Just don't—I'm asking you," I press through tightened lips. I feel sick.

Unable to take his mean provocations any longer I reach for a chocolate éclair and bolt toward my dressing room. Jesse James leans against the railing with an eerie expression that rivals doom. Then he smiles.

Gripping my tote, I creep down the yellow-brick hall and tiptoe toward the A Suite. Sam is in his booth watching monitors while Smith the Director positions the actors on set below. I lean against my door and watch him work, wondering what he's thinking. Our eyes lock when he looks up to see me studying him. The corners of his mouth turn up into a wishful grin. He winks. I click my heels three times and secretly wish I could press rewind.

Chapter 28

I AM SO HIGH.

My runner's high kicked in somewhere around mile four. Boom. Boom. Boom. Boom. The pulse beneath my feet is in sync with my heartbeat. Boom. Boom. Boom. My eyelids are half closed and my lungs are wide open. *I am a machine.* My body is at war with my own mind. *My mind is losing.* The sweat trickles into my mouth from my upper lip. I glance down at the treadmill: 8.72 miles. I run harder. The fact that I've burned in excess of eight hundred calories makes me feel stronger. In control. The thought of Jesse James—*not so much.* My legs begin to burn. I run anyway. Boom. Boom. Boom. I run from yesterday. I run from today. I run tomorrow's lines in my mind to the rhythm of my Nike Frees against the conveyor belt. Limp Bizkit screams in my ear. *HE DID IT ALL FOR THE NOOKIE!*

I try to bury the second half of the day I've had somewhere behind mile nine. Jesse's veiled threats came back to scare me every time Smith the Director yelled "CUT!" "How badly do you want your job, Sexy?" he'd said without elaborating. "How bad, Sexy?" he'd said without hesitating. It was his afternoon song. I couldn't figure out if he wanted me to service him, to be his Pretty Woman, his beck-and-call girl. I fill my lungs with air, completely aware that the last two cigs I'd smoked were beginning to slow me down. *Smoking sucks. I needed that seventy-five bucks.* I extend my stride and settle into a painful glide. *That came out of my iPhone fund!* My fight-or-flight tells me to run. Kanye tells me to run—HARDER, BETTER, FASTER, STRONGER. I run, even though I know I can't outrun The Outlaw. I run until my mind finds . . . BLISS. *That's it! I'm done!* I flip off my iPod and kill the treadmill. I step down from the workout ledge and buckle over, sweat pouring from my head. I am an absolute mess, my lungs pound feverishly against my chest. Boom. Boom. Boom. Endorphins rush through me, and in that moment I resolve to accept Jack the Rat calling me a "slut" and/or a "whore" much more—much more than I can ever accept Sam receiving an anonymous email, a phone tip, text message, singing telegram, or Morse code memo about me going down on his Golden Boy—not once, not twice, but according to Jesse James the Outlaw, FIVE MANIC TANTRIC TIMES!

Chapter 29

INT. SWEETHEARTS, INC. OFFICES—EVENING

After finishing another late night at the office, Lacey Madison is at her desk gathering the last of her belongings. The opening shot is a tight one of her hands packing her bags. Camera pans out to reveal her face. Audience sees that she is tired but still beautiful. A wide shot of the office shows Blake standing in the doorway watching her, undetected.

BLAKE (*sneaking up behind Lacey at her desk*): Hey you.

LACEY (*caught off guard*): Blake, what are you doing here? It's almost eight.

BLAKE (*moving into her personal space*): I could ask you the same thing.

LACEY (*visibly nervous; trying to keep her cool*): I work here. But I had some things to finish up.

BLAKE (*seductively touching her cheek*): Lining up interviews for me, Lacey? My spot on *Oprah* or *Letterman*?

LACEY (*trying to remain professional*): No, Blake, some personal matters.

BLAKE: Well, I just wanted to personally drop off these new comp cards. And truthfully I was hoping I'd run into you, especially after what you said last night at The Porsche Club.

Blake strokes Lacey's hair. She steps away from him.

LACEY (*quizzically*): But I wasn't at The Porsche Club last night. I was here—working late again, until eleven.

She turns back around to her desk.

BLAKE (*unfazed*): Okay, Lacey, if that's how you want to play it.

He grabs her around the waist and slowly spins her into his arms. She tries to push him away but he holds her tighter. He nudges her hair behind her ear and lets out a soft sigh.

LACEY (*with trembling voice*): Blake, wh-what are you doing?

Trying to remain focused, she nudges him away and smoothes her skirt down.

BLAKE (*unyielding and determined to get his point across, he crosses to her and whispers in her ear*): I feel what you feel. What you said last night is true; we shouldn't deny ourselves. You were so right; no one needs to know, especially Bliss.

LACEY (*confused but clearly turned on by him*): I, I don't know what you're referring to. I told you, I was here until eleven.

He grabs her waist with one hand and the back of her neck with the other and kisses her.

Blake pulls away from Lacey, assessing her response. Her eyes are closed and her lips are slightly parted. He smiles as he bends down to kiss her again, this time lustfully, with obvious heat. She engages him back.

WTF! I feel Jesse James's tongue thrashing around in my mouth and somehow it doesn't entice me to collapse into the throes of passion. All I can think about are the frightening words he jabbed me with yesterday. *How badly do you want your job, Sexy?* As the camera closes in for a tight shot of our mouths I try my best to focus and remember my blocking. I angle my body against his. *How badly do you want your job?* What I want is to kick him in his naughty place; instead I channel all my energy into my new religion: forcing a boner to cameo in five, four, three—*YAHTZEE!* I drag my fingers through his hair and dig my fingernails into his skin. I simulate seduction with a soft sigh followed by a throaty moan. His poky prick stabs into my pelvic bone. I shriek into his mouth when he gropes my A-cup.

"And cut!" Smith the Director yells.

"Cut!" Jack cosigns, with bugged eyes.

I hear the PA switch on. "Um, that was—" Sam rasps before clearing his throat. Everyone looks up, at nothing in particular, awaiting the Voice of God to bestow his opinion upon us. "Quite heated." He shuts off the PA then turns it right back on again. "We're done," he finishes.

"You wanna shoot one more for—" Smith questions him.

"NO!" Sam yells, with urgency, clearly frazzled. "No, uh, that won't be necessary. I'm pretty sure we got it," he says with forced frankness.

"We're moving to the docks, people. Scenes twenty-five through thirty-three. Scenes twenty-five through thirty-three. Need Aleksandra and Diesel to set, plus background, please," the girl over the intercom orders robotically.

I smile down at my tangerine satin Stuart Weitzman stilettos. They smile back. *Things just got interesting!*

Chapter 30

"What the hell was that?" Jesse James rushes me as I step down from the prefab PR office suite.

"I don't know what you're talking about." I'm flying through the air, headed straight for the stairs.

Thrilled to be done shooting for the day and coming down off a massive actor's high I try to stay calm and not let Jesse see me sweat through my Mrs. Butterworth foundation mix.

"You know exactly what I'm talking about. You fucking tried to rape me out there."

"Are you serious?" I feign innocence, but glance back at the diminishing bulge in his pants. Jesse is on my heels and I am determined to escape the wrath of his heated hard-on.

"Don't play dumb; you weren't supposed to, uh, engage me like that."

I rush through a flurry of actors and take the stairs two at a time. "I don't think I took any unnecessary liberties. I was just doing what I thought the scene called for. I'm sorry if you weren't prepped, or if I caused you any, um, embarrassment."

"I can handle my own."

I stop at the top of the stairs and about-face in front of his glare. "Then what's the problem? No one seemed to mind." I study his anger, dismissing the possibility of us ever becoming frenemies. "I thought you were great—smooth, dynamic, sexy—"

"Don't push me, Kennedy. You're in no position," he warns. "One confession to God is all it would take for—"

"Then what do you want from me?"

Before he can answer Izzie motors down the hall and interrupts. "Wow, Kennedy, that was awesome. You guys were mooo-ey H.O.T."

"See." I throw Jesse a faux smile. "You were mooo-ey HAWT."

"Oh, and Kennedy I've got your—" I hold up one finger to her, relieved to have the station break.

Jesse James narrows his eyes at me and whispers something under his breath that sounds eerily similar to a voodoo chant I'd heard on *Charmed* last night. I can feel myself start to unnerve just before he storms off, leaving me shaking in my shiny shoes.

"Sorry, Izzie. You were saying?" I force a recovery.

"Your revised script." She hands it to me. "Quite a few changes and some veeeddy interesting new scenes. Just wanted to give you a heads-up."

"New scenes?" I say, flipping through the pages and hauling ass down the hall on a mission to get to my dressing room.

"Yeah, tons," she says, keeping up. "More lines—more screen time. Looks like a *Face/Off* storyline. Think Travolta before the hair plugs, circa 1997."

Face/Off?

"Not his best work, but . . . or maybe it's twins; either way, you're showing up in *dos* places at *uno* time."

If only everything in my life could be explained away so easily, I'm thinking when she turns to skip away.

"Looks like somebody's name just got slipped into a Soapies slot."

Chapter 31

"Who is it?" I scream at the obsessive knocking on my door. I shove my leg into my cowgirl boot and grab my tote.

"Open the fucking door, *LAYYY-SEEE MAD-I-SSSUN!*"

BLISS!

Fight or flight. FIGHT OR . . . I survey the room.

"You know I can hear you!"

"Uh, one second."

When I swing the door open, the tip of her pointy nose is red and despite the muscle glue in her forehead, I do believe she's trying to scowl.

"What the fuck was that?!"

"What?"

"You know exactly what I'm talking about, Lacey Madison."

Conversations around here were like a very bad game of Password. And I needed more clues.

"You were all over him. You tried to suck his face off. None of that was in the script—"

"Uh, I was just—"

"—that you were supposed to have *studied*. These are THE SOAPS! THE SOAPS!" Her fists are balled and she's stomping her heels into the concrete floor. "We don't operate on whims around here. There's clearly a difference between a polite peck and a vacuum session. Why don't you just blow him already?!"

"I was just—"

"And FYI, he's so not into you. He's sooo NOT—"

"But—"

"—even aware that you exist. You're not even his type—you're b—, you're b—"

"Brunette?" I fold my very brunette arms over my chest.

"Watch your step, *LAYYY-SEEE MAD-I-SSSUN*. There's only room for one Queen Bee around here so keep your honey for the boss's BJs."

I gasp. *The nerve.*

"That's right, suck him off all you want, but stay away from J.J.—if you know what's good for you!" She runs her tongue back and forth over her gums. "But I'd be very careful if I were you; you're playing with fire and you don't even know it," she scoffs. "You're not in reality TV anymore." Bliss snorts so hard her left nostril caves in. Then, as if on cue, it pops right back out.

I flick the lights off and ease past her, forcing her to back into the yellow-brick hall. Shaking my head at her irate performance, I try to tune out the rest of her flagrant threats and wicked warnings. "I'll get you!"

This bitch is nuts. Coke-rages and balloon tits and delusions of grandeur—OH MY!

Chapter 32

TGIF.

"To your first official week on your first soap opera finally being complete," Hannah raises her Naughty Girl, a dark chocolate banana martini, in the seductive air for our first toast of the night.

Hannah, Britt, and I are posted around the posh pool at Plunge, the sleek fifteenth-floor lounge at Manhattan's decadent meatpacking district hotel, Hotel Gansevoort. We'd synced schedules and Hannah had penciled us in for Rihanna's *Naughty Girl* magazine cover party.

"That bouncer outside is ferosh. Asshole might as well make folks whisper a password outside the bathroom stall of The Hog Pit across the street, blindfold them through a secret sliding door, and force them to crawl through the Underground Railroad just to get a fucking drink," Britt rages.

"But you said he was cute."

"Yeah, he could get it." Britt picks up her Nasty Girl, a raspberry-infused piña colada martini, and raises it to us. "Now congrats, Annie. And I was starting to think you weren't woman enough to stomach it through your first week."

"Barely." I sip my Natural Girl, a key lime pie martini that's been rimmed with granola. "But I'm gonna have to step up my endurance game. Sam wasn't playing about me having more of a presence on the show." I bite into an oats and honey crunch. "Might be playing a dual role."

"Dual?" Hannah inquires while waving at Tru Records's head of A&R.

"Maybe twins, maybe long-lost sister, maybe a coincidental look-alike or victim of a Face/Off," I muse, rubbing my hands together. "They're just introducing it—have no idea where they're going."

"Well then, let's toast to you having no idea where the fuck you're going." Britt clinks, crossing her thigh highs beneath her cobalt blue Stella sheath.

"To more screen time and to you living out your dreams," Hannah gushes. "From soap star to superstar! Like Anne Heche and Ricky Martin!"

The night is buzzing with the perfect blend of hipster sophisticate in the Miami-esque scene. The Urbanatti, the movers and shakers and the wannabe hit-makers in every sector of "The Biz," is present and accounted for, drinking in the vibe on the lavishly landscaped rooftop garden and bar. Their ritual dance continues as some mix and mingle while others too-coolly prance. Newbies hold up the periphery, casually checking out the panoramic views of the city. The scene is toxic.

Although Hannah had to make an appearance for work, Britt had begged to tag along to wallpaper the night and see what trouble could be found. "I heard this is going to double as her engagement party," Britt rumors, checking out the gaggle of barely dressed, beautiful broads going gaga over the Cover Girl's beau.

"To Chris?" I inquire, without thought.

"No, Neyo," Hannah pitches to Britt.

"Oooh, how *you* doin'?" she swings. Britt surveys the premises, settling on her prey. She points through the glass divider into the Super-Duper VIP space sectioned off by an entourage of palm trees. "Spotted: Rihanna's nirvana," Britt capers, stirring her Nasty Girl with a sour cherry. "Chick is the biz-ness."

"Chris, you betta watch your girl," I say, almost spilling my last sip onto my Tori Nichel backless dolman-sleeve silk-jersey rocker dress. I pound it back and stare into my empty glass before motioning to the server for another. "She's been munching lately." I laugh, prepping for her inevitable retaliation.

"And blackout sex with your costar, THE WIGGER?" Britt challenges, rolling her eyes.

"THE OUTLAW!"

Britt was right; his suburban swagger had definitely been Diddy-fied somewhere along the way.

"Jerk threatened to tell Sam about us."

"What did he say?"

"Not enough. I can't figure out what he wants; he's not holding anything for ransom."

"Except your job." Hannah points out the obvious.

"She can't get fired for sleeping with Eminem, the house

wegro." Just as the waitress sets my next Natural Girl on the table, Britt picks it up and slinks away. "Ella, ella, ey, ey, ey . . ."

"Hannah, you absolutely canNOT tell Britt what I'm about to tell you. She would rip me a new one. And I can't handle any more drama right now, especially not from her."

"Pinkie swear, Sweets."

"It's just that I really need to focus on work—and keeping Bliss and Jesse James at bay. The worst thing that could happen is if Sam finds out about us before I have a chance to tell him myself, especially with him giving me such a big opp with this new story-line."

"So you are going to tell him?"

"I don't know. Either I have to tell him or make sure he doesn't find out from Jesse. I would totally die." I huff. "And the truth is I don't want him to look at me differently. I like the way he looks at me."

"A crush, huh?" She nudges my knobby knees.

I turn back to my BFF. "Is that, like, three scoops of wrong?"

"He *is* your boss, Sweets."

"But is it still so wrong if he's throwing me rhythm in return?" I blush. The water ripples as muffled music pumps from the underwater speakers.

"Spill!" she orders, acknowledging the editor of *Naughty Girl* across the pastel-lit pool.

"Well, I kinda upgraded an on-screen kiss with Jesse and sorta popped a tent in his pants," I sheepishly admit. "Jesse was not happy about it, neither was Sam."

"You're *inviting* trouble?!"

"Well, no, not really. It worked for the scene but Sam didn't sound like a happy camper when he wrapped."

"And making him jealous moves you?" she presses, tapping into the keys on her CrackBerry, mumbling something about Rain being late.

"Nooo," I deny.

"Sweets?!"

"Well, maybe—a little."

"I hope you know what you're doing. That kind of girl power needs to be stifled." She stands up abruptly, flips her hot hair over her shoulders, and tugs at her superskinny winter-white leather pants. "Now come on, you need to meet the editor; you're ridiculous *Naughty Girl* material."

Am I?

Chapter 33

Mondays have always been pretty religious for me—a brand spankin' new chance to start a fresh week, no matter what deals were made with the devil over the weekend. Although my weekend had been spent innocently running lines in my living room and running miles on the treadmill, somehow I'd been forced to sleep with Lucifer by the middle of the week.

This past Monday morning when I arrived at H&M (Hair and Makeup) Trinity preached me the gospel. "Word around Destiny is this new 'CLONE' storyline means Soapies and Emmys for a select few of us." *Us? Me? Sleeping with the Emmy?* I knew better than to get my hopes up but I was still tickled pink. Bliss, on the other hand, was bitter green. "Have you all gone fucking mad!? This is my year to win! My year!" she'd yelled at Jack the Rat as I whizzed by with my head buried in my revised sides. "You're playing with fire!" she'd hissed at me through the air, her clip-on lowlights and highlights streaking through her hair.

Later that afternoon I'd been slumming it in the smoker's lounge (read: between two garbage cans in the alley), and had sensed that I wasn't alone. Sam had been watching me from the top of the fire escape. "I thought about you this weekend, Gorgeous," he said after inviting me up to his world. When I pressed him about my character(s), he only commented that the writers were scrambling. "We should go for drinks and discuss it." It was all I remembered him saying, the only thing that had really mattered. "Don't you have an office?" I yelled back as I ran down the fire escape in a rush to get back inside.

On Tuesday he slipped a note under my dressing room door:

Dinner? The Waverly Inn?
Check a box: YES ❏ *or NO* ❏

I leaned against the wall and stared at the words. *I couldn't.* Later, one of the many times when I walked by the control booth, I peeked into the window and watched as he meticulously monitored the action on set below. He glanced up and winked. *Could I?*

By Wednesday, the coast seemed clear so I ducked out into the smoker's lounge *alone.* I realized that puffing in peace wasn't all it was cracked up to be. But when I stopped by the wardrobe den to try on my digs, a note had been shoved inside the pocket of my cropped Cavalli pants.

Le Parker Meridien . . . Breakfast at Norma's?

I inspected the cluttered room. No one was paying me any mind. I pressed the note against my chest and lost my breath that time. Marge peeked up from pinning my pants. "You okay, dear?" I nodded my head. "So it seems good things are in store for you," she predicted, just before I glided down the hall toward Studio 26. But Jesse James scared me straight that midweek morning when the doors to Destiny slammed behind me. He'd dropped a CD into my tote and said "I've seen you in pictures with the head of Tru Records." I pulled the CD out of my bag and held the ransom in my hands. "See, Sexy, I'm a triple threat and the time has come for you to broker my record deal. I want to be bigger than Justin Timber—" I stared at the CD. Scribbled across the case was "THE OUTLAW" (pinkie swear! I couldn't make this up if I tried).

But it wasn't until this morning that I finally began to feel like I was actually finding my way. Jesse aside, my fellow thespians were gradually growing bored with me and were digging for someone else's dirt. I never thought I'd be so happy to be passé.

After my last scene today, I'm doing my usual dance out of Destiny when Izzie stops me and says, "You were really good out there. You picked up the blocking faster today than you have these past few weeks. You're gonna be a big star, ya know." I step onto Cloud 7. Then Smith grabs my ear. "Good job, kiddo; you're starting to find a good groove out there. Keep it up. See you next week." I hop onto Cloud 8 and glance up at Sam's booth. He tosses me his approval. He hasn't stopped smiling since Smith yelled "CUT!" I smile back—and float right up to Cloud 9.

"If you want to continue that love affair, I suggest you take me seriously and pass off my demo to your friend," Jesse abruptly interrupts. I slam the door to my dressing room with his words playing on repeat in my mind. *I expect to hear from her this weekend about my record deal.*

Exasperated, I press my head against the door. I knew I couldn't work this way. Even if his music didn't suck (and it totally does), he'll always hold this over my head. It's clear that I have to confess my sins to Sam. I only hope my penance doesn't run me out of a job.

The only relief in sight is that it's quitting time and that I don't have to report back to Destiny until the beginning of next week. I'm stuffing my crap into my tote when out of the corner of my eye I spy a big pink box watching me from the ottoman. *Magnolia's cupcakes.* The box is filled with an assortment of flavors—six rows of five with no two flavors the same. All have been doused with an extra sprinkle of sprinkles.

"MOOOOO." I ignore the heifer and go for the high fructose, running my finger over the tops of the sweet treats. The hodge-podge of flavors melts in my mouth and I feel a tingle flush up my spine. I'm deeply entranced in a sugar rush when I spot the note:

> *I picked you up some REAL cupcakes. I made sure each one was given an extra serving of Magnolia's Special Sprinkles.*
>
> *Enjoy! I won't tell anyone.*
>
> *P.S. Join me tonight for a REAL steak. Be ready at 8. I'm not taking no for an answer.*

Chapter 34

"It's almost seven thirty, Sweets, what're you going to wear?"

"I never have this problem, Bug; I don't know what's wrong with me," I say, throwing the Heatherette tutu dress at the wall. Britt ducks and it lands on the cluttered handlebar of the state-of-the-art treadmill. "I can't even think straight." I fall back onto the bed and stare helplessly at the ceiling.

"Unbelievable! It takes those crazy bitches on *The Bachelor* longer to fall in love with some hand-picked prick than it's taken you to swoon over this dude."

"I'm not swooning," I lie. "We're just going to talk. He said he wants to go over what's happening with my character." I look away from Britt. "And I want to talk to him about a few things, too."

"I call bullshit," Britt blares, sashaying out of the room.

"She's not swooning," Hannah yells after her, fibbing for me, her fingers crossed behind her back.

Still in my black lace La Perla bra and thong set, I pull up a seat in front of the vanity and clip my garter to my thigh highs. I look at my reflection in the mirror: Kennedy, the beautiful disaster. She has to purge her soul tonight. "So what if I do like him? It doesn't matter anyway," I say into the mirror as I blot my T-zone. *You're right; it won't matter, not after you tell him everything you've done. He'll never look at you the same.*

"Let's just keep it grown and sexy up in here tonight, all right," Britt bellows, barging back into the room with an enormous piece of my red velvet cake toppling over on a Martha Stewart serving platter. "I wouldn't tell his rich ass shit!"

My mouth dries and I cannot move my tongue. "Wh-wh-where did you get that?" I stare at her pouty lips as she chews in slow motion.

"Oh, kill it, Annie! We all know where you stash your binge-and-purgers."

Hannah looks away when I glance at her. She's holding a BCBG Runway dress and a Gucci smock that look almost identical.

I shrug with indecision. "I don't know what to do."

"You need a look that says you're going there to discuss business and to extend him the courtesy of telling him about Jesse James—and nothing else!" Hannah declares, as she stands still dangling both dresses in the air.

Instead, I stare at the plate of cake in Britt's grasp and my fingers twitch to swipe at the cream cheese frosting. Hannah dangles the dresses again. I snap out of it.

"Neither," I say, pointing to the badass body-skimming Balmain dress in the corner.

"Purrrfect! A fine blend of subtle belligerence."

"I say fuck it!" I turn my head to Britt. "Don't tell him a goddamn thing; make him bring the info to you and then deny it ever happened. Deny! Deny! Deny!" Britt shakes her head from side to side. "It's not like Blond Boy has any proof anyway! And you're getting handed a shot at a fucking Emmy performance. As if?!"

"Don't listen to her, Sweets." I turn my head back to Hannah. "You have to be honest from the very beginning, especially if you're going to be working with him for the next eleven weeks. Just put it all out there and be prepared for the consequences," Hannah urges.

"What kind of fuckery?!" My neck snaps back to Britt. "Then when he leaves your ass stranded somewhere in the Boogie-Down don't say I didn't warn you!" Britt runs her tongue across her lips to catch the icing hiding in the corners of her mouth. She looks up from the cake and into the confusion in my eyes. "The Bronx, Bitch!"

Right.

"Look." My head twists back to Hannah as she pulls out my fave pair of to-die stilts. "Just ease into it, tell him gently and use your best judgment."

"She's green." I about-face back to Britt. "If she would've been using veteran judgment, she never would've given a complete stranger her house keys with directions on how to get to her shriveled up G-spot."

"Don't worry." I spin back to Hannah. "He's not gonna fire you."

Dizzy, I take the bottle of bubbly and turn it upside down, guzzling the last quarterful.

"This cake is hittin'," Britt smacks. "Now, I fucks with this right here."

When the clock strikes 7:55, I catwalk into the kitchen, open the door to the fridge, and slink through the veggie bin to get at a sliver of leftover red velvet that hasn't stopped screaming my name.

"What'cha doin'?" Hannah pries.

It's calling me. I shove the spinach and sprouts back into place and grab my pack of smokes instead.

"You don't need any crutches tonight." Hannah snatches the box of cigs from me. "You're going to be fine." She glances over her shoulder to make sure Britt isn't lurking.

"I'm not so sure."

"Well, you got a box of cupcakes from the best bakery in all of New York. And we cannot forget that fabulous and very coveted dressing room. And why?"

I look at her quizzically, waiting for her to stop waving my ciggies around as she talks.

"Because he wanted to make you happy. How did you say he put it? He wanted to make it better for you! Clearly he digs you and—"

"Shhh." I look over her shoulder.

"Give the man some credit, Sweets," she whispers. "Even if he's pissed at first about your tryst with Eminem, you can't deny that you two still have some sort of connection. So, don't force it; let it take its course. At the end of it all you two could be exactly what the other one needs. And you look beautiful, by the way, my refined rocker."

I pick up the ringing phone. "Yes, okay. Tell him I'll be down in a sec." I flush into the mirror. "Thanks, Bug, but why do I feel like I'm going to prom and to the Inferno all on the same night?"

"It's been way too long since you had a boy come calling," she sings into my ear as she hugs me gently. "And no one's judging."

"Thanks for that."

I grab my clutch and keys and head toward the door. But before I can escape, Britt switches into the foyer, licking her sticky fingers. "Brazilian?"

"Check."

"Then don't take less than a grand!"

Chapter 35

When I step onto the sidewalk I drink Sam in with my eyes. He's leaning against the car with his arms crossed over his chest exuding casual power (you know the effortless kind that only those who possess it can convey). We lock stares as I glide toward him, the tight thigh-grazing mini-gown tickling my skin. I can't help but notice his dimples boring holes into his cheeks as he smiles at me. His skin radiates a glow from a man-facial that I'm convinced has been checked off his "to do" list today.

As I amble into his personal space I fight the urge to brush the back of my hand against his nearly clean-shaven face. Instead I look into his bold eyes, blinging daringly against the crisp white shirt under his perfectly tailored Armani suit. And at that very moment I know I'm in trouble!

"You look amazing," Sam says, reaching out for my hands. He takes them both, raising them to his lips and stealing a few kisses from each of them.

"Thanks."

He steps away from the car, opening the door as I slink in. Wearing a very comfortable grin, he nods approval at Winston.

"So, where're we headed?" I ask, caught in the seductive fog of his pheromones and cologne as we ease away from the corner.

"It's a surprise."

"Well, then I hope I'm prepared for whatever it is."

"Don't worry, you're perfect." He takes a moment to stare through me until he realizes what he's said and promptly turns to look out the window. "What I mean is, no matter what we get into tonight you're dressed just right."

Oh.

"Not that I don't already know what we're doing; I've got it all planned out."

"And you don't wanna share any of that with me?"

"Nope, not a chance."

"Okay," I say, and sit back into the heated seat, prepping myself to just enjoy the ride while my stomach turns somersaults inside. The daunting task of being honest with Sam about Jesse is torturing me.

"You want a drink?"

"YES!" I scream before I can adjust my levels.

"Champagne okay?"

I nod into the thick air between us.

"To a great evening," he toasts.

"Yes, a great evening," I concur.

Enormously unladylike, I gulp down the tonic.

"Wow" is all Sam says after taking a more appropriate, rather metrosexual sip. "More?"

"Please."

As the champagne fizz sizzles over onto my fingertips, I instinctively switch hands and slip them, one at a time, into my mouth. Having sucked the stickiness from a few fingers I realize Sam is staring at my lips. Before I know it he leans across the seat and kisses me softly. I freeze, unsure of what is happening as the car picks up speed.

"I'm sorry," he whispers, inches from me.

"It's, uh, okay," I manage.

"It's just that I've been wanting to do that every time I look at you." He reaches out to touch my mouth. His rapid breathing encourages me to keep up.

"Uh-huh," I hear myself murmur.

"You've got this thing about you."

"Thing?"

"I can't really explain it," he says, smiling slyly. "You've got this way and you don't even try."

I lick my grin. A faint throb begins to push its way up to my lips from the heat in my hips. I'm breathing as fast and as hard as he is now. He sets his glass down on the sidebar behind me and moves closer.

"Sam."

"Yes." He sighs.

"I, uh, need to tell you something," I manage, as Hannah's voice resonates in my mind instructing me to be honest.

"Yes?" He smooths my hair behind my ear.

"Uh, well . . . thank you for tonight." Britt's warning wins out over Bug's as her nauseating voice urges me not to tell him "A GODDAMN THING!" With no idea how I'm supposed to resist his persuasion, I permit myself at least this. "In case I forget to tell you later."

"You're welcome, Gorgeous."

He breathes into me and our lips touch again. I chart his gaze from my eyebrows into my eyes, past the tip of my nose and down to my lips. He leans in to kiss me again, but stops, awaiting permission. In that micro-moment, I align myself with the red devil resting on my right shoulder and seek refuge in the shadows of what is sure to be my doom. Closing my eyes, I prep to taste him again. His lips are soft and invite me back for more.

"Sam," I moan.

"Yes?" he whispers into my ear.

"I really do need to tell you something."

He pulls away. "What's wrong?"

"I, uh, don't think—"

"I know, you're right; I'm sorry." He eyes me hungrily.

WOW! I'm thinking, when a big fat elephant, now squished between us, thrashes his trunk at me. He snorts into my ear, mocking the big fat liar that is Kennedy Sun Lee.

"I don't want to rush you, Gorgeous."

"It's fine, really," is all I can utter without choking on his sincerity.

"You sure?"

"Uh-huh," I say shamefully.

Sam sits back and interlocks his fingers in mine. "What am I going to do with you?"

Unable to respond, I turn to look out the window, resigning myself to this double date. Table for four for my boss, a little red devil, a big fat elephant, and me.

Chapter 36

The ride is packed with sneak peeks, enticing smiles, and playful winks from across the backseat. And when we finally turn into Central Park off West 67th I know I'm in for an unorthodox treat.

"Tavern?" I note.

"Uh-huh, I love the park." Sam looks out the window. "I'm going to feed you first but that's all the information you're getting out of me," he says as Winston pulls up to Tavern on the Green. Two maître d's are standing outside the entrance awaiting our arrival. Sam nods as Winston lowers the divider.

"Right on time, sir."

"As always, Winston. Thank you."

"You ready?" Sam asks.

"For what exactly?"

He leans over and quick-kisses my cheek and whispers into my ear. "To lose yourself in your very own fantasy."

Before I can question him, Sam grabs my hand and escorts me from the car. As soon as I step out, I'm overwhelmed by the festive lights and accessorized trees that resemble something out of a wonderland. The wind kisses my cheek and I quiver. Sam pulls me into him and ushers me up the walkway. An older gentleman takes our coats and we follow the maître d' and the Captain through the maze of palatial rooms, each one replete with infinite mirrors and ornate chandeliers. I'd been to Tavern on the Green before but it was with the Brats for a private party Max had scored us invites to. That evening had been beyond packed with hot and sweaty trust-fund foolishness. Except for the views of the park it could've easily been mistaken for a different place in an altogether different time.

"Been here before?" Sam asks as we enter the Terrace Room.

"Nope."

I gawk from the stunning glass pavilion that overlooks the park. It twinkles back at me. The room is bejeweled with outrageous Waterford crystal chandeliers that hang from a decorative ceiling, a crisscross between kitschy gaudy and regal royalty. I fancy my mouth is hanging open when Sam eases up to me and says, "All for you." In the middle of the pavilion there's just one single table that's sparkling in its own right. It shimmers in white layers of candlelight. I think, *All for me.*

"My favorite is the terrace. C'mon," Sam says, grabs my hand, and pulls me into the private garden lit only by more bundles of votives propped up and down the patio. The flames flicker in the wind, surrounding the trees that support lines of dangling Chinese lanterns that whisper to me as they sway about, "All for you."

"I see why it's your favorite."

"Yeah, well, the chief executive is an old friend of the family. I know where all the bodies are buried." He chuckles and his cheekbones jut out as if someone sculpted them in perfect symmetry.

"I love it."

"Great, then that's one hard-earned gold star for Sam," he says and leads me back inside. "Now I know you're a meticulous eater so I took the liberty of designing a special menu exclusively for you." He pulls out my chair and I look up at him in surprise.

"Exclusively?"

The sommelier greets Sam in French, placing two wineglasses between us.

"Thanks, Jacques," Sam offers, testing the red bordeaux and nodding.

I fold my hands and eye Sam.

"He's another close personal friend of the family. Jimmy and I go way back."

"Uh-huh."

"We actually went to school together—undergrad. I put some money into a bistro he opened on Restaurant Row."

"And?"

"Bygones," Sam says, and winks at me, raising his glass for a toast.

We enjoy the rich red and soak each other in.

"So you think you got it right—my dinner tonight?"

"Let's just say I hope so. With the PETA logo attached to your cowgirl bootstraps, I knew not to start your evening off with the ribs-'n'-bibs or their critically acclaimed lobster bisque."

"That sounds good."

"Tastes even better, buttery and sweet; melts on your tongue."

I grab the back of my neck when big fat elephant sitting in the seat between us smacks me across the head.

"This room is beautiful," I compliment, drowning out the more ethical side of me when a nondescript jazz band cranks sultriness from the corner of the room. "You thought of everything."

"They're friends of the family, too, believe it or not."

"I choose not."

"Okay, you got me. So maybe I've never seen them before," Sam says as the maître d' places the lobster bisque with tarragon crème fraîche in front of him.

"I should've seen that one coming," I tease, as I watch his eyes glaze over at its perfect presentation.

"Well, you've got chilled gazpacho with tomato, cucumber, onion, and sherry vinegar." He rubs his hands together. "Incredible. Now eat up. I need you to have all your energy tonight."

"Is that right? What're we doing, rock climbing in the park?"

"I'm not telling."

"Dancing under the stars?"

Sam stops eating his bisque and stares at me.

"That's it, isn't it?"

"So, Kennedy," Sam begins, ignoring me.

"Yes?"

"Can I be direct?"

"You don't think you've been direct all night?"

"I mean about you." He takes one last spoonful and before he can push the bowl away, the server scoops it from the table and disappears.

"Sure, I guess," I say, suddenly reunited with Guilt and Shame that must've been on a bathroom break.

He sits back in his chair and takes a sip of his wine. The edges of his grin begin to tune back in and I immediately feel relief. "What do you wanna be when you grow up?"

"Huh?" I ask, forcing down the cold soup, guesstimating the caloric value of each swallow.

"When you grow up, what do you want to be?"

"I am grown-up—at least I think I am, except for a few occasions when I've been around you and I've gotten a little more *Superfudge* than *Wifey.*"

Sam wrinkles his brows.

"Judy Bl—never mind," I continue. "Let's just say except those few occasions when you've taken me back to the fourth grade."

"Why's that?"

"Schoolgirl stuff."

Sam puts his glass down and narrows the space between us.

"Ms. Lee, do you have a fourth-grade crush on me?"

"This time I'm not telling."

"Okay, fair enough," he concedes. "So back to my question. When you grow up . . ."

I push the soup away and look around the room. When I look back down at the table, the bowl is gone. I think carefully about his question. His glance confirms that he is quite serious about his inquiry, so I swallow and readjust my focus.

"Well, I want to be an actress; it's all I've ever really wanted to be. I took the Doctor/Lawyer/Indian Chief route after undergrad and bided my time in med school before putting it all on the line and going after what I really wanted." Sam hasn't moved—has barely blinked. "My sister and my best friend have supported me, emotionally and financially, and have been in my corner since the moment I made that crazy career move."

"What about your parents?"

"What about them?" I look down at the linen tablecloth. I'd kill for half a puff of a cig right now.

"Did they support you and your choices?"

"My parents—" Keenly aware that the soup is settling in my belly, I look around for the loo. "My parents, uh—" I suppress an uninvited gag reflex. "Well, when I told them I was quitting they sort of disowned me."

"Your parents—"

"Yeah, they stopped speaking to me. Kinda cut me off—didn't talk to me again until my first magazine spread in *XXL*." I breathe back into the moment. "It was a June issue."

Sam reaches across the table and grabs my hands to stop them from fidgeting with the velvety petals on the rosebuds that have been intricately woven into the candelabrum.

"We don't have to talk about it if you don't want."

"Okay."

"But I do think that they should both be proud of you now; you've obviously made some good choices."

"Yeah, well, Racquel died a month before the magazine came out."

"Racquel?"

"My mother; her name was Ae-cha, but she was a bit on the dramatic side and she had this thing for Raquel Welch so . . ." I stop talking.

"I'm sorry."

I finish my bordeaux, and it's refilled before I can deal with the dormant emotions wrestling themselves awake.

Sam puts his fork down and rests his hand over mine. "I'm glad you're doing what makes you happy. And you're good at it—very good. And I should know—I hired you!"

I smile through the strange unfamiliar feelings and press on. "I'd be lying if I said it hasn't been hard. This business has been tough on my ego. But one day modeling fell into my lap, and I wasn't about to walk away from the free clothes and the exposure—especially not the free clothes. Still my worst vice." I gulp down my wine and choke on it when big fat elephant smacks me against my back. "But acting is what I really want; it's all I've ever really wanted. When I got the courage to walk away from the med school blueprint, I snatched my student loans and never looked back. I guess you could say becoming an actress is my dream."

"But you're already an actress, and on a rather hot soap if I do say so."

"Yeah, and I'm so excited to be part of the ANS family, don't get me wrong . . . but when I grow up . . ." I lose myself in the light show already in full blast over my head in the bouncing beams inside the multitiered chandelier.

He doesn't push me.

"When I grow up I wanna go to my film premieres and tell reporters on the red carpet how amazing it was to shoot the movie, how I adored the script the first time I read it . . ." I drift off.

Sam doesn't say anything, but watches me from across the table.

"When I grow up I want to do something Oscar-worthy."

When my attention finally returns to our table, Sam is smiling. "Did you know they filmed *Ghostbusters* here?"

"Uh-uh, didn't know that."

"And *Wall Street*," he says, as his New York shell steak arrives. "This place used to be a sheephold; it used to house sheep. Can you believe that?"

"From sheep to ghosts."

"From soaps to the silver screen," he says, and raises his glass to mine.

"Well, that's exactly what I want to do, you know, when I grow up." I'm still laughing at that lofty prospect when the waiter places my plate in front of me.

"And you will; I have no doubt in my mind." He studies my dinner. "Now eat; you've got tagliatelle, roasted eggplant, and broccolini."

"You did good."

"Another gold star?"

I nod.

"Good. I aim to please."

And that's just what I was afraid of.

Chapter 37

"You wanna take a walk around the grounds?" Sam asks after I finally convince him that I can't eat another bite.

"Sure." I fancy a walk is just what I need to clear my head and

ease into a convo with him about my freak show with his leading
man.

We slip into our coats and Sam leads me onto the patio. "Enjoy
your dinner?" He reaches his leather-clad hand out for mine.

"Yes. Thank you for going to all the trouble."

"It was no trouble."

We duck through a tree-covered archway. The winding cobble-
stone path comes to an end a few paces away from a horse-drawn
carriage. "It's not dancing under the stars, but—"

"It's better." My jaw drops.

"You okay with horses?"

"Love them; one of my favorite things."

"You ride?"

"When I was younger. My father bought me a horse; one of the
times he wanted to make up for something Racquel did." I stare at
the horse and carriage. "Midnight—a Gypsy Vanner mare."

"Beautiful breed. Where is—"

"Colicked in her stall and didn't make it, six months after I got
her."

Sam pulls me into him.

I look away from the horse. "I cried for a week."

He kisses my forehead. "How about a ride tonight?"

"I haven't been riding in forever."

"Not even in Central Park? It's every horse lover's duty to take
the reins through the park." He helps me into the carriage.

"This'll be a first."

"A first?"

The carriage driver hands Sam a blanket and pours two glasses
of champagne.

"Tonight we'll relax under the stars, but I promise to take you
riding." He nuzzles my ear. "Very soon."

"I'd like that."

"Good." He pulls me closer. "I hope it's not too cold for you."

"I don't feel a thing," I say, honestly, soaking in the scene. I look around into the crisp November air. The psychedelic hues burn bright with fall foliage. Dirty reds, stark yellows, burnt oranges, and forest greens light the narrow path in front of us.

The ride starts off without a hitch. After a few hoof clacks around a cluster of late-night walkers, I feel an indescribable pressure bearing down on my shoulders. *Crap!* Big fat elephant hoists itself around my neck.

"Sam, I really do need to tell you something."

"I need to tell you something, too," he says, and wraps his arm around me.

"Okay," I hesitate, watching a runner pace by to the same rhythm of the horses' hooves syncopating against the ground.

"I really enjoy being with you, Kennedy; somehow you always have me thinking about what's really important. Watching you work these past few weeks has been good for me. It's been good for everyone else, too—they've all stepped up their game." He lifts his arm to run his hand through his hair. "Smith loves you, and the writers are scrambling with storylines to maximize your screen time." He stops talking and looks away.

I look up and marvel at the perfect archway the trees make, bending over backward to extend their branches over us.

"I know I probably shouldn't be telling you that but I'm sure you've noticed the changes and revisions to your scripts by now. They're excited about what you add to the show. And they're right; when I'm in the booth I can feel you through the lens. Your passion is infectious and it's made me really reevaluate what makes me feel that way—you know, passionate." He takes a sip from his glass and turns his body to completely face mine. "Last week when we were in the car you asked me what I'm passionate about, what I'd really like to be doing with my life. It honestly made me think." Sam laughs, and then takes a deep breath as he looks over the edge of the buggy. "Actually I haven't stopped thinking about what *should* be driving me since you asked me that."

"That's good, right?"

"Yeah, I think so." He pauses. "Scary, too."

I don't say anything as I wrestle with my own fears.

"What I mean is that no one else has really made me look at myself—I mean really look and ask those questions that force me out of my comfort zone."

"There's nothing wrong with that—making time to reflect that way."

"Yeah, but I don't do it nearly enough." He studies my reaction carefully. "Watching and listening to you has been eye-opening; you're going after exactly what it is you want out of life, and you're doing it on your own terms, without taking any shortcuts. You're not using anyone or getting ahead by—"

"I know what you mean, but Sam . . . ," I say, unable to listen to the next words that are about to forge from his mouth. I feel like a fraud. A fiery orange leaf flutters to the ground. Frantically, I try to devise a verbal strategy and find the exact words I'm going to say to him. *Just put it all out there and tell him what I did before anyone else has a chance.* "Sam, I should really tell you something—before you go any further."

"Let me finish first. Please, it's very important." He squeezes my hand. "Then you can tell me whatever it is you have to say and I'll give you my undivided attention. I promise."

"Go ahead." *When he's done I'll just count to three and spit it out! I FUCKED JESSE JAMES!*

"You know how I asked you what you wanna be when you grow up?"

"Yeah," I say, as my stomach is being tossed around the spin cycle.

"Well, after giving it a lot of thought I know what I want to be when I grow up, too."

"Okay."

"And I want to tell you."

"All right." *I HAD SEX WITH JESSE JAMES.*

He clears his throat and readjusts his long legs in the cramped space. The horse stops at the fork in the road. "Kennedy, I want to make a movie." He exhales through his words like they've been stuck to the tip of his tongue. I sit still and wait for him to continue. He doesn't.

"I think that's great. You should definitely—"

"I mean I already have a script."

"That's even better, right?" *It's now or never. I BANGED JESSE JAMES? No way; too Velveeta.*

"What I'm trying to say is that I have a script that I've been holding on to." He clears his throat. "Let's just say I acquired it a few years ago, and well, I'm ready to produce it and"—he squeezes my fingers—"and I think you'd be perfect for it." The horse goes left—way left.

"What!?" My body jolts with the buggy and I almost spill the half-empty glass of champagne all over him.

"It's this romantic espionage thriller with comedic undertones." He shifts into overdrive. "It's *Charlie's Angels* meets *Kill Bill* meets *The Bourne Identity* meets . . ." As he explains I stare past him, watching the picturesque park pass in my periphery. "The theme is a little dark at times, but I think it's brilliant and I'm convinced that you'd be perfect."

"For what?"

"The movie." Sam flexes his eyebrows and continues. "It still needs a little work and some of the window characters need to be fleshed out because they aren't—"

"But—but—"

"You don't have to answer me right now, just say you'll think about it."

"But, Sam, I've never done a feature. Wouldn't you want someone with a big name to put you on the map, especially your first time out? Nobody even knows who I am." The horse begins to pick up speed and the skinny branches on the trees whiz by.

"I know; but weren't you the one who said when you grow up—"

"Yes, of course, and it sounds like something amazing. But I don't know. Really, wouldn't you want to have some big box office star like Angelina attached to your first?"

"Yeah, maybe if I hadn't already seen you—and your work. Besides, I like discovering the next big thing, that's one of *my* things, remember?" Sam begins to settle into his excitement.

"And you think I'm it?"

"I told you that already. You need me to say it again, because I will. You're it, and I'm just glad I found you before anyone else did."

"I guess I just don't know what to say."

"Say you'll read the script."

"Of course I'll read the script!" I laugh. "I'd be crazy not to."

My stomach starts to spin in the opposite direction as I digest the life-changing conversation.

"My film company's just been sitting stagnant, and after last night I couldn't figure out why. I couldn't come up with one good reason why I wasn't moving on this project and then it dawned on me." He rubs his leather glove against his chin and cocks his head into my train of thought. "What I needed was you."

"You can't be serious." I shake my head in shock. Big fat elephant thrusts his trunk across my face. I duck.

"I'm dead serious; two things I don't joke around about—my money and my business." He grabs my shoulder and steadies me. "You're what was missing."

My eyes dart around his face until a smile takes hold of mine. "I'm at a loss."

"Say you'll at least consider it and just read the script. We can talk more about it when you're done."

"Of course, Sam. Of course. I'd be honored."

"That's exactly what I wanted to hear," he says as his cheeks flush red. "It's on my desk at home. You up for taking a detour to my place?"

"Uh-huh," I say, on autopilot.

Sam redirects our carriage driver and rings Winston on his cell with alternate coordinates. The rest of the buggy ride blurs by while each tree in Central Park rustles in the night's breeze and reawakens every sleeping dream inside me.

Sam raises his glass in the chilled air and wraps his other arm around me. "From soaps to the silver screen."

Chapter 38

One Fifth Avenue.

"Thanks, Winston," Sam says, as he helps me from the car in front of his apartment in Greenwich Village. I struggle to over-hear as he gives Winston directives for the remainder of the evening.

"No problem, sir," Winston says, nodding before shutting my door.

"Good evening, Mr. Cohen," Sam's concierge greets, as we enter the building.

"Evening, Gus," Sam returns.

"Beautiful evening, huh, Mr. Cohen?"

"Yes, Gus, it sure is." Sam grins and grabs my hand, leading me through the lobby and into an elevator.

"I bet you get a lot of 'beautiful evenings' when you bring women back to your apartment to 'look at scripts,' " I tease into a typical female's fishing expedition.

"I get my fair share," Sam teases back.

"I just bet you do; that line has to work on every actress in Manhattan and some in Jersey, too."

"And in Connecticut and Delaware and—"

"Okay, enough! I can't take any more."

"You started it."

"I should probably tell you that my place is pretty minimalist and lacking in many areas, so try and look past all that. Just don't judge me," he says, as we exit the lift.

"That's all you got? That's your pre-party panty-dropper speech?"

"Not unless they're fucking for tracks."

"Touché, Mr. Cohen. Now please hurry up and open the door. I've had to use the restroom since our horse peed a new pond in the park."

"Why didn't you say something? Down the hall, second door on your right."

I pull out my cell as I hightail it to the loo. "YOU'RE WHERE?!" Hannah screams through the cell, as I perch myself on the toilet.

"I know; I can't believe it either. It all happened so fast—one minute he was talking to me about Racquel and the next he was asking me to star in his movie. Now we're back at his place to look over the script." I glance at the encased tub across the totally major bathroom and lose my thoughts in the marble floor.

"Did you tell him?"

The line is quiet for a few. "No," I finally force the words from my mouth. "I know you're gonna get all Disappointed Diva on me, but I just couldn't—not after he sprung *that* on me."

I await her response.

She doesn't offer one.

"Really, I swear I was gonna tell him right after he wanted to tell me this really big important thing. I had no idea that *this* was the thing!"

"Okay, if you think you know what you're doing then—"

"No, I don't know what the hell I'm doing, but how was I supposed to tell him *that* after *this*?"

"I really don't know, Sweets; I'm just trying to stay focused on the big picture here, and all I know is that it starts with *that*."

"I know, me too; but if I tell him that now, there's no way he's still gonna want me to do *this*."

"I guess I can understand that then."

"Shit! What would Jesus do?"

"Well, He wouldn't do *that*."

Chapter 39

"Everything all right?" Sam asks, as I turn the corner and stalk straight into him.

"Perfect," I lie when I spy big fat elephant getting cozy on Sam's sofa.

"Good," he says and hands me the script from behind his back. "I believe this is for you."

"LONDON'S LOVE." I read the big bold-faced block letters on the title page.

"It's a play on words; London is her name and it's where this big action sequence that's part of the climax takes place." He bites down on his lips and smiles, completely psyched.

"I like it." I roll my eyes at big fat elephant and shoo him away. "London is one of my favorite cities; I can even get past the grouchy weather."

"Well, we'll definitely be spending a lot of time there if you take me up on my offer and agree to get to know her better." He slides his hands into his suit pant pockets. "I think you'll love

London; she's got real depth and strength, but she's vulnerable at the same time." He reaches out to squeeze my forearm. "It would give you a chance to show some nice range, too."

"You haven't even heard me read or seen me screen test for this."

"You've been doing that for me the past few weeks." He touches my chin with his fingertips. "I know it's a lot. Have a seat and I'll get us some wine. Flip through it, start reading it, put it up to your head and see what osmotic vibes you get from it." Sam walks into his chef's kitchen laughing and I decide to venture around the massive living room and gaze out the floor-to-ceiling windows instead. The sheer curtains are gathered with thick ropes that have been tied into captain's knots and wisp into billowy bundles against the hardwood. The city is still alive beyond the window-panes and looking down from the fourteenth floor onto the so-phisticated Manhattan mayhem below excites me. He whistles a melody from the kitchen. Tuning out the raging horns from the entourage of racing cabs outside, I turn away and notice the ab-stract artwork hanging in Plexiglas along Sam's walls. They are breathtaking, I'm thinking, when I stop to study several oversized photographs of famous jazz musicians hanging reverently around his majestic black baby grand piano.

"Nina Simone and Charlie Parker are my favorites," he says, from the island next to the Sub-Zero.

"Are those autographed by them?"

"They were special gifts," he explains, walking up behind me with a glass of red.

"You think?" I turn around straight into his arms. "Ooh, sorry," I manage, stepping back.

"It's all right," Sam says, still smiling. "I got to see Nina before she died; took a trip with my dad and uncle to France and we stopped over in Carry-le-Rouet. My uncle Pete used to play with her from time to time." He stops talking. "The one of Charlie

Parker was passed down from my father. He loved Dizzy more, but I've always been a Charlie P. groupie."

"So you play?"

"I stroke the keys some," he teases.

I move aside and swing around to remove Sam's suit jacket.

"Thank you," he says, with unintended seduction. "Just throw it over the sofa," he directs, taking a seat at the piano and unbuttoning the second button on his crisp shirt.

I toss his jacket over big fat elephant's head.

"What would you like to hear?"

"Surprise me."

"Okay, come sit next to me." He pats the bench, motioning for me, but before I can take my place beside him he is already entranced in a song my papa would play on the phonograph when he thought no one was listening. Sam's eyes are closed and his fingers are massaging the keys like they are the dough to his culinary masterpiece.

"Know this one?"

"Uh-huh," I say, allowing myself to revisit the little girl perched as close to Papa's "Private Room" as possible, listening as his giddiness traveled through the space beneath the door and into my ears. Sounds of happiness sneaked under the door from his prized eight-tracks and pristine records and the peculiar stench of his special grass as he found solace in his room—away from Racquel, and even farther away from me.

"Who is it?" Sam asks.

"Fats Waller, 'Ain't Misbehavin'.' "

Sam stops playing.

"Don't stop; I like it." I sigh.

"I'm impressed, Ms. Lee."

"So am I, Mr. Cohen," I agree, and close my eyes again as his fingers tickle the ivories, but this time Sam's face is the one superimposed behind my lids.

The music stops again and I feel him staring through me.

"What's wrong?" I ask, both excited and afraid of his answer.

"I don't know what to do."

"I don't understand."

Without taking his hands off the quieted keys, Sam leans into me and brushes against my lips once, then twice, and then a third time. From the inside out I feel myself quiver.

"Now what?" he asks.

I reach over and cup his warm face in my hands this time and look deeply into his dark eyes that are framed by his long lashes. They blink back at me and his dimple emerges through a sly smile. "Now I kiss you back."

And I kiss him so sweetly deep that I think my body will ignite right there beside this incredible man who I am fully aware is my Big Boss and the producer of a film that could change the course of my life. And I still don't care.

I kiss him more tenderly and passionately than I can remember ever kissing a man. And I am fully aware that I'll have to be back on set with him next week with the weight of the soundstage on my shoulders right next to Big Fat Elephant, who I am deciding to outright ignore tonight.

I kiss him with an intimacy that makes him clutch my back and moan in abidance. And I am fully aware that there will be severe repercussions resulting from my many indiscretions, just as I am aware that I have refused all opportunities tonight to take responsibility and own up to my many mistakes, no matter how multi-orgasmic they may have been. And I still don't care.

I indulge myself in his erotic tongue massage and feel my body get wet all over as thoughts of straddling him race through my mind. Because just for one night I want to feel the passion of someone who believes I am everything they are looking for: their star, their undiscovered jewel, their Next Big Thing.

I pull away gently to slide my dress up and straddle him on the piano bench in the living room, while the greatest jazz musicians to ever breathe life into music watch as I get right down to my very own mind-blowing Misbehavin'!

Chapter 40

"We don't have to do this, Gorgeous," Sam cautions, through hushed heavy breathing.

I am digging my fingernails into his back when I come up for air, barely holding on as he slides his tongue across my collarbone. "I know, but what happens if we both *want* to."

"This isn't what I had in mind when I asked you over to look at the script," he affirms.

I giggle into his ear from the tickles making their way down my shoulder blade with each soft kiss he leaves against my skin.

"Okay."

"There's a lot at stake here."

"Okay."

Sam is smiling when he pulls me from the cradle between his neck and his chest, and although I try to regroup, I find it impossible to make the electric surges go away.

"Okay, what?" he whispers into my skin.

"Okay . . . then we better make it count."

He wraps his arms underneath me and lifts me from the piano bench and into the air. His carrying me down the hall and into his bedroom is just as sexy as my straddling his lap on the piano bench, feeling his hard body pressed against my breasts while I swiveled my hips in a melodic rhythm in perfect tune with his. He eases me onto the plush comforter, still kissing the sensitive skin beneath my earlobe. My body begins to slowly spasm. He slides on top of me and stares into my eyes. "Baby, are you sure? I don't want you to feel pressured about this at all."

"I'm sure."

Sam licks his lips and his dimple joins us. "And you'll respect me in the morning?"

"Yes," I whisper at him through a slick grin, feeling his body take shape through his clothes against my skin. My eyes shut under the weight of the heat between us, and I wrap my arms around his strong waist, feeling the energy from my fingertips as they trace the definition of the muscles in his back. Sam leans into me again, this time kissing each of my lips with deliberation.

"I could kiss you all night."

"Then we'd never get to the good part," I tease.

"It's all the good part," he clarifies, sliding my dress away from my shoulders.

Impulsively I scoot out from under him and wriggle myself from the king-size bed.

"Where're you going?" he quizzes in his raspy voice, rolling over and following my every move with hungry eyes.

Without saying a word, I turn around so he can unzip my dress. "Oh," he voices understanding. "Now what?" he inquires after obeying the nonverbal cue.

"Now you relax and I take it off for you."

"I see," he says, leaning back on his forearms, kicking off his Ferragamos. I let the dress fall to the floor to reveal my black lace garter.

Sam draws me into him with strong arms and a wily smile, and guides my hands up to the few remaining fastened buttons on his shirt. I undo them, leaving a lovebite on his neck after each one. He stands over me, slips out of his undershirt and unbuckles his pants, letting them fall to the floor beside my dress. As the belt rattles against the Brazilian oak, I feel my nerves shake as I am standing in front of Sam, all but naked and totally exposed.

"You still sure, Gorgeous?"

I nod my head, and he carelessly turns down the bed and relaxes into the sheets. I inch toward him with more fear and excitement than I've ever felt with a man. I exhale slowly, and he pulls me into him and kisses my lips between unhooking my garter and bra.

"You're beautiful."

I try to focus on his words.

"I want to taste you and feel you and—" He craves into my breasts, taking turns kissing each of them. I zone in on his lips, watching them caress my nipples. Then Sam bites down gently before cupping each inch of them in his hands and sucking them heatedly.

"I'm glad you're here."

"Me too," I concede, completely getting lost and spiraling out of control as Sam tours my torso with his tongue, ending just below my navel.

"Open your legs."

He lowers his head between my thighs and licks his lips. "Now watch."

I lift myself onto my forearms and slide into erotic reverie as he licks and sucks me at various speeds toward differing degrees of ecstasy. Just when I thought I was going to lose my air altogether, he looks up at me, licks his lips again then slides his fingers inside me. I tense and purr myself into a stupor.

"I can feel you throbbing," Sam says, narrowing his eyes between my thighs. Sliding his fingers from inside me, he sucks them clean. "You taste better than I imagined."

I collapse onto the sheet and feel my eyeballs roll into the back of my head when he bends down for more.

Through incessant moaning and carnal groaning I grip the sheets with one hand and run my fingers through the back of his damp, wavy hair with the other. As the tension builds around all my insides, I clutch him and surrender my hips to him.

"I need—"

"Yes, Baby, what do you need?"

"I need—"

"I'm listening," he says, licking lost juices as they make their way down the inside of my thigh.

"I need—"

"Anything you want!" he confirms.

"I need to feel you inside me right now."

He takes a break from my tongue bath and laughs coyly. "I think I can make that happen," he assures and gets up to grab a few condoms from the cherry oak drawer in his antique armoire. "Is there anything else you need?"

"No, not that I can think of," I answer, dazing in and out of consciousness.

Sam is standing next to the bed and as I'm watching him I become entranced when he takes off his boxer briefs to slip on a condom.

"Wow," I hear myself utter under my breath. I don't realize he's heard me until my eyes travel over his body and into his smile, savoring each amazing inch of him. "What am I going to do with you?" I let myself ask.

"Enjoy me."

I make room for Sam to inch into bed, and as he positions himself over me he stares past my pupils, lingering in a gaze that feels like forever. I close my eyes and wrap my arms around his back, feeling the touch of his lips as he slides into me. I let out a soft moan as he takes his time and stretches me out to fit tightly around him.

"Take all of it," he orders me, licking my lips.

I moan into fulfillment and within seconds we are rocking to the same rhythm, riding with the same beat. For what feels like an eternity I am taking and receiving him with ease that makes me feel like my world is complete.

"Thank you."

"For what?" he whispers into my ear, still sucking my earlobe and penetrating me into an orgasmic oblivion.

I wrap my legs around his back and hear my panting crescendo toward rapture.

"For everything," I manage as my limbs go limp.

Sam scoops me up into his arms and rubs the tips of his fingers along my hairline before brushing them against my lips.

"You're welcome."

Chapter 41

An hour later my body erupts out of a soft slumber when I hear myself snore. I peek through my lashes and smile into Sam's eyes.

"Were you watching me sleep?"

"Yes," he whispers. "I needed to make sure the bedbugs didn't bite."

I stretch. "Sorry; I must've dozed off." I rub my eyes gently.

"You're just as beautiful when you're asleep as you are awake." He bends down and kisses the tip of my nose before brushing my lips with his. "Close your eyes." He reaches for the nightstand behind him.

"Huh?"

"Close your eyes. There's something over here for you."

I shut my eyes and inhale a familiar sugary sweetness before tasting the chocolate caramel icing on my lips. Sam pushes his index finger into my mouth and my toes curl. I suck his fingertips raw until all the icing is gone.

"Keep them closed and open your mouth," he orders, and again I obey. The moist sweet cake melts in my mouth.

"Ummm, can I open them now?"

"Yes," he allows. Sam is holding what little is left of a chocolate caramel cupcake. A mound of strawberry sprinkles is scattered on the sheet beside me.

"The sprinkles are my favorite part."

"I know."

"What's it doing here?"

"There's a whole box in there for you."

"But when—"

"While you were sleeping; I had to put Winston to good use. He was glad to do it; he didn't plan on being idle all night anyway. I really did have plans for us, you know," he says, feeding me cupcake crumbs.

"And what were those plans? You can tell me now; it doesn't look like we're gonna make it very far tonight," I say, reaching over to trace my finger over his defined ab muscles.

"I don't know if you can be trusted with that kind of information." He licks the leftover crumbs from my mouth. "That *is* good."

"C'mon, tell me," I plead, rolling over into his chest.

"Okay, Gorgeous." He moans. "Whatever you want; my Black Card and bank account numbers, too."

"Let's start with tonight's canceled plans."

"Not canceled, just postponed."

"Sounds promising."

"I would hope a private Prince concert for your birthday sounds a little more than promising."

"Prince?!"

"The Artist Formerly Known As."

"A private—"

"Yeah, and a few of his close friends and maybe a few of mine." He smiles over at me. "From time to time he does these exclusive listening parties, just real intimate at his loft downtown to try out some of his new stuff."

I kiss Sam's neck. "Oh my God! I love Prince. But how—"

"Let's just say I've got a few connected friends."

"Of course."

"I'm sorry you didn't get to go. I know we got a little sidetracked but I'll make it up to you. I promise," he says, and kisses my damp forehead.

"It was worth it." I lean into his body and indulge in feeling him against me.

"I'm glad you think so. You know, it's not easy competing with a legend like Prince."

"You have nothing to worry about; you're already in a league of your own," I admit, and reach for a condom on top of the nightstand beside me. Excited to be fully reinvigorated, I climb on top of him. "And there are many more perks that come with that job."

Sam wraps one arm around my back and cups my ass with his hand. He kisses my chocolaty mouth thoroughly before pulling away. "Then I think I'm going to love this job."

Chapter 42

The sun streaks through the bedroom window and I reach across the sheets into the realization that Sam is not there. I wince through the sunlight and grab his dress shirt that had been slung across the chaise longue next to me. Fastening the middle button,

I walk down the hall and through the living room. I recognize the smell of assorted breakfast bingers.

"Well, good morning, Gorgeous," Sam says, already seated at the dining room table flipping through the *London's Love* script.

"Morning." I look around the room and focus on the sofa, thrilled that big fat elephant has decided not to join us for breaky.

"You looked so beautiful and were sleeping so soundly when the alarm went off that I decided not to wake you."

In my AM reality I am anything but torn between last night's decision to not make mention of Jesse James and today's resolution to abide by Brittany's "Deny! Deny! Deny!" There's just no going back now.

"How did you sleep?" Sam motions for me to join him at the table.

"It was one of the best sleeps I've had in a while; I slept tight and the bedbugs didn't bite."

"Must've been after I chased them all away. I hope that encourages you to sleep over again." He stands to pull me into him and hold me close. "I'd like to see more of you." He bends down and kisses me on my forehead and loads my plate with an egg-white omelet filled with asparagus spears, tomato, and goat cheese, and two pieces of thick French toast. "Now, they say breakfast is the most important meal of the day." I stare at the plate. "Courtesy of Chef Armand."

"Chef?"

"Best on the island—you just missed him."

"It looks, uh, amazing. Thank you."

Sam sits down and watches me.

"You've already thanked me—just by being here."

I take a tiny bite of French toast and a sliver of the omelet. "It does feel nice."

Sam closes the script and rubs his hand against his chin. "So does that mean that you're not afraid of what people are going to say anymore?"

"I didn't say that."

"You can handle it." Sam cuts into much more of my omelet and feeds it to me. "We can handle it!" he says definitively, and wipes my mouth with his napkin. "So, Gorgeous, I know you don't have to be on set again until next week, which is good because I want you to look through this." He hands me the script.

I snatch it from him and hold it tightly. "I've been looking forward to this since last night. I can't wait to read it."

"Now remember it's not perfect yet; there'll have to be some rewrites but you should be able to get a good feel for it," he says, pulling me out of my chair and onto his lap. "While you were getting your beauty sleep I firmed up a few meetings out in L.A." Sam finishes the glass of juice in front of him and pushes his plate away. He wraps both his arms around me. "I made some calls to some friends of mine who are studio execs and to some potential investors as well. I'm gonna fly out over the weekend and we're gonna talk it over on the course." He shakes his head. "My golf game has really been suffering lately. I'll have to tighten that up before I get on that plane." He kisses my lobe then whispers into my ear, "You up for a quick trip to L.A.?"

"Are you serious?"

"Of course; we're in this together now."

"Sam, I don't know what to say."

"Say you'll come with me. Hell, say you'll take the part; it's a perfect career launcher for you."

"Can I think about it?"

"Think fast. Plane will be gassed up and ready to leave first thing tomorrow morning."

"That was quick."

"Well, if we're gonna make a movie I need to raise some capital and we need to find London a good home. The good thing is there's already some interest. Most of my friends that I reached out to all said the same thing."

"What? That you should have been doing this all along?"

Sam laughs. "Yeah, something like that."

"And they're right, you know."

"And they all wanna see this 'Next Big Thing.' " He grabs my fingertips as I watch him nervously. "They're going to love you, Gorgeous."

I stop chewing and put my hand over my chest; it's speeding a million miles a heartbeat.

Sam's BlackBerry starts buzzing beside a stack of newspapers and trades. He picks it up and shoots off an email. "I'm only putting the best team together on this—shooting it off to a few agents as we speak."

"You know who you want cast already?"

"I've got a few people in mind, just want to make sure they get a first look."

"Anyone I know?"

"Well, let's see . . . there's Paul Walker—"

"He's a cutie."

"Oh, he is, huh?"

"Well yeah, but you're super-*muy caliente!*"

"Much better." Sam hugs me and I immediately sigh into disbelief that I've ended up here and pinkie swear to myself that I won't let him down, no matter what it takes, even if a few unmentionables and a big fat elephant have to be buried six feet under me.

"I'm glad you're here. You've made me open my eyes—about a lot of things, and I'm excited about what comes next."

I open my own eyes and look at the plate of food he's prepped and feel my stomach double dare me. *"Mooo!"* Skinny Cow yells. Feeling fierce and in control I tear off another piece of the French toast anyway.

"So, I've gotta get to set. After work, my assistant, Libby, scheduled drinks at the Mandarin with my partners to go over everything," he says, watching me intently. "What's on your books for today, besides a date with London?"

"Fridays are usually workout days, and since I don't have to be on set I figured I'd try and get back into my routine. Besides that, just scripts."

"Sounds good," he says, standing to take off his undershirt. "Gotta jump in the shower, but I'd love it if you hung around for a while. You can help yourself to the sauna or the whirlpool while I'm gone." He takes my hands.

"So sweet, Sam, but no; I think I should just head home. You kind of wore me out last night." I stand on my tiptoes to kiss him lightly on the lips.

"You kiss me again and I won't be held responsible for what happens next." He nuzzles my ear and slips his hands underneath his shirt that I'm wearing and caresses my ass with intention.

I close my eyes and inhale, already lost in his touch. His skin pressed against mine is a temptation I'm fully aware I can't fight, at least not if my goal is to win. "What are you doing? I thought you said you had to get to work?"

"I think that'll have to wait," he says, leading me back to the bedroom. "There's some business I need to handle here first."

Chapter 43

"Hey, Gorgeous," Sam says an hour and a half later, with only a towel wrapped around his waist. He drips water from the shower over to the bed and I watch as his chest glistens when the sun spotlights it. "You look like you've got something on your mind." He bends down over the bed and traces his finger against my lips. "You sure you're okay?"

"I'm sure," I lie, thinking this isn't exactly how I imagined my Friday morning playing out.

"Listen." He sits down, intertwining my fingers in his. "I know this all happened so fast, but here we are."

"Here we are."

"Yes, Kennedy, here we are." He kisses my forehead. "And now that we're here, this is right where I want to be."

"Okay." As new and as raw as this morning-after thing is, I shudder at the thought of not being with him.

"Okay," he says, getting up from the bed and shoving a small towel through his wet hair.

"Maybe I will take you up on that offer for a little Jacuzzi time. A soak sounds nice."

"Good, that's what I like to hear." He slips into a pair of perfect jeans and a button-up and throws some product in his hair. As he emerges from the bathroom I think he could just as easily be coming from a photo shoot.

"You look delicious."

"Delicious? Wow! That coming from you—a model slash day-time soap star slash future film starlet?"

I shove the covers over my head. "Not this morning!"

Sam pulls at the sheets and sits on the edge of the bed beside me. "You look sexier this morning than I've ever seen you look." He kisses me with his eyes wide open. "So I was thinking"—he reaches into his music stand and sets a Prince CD on the end-table—"if you're not too busy later I'd love to take you to dinner. A late dinner after my meetings, if that's okay."

"I'd like that." I grab the CD.

"Good." He brushes the mess of curly hair from my face. "There are a few things I want to talk to you about, some things I think we should discuss." He rubs his thumb across my eyebrows. "We can do that over dinner; how's Mr. Chow's sound?"

I sit up on my elbows. "Good."

"I just want to make sure that we're on the same page with each other, especially after last night—and this morning." He smiles.

My heart feels like it's going to combust and for the first time today, I'm completely craving a cigarette.

"I don't want to be with someone who isn't honest with me, someone who *can't* be honest with me." He stares solemnly through me. "We need to start this thing the right way and there are some things we need to talk about." He exhales. "The truth is a funny thing; it has its own agenda and when it's ready to come out, it does just that." I watch Sam's glance slip sideways and big fat elephant rejoins our relationship, nodding in agreement behind Sam's head. "Do you want to do this with me and see where it goes?"

"Yes," I hear myself murmur.

"Then we definitely need to talk, don't you think?"

"Okay." I sink back into the sheets.

"Call you later, Gorgeous."

"Okay." I sink deeper.

Sam grabs his keys and wallet from the armoire. "Now you've got some homework: read the script carefully, get some rest, and be ready for dinner around nine."

"Okay."

And deeper!

Chapter 44

The Jacuzzi is a perfect ending to an incredible morning, I think, descending into the mountain of bubbles that has filled the tub around me. The jets drown out "Little Red Corvette," playing on the stereo, cranking me into my very own morning-after Prince concert. I sink deeper into the hot water and close my eyes, wondering what it would've been like to sit on Prince's chaise lounge, watching him trick out his own jam session. "But it was Saturday night/guess that makes it all right . . ." I snap my fingers—"What have I got to lose"—and sing along as Prince eyes me from across the room. "Little Red Corvette . . ." I gleam back at him and buzz into the bubbles. *Dunt dun duh.* I juke into the air around me with my imaginary microphone, sloshing water everywhere as I groove to the beat.

When the water begins to cool, I wriggle myself from the suds to turn up the temp in the tub. I freeze when I think I hear footsteps. They are clacking down the hall straight toward the bedroom.

"Hello!" I yell. "Did you forget something?"

"Yes, I believe I did," her English accent screeches. "MY HUSBAND!" A tall, stunning blond woman with piercing blue eyes barks at me as she stalks straight through the doorway of the bathroom.

"OHMYGOD!" I swish back into the water, seeking cover beneath my bursting bubbles.

"So, I reckon you're the flavor of the month," she says bitingly, her British pitch overpowering my fizzling suds. The woman positions her hands on her slim hips and takes her time taunting me with a demeaning stare.

Unsuccessfully, I try to cross my legs over my midsection and strategically gather the bubbles around my erect nipples. "Who are you?!" I squeal into the air, my heart pounding over the Jacuzzi jets.

"No, hon, I think the question is who are *you*?" She looks around the bathroom as if the answer to her question has gone into hiding. "I'm the Mrs.—Samson's wife!"

"His wh-wh-what?!" I sink farther into the tub and wrap one arm around my chest and the other over my crotch.

"His wife, Mercedes!" she stings, taking a step closer to the tub. "Don't play coy! You know who I am!" she challenges, flipping her very platinum hair over her shoulder.

"What are you doing here?" I ask, realizing that question should be thrown right back at me.

"No, what are *you* doing here?!" she demands as she peers at the bed. The covers and sheets are in disarray and tell tales of how our time has been spent. "You're not Chef Armand, you're not Libby, and I can see that you're clearly not the maid, Althea—although you very well could be a relative. I've warned him about hiring the darkies." (Does she not know our president is a "darky"?) Her stare chills me through the tub and I shiver, knowing she is sizing up every exposed inch of me. She moves closer and I wonder if she's going to get in and join me.

"Do you even have a green card?" She smirks, lowering her tweezed brows and straining her eyes into a standoff.

"I'm—I'm Kennedy," I say meekly.

"Where is my fucking husband?" she demands. "Where is he?!"

"I don't know. I mean, he's at work. I mean—" I stammer through shock and confusion and straight into fear.

"Let me guess; you're the new girl on set."

"I, uh—" Realizing that Mercedes has no intention of leaving me alone to gather myself or my clothes for that matter, I clumsily reach for the towel on the floor. Before I can grab it, she has smushed her Jimmy Choo onto its edge and is slowly sliding it away from me.

"You must work for him. Correct?"

"Yes," I say, slinking back into the tub. "I didn't know he was married. I mean, Sam never said he was married."

"Sam? You mean Mr. Cohen, don't you?" she barks.

"Look, if you wouldn't mind," I say, trying to reclaim my personal space. "If you really wouldn't mind!" I nod down to my nether lands.

Mercedes' face tightens as she continues to ignore my request for a tits-'n'-ass timeout! "Where in the bloody hell is my husband?!" She stomps her foot against the marble. "Where the fuck is my husband?! And why are you still in my goddamn bathtub?!" she screams.

"I'm sorry," I confess, growing more afraid of this woman by the minute.

She grabs her keys and fumbles through her Balenciaga for her cell. "I'm calling the police," she threatens.

"I didn't know he was married. He never mentioned you!" I finally blurt aloud and stand up in the tub. The air hits my nips and they harden like cement. *Ow!* Mercedes' mouth drops as she stares at my Brazilian in her bathtub in the buff. "Excuse me," I say, and rush past her with my head down, searching for my panties and bra.

"Let me guess. He took you on a ride through Central Park," she begins, whipping herself around to follow me, unloosening the belt on her winter-white cashmere coat. I freeze, naked and immediately empty inside. "Then what? He told you he had a script he wanted you to read? Something you'd be just perfect for, I'm sure," she jeers. I can feel the stinging from the tears that have decided they want to sit still in the edges of my eyes until I can't see through the blurs enough to fasten the straps of my stilettos.

The tears finally fall without my permission, but everything of the last forty-eight hours is now a blur.

"What's wrong? You can't be so naïve to think you're the first little actress that he's pulled this stunt with when I've been away on assignment." She folds her arms across her chest and I wipe through my fog to get a good look at her, this time with particular purpose.

"Oh my God! You're Mercedes!"

"Dah-ling, are you slow?!" She frowns with annoyance and shakes her head. "Not another twit!"

"The supermodel, Mercedes Gold!" I conclude under my breath.

"Yes! And you're the new girl who's still in my goddamn bedroom!"

I try to compose myself, eyeing the bejeweled cell phone in her hand. "Shit!"

"He has a thing for the minorities, you know," she quips. "But he is good, isn't he? Made you feel special, think you had a chance. You probably thought he was going to whisk you away from your little insignificant world and introduce you to the finer things. Thought he was going to help you break through the ranks, escort you into the inner circle of the upper crust, let you sit at the table with old money." She twists her mouth up. "Think again; he was just having a little fun with the help. It's one of his things."

Where is my purse? Where is my purse? Where is my fucking purse?

Mercedes is on my heels when I storm out of the room, not able to run away from her fast enough. I spy my clutch on the other side of the sofa, right next to her Gucci luggage set. I am unable to move. (Flashback: I was an alternate once for a Carolina Herrera show Mercedes walked in Paris. She'd been the muse. I never got used.)

"How long have you been fucking my husband?" she yells at me and latches on to my elbow.

"You need to have this conversation with him."

"I'm asking you!" She squeezes my arm tighter.

I fight to pull away from her. "With him!" I scream, barreling at her with malice.

She releases her hold on me. "Did he go down on you? Make you cum in his mouth?"

"Shut up!"

Mercedes takes a step back and covers her mouth with her palm. "You didn't know," she finally resolves. "You really didn't know he was married, did you?"

"I told you I didn't know." I am wet all over from the half-ass air-dry I was forced into, the sweat from my sudden state of terror, and the tears that are now gushing down my face onto my pretty dress. I fight to wipe them away as fast as they fall.

"Do you love my husband?" she screams at me as I run for the door, leaving *London's Love* alone on the breakfast nook to fend for itself. When I don't respond she hurls the words at the front door as I make a fast break for it. "Do you love my husband?"

"I don't even know your husband!"

Chapter 45

"Mercedes fucking Gold!" Hannah shakes her head, sitting beside me on the bed. "Well how the hell were you supposed to know the asshole was married? There's just no way you could've known." Hannah consoles through the pillow that is smothering my face. "Such a fucking asshole!" She rubs my back gently. "And don't people wear wedding rings anymore? When did that shit change? So Hollyweird, so cutthroat, so devious, so . . ." Nudging me over in the bed, Hannah slides in beside me. She takes a few deep breaths and struggles to calm herself. "Is there anything I can do?" she whispers in my ear. "Anything at all?"

"Don't tell Brittany," I cry into the sheets.

"Done! Don't give that another thought," she promises. "At least you used a condom." She snuggles up beside me and peeks under the pillow that's been swallowing my head. "Right? Right? Sweets, right?!"

I nod.

"Whew!" she exhales loudly. "So, you wanna talk about it?"

I don't nod.

"You know I love you, right?"

I nod.

• • •

Later that afternoon, after I'd cried through thick layers of embarrassment, disappointment, and anger, I inhaled the rest of the red velvet cake and half a pack of smokes.

"Are you gonna get that this time?" Hannah calls into my room when she hears my cell ringing for the fourth time in the last half hour.

"Why should I? I have nothing to say to him."

"What about dinner tonight? Are you just not gonna show? Not gonna give him a piece of your mind—nothing at all?" She pokes her head into the bedroom, her voice climbing an octave with each press.

"I'm sure he'll figure it out."

"You don't wanna at least hear what he has to say?"

"Nope, I feel like Mercedes said it all, and she did it so eloquently, 'Get the fuck out of my house. . . . You've been fucking my husband, you twit. . . . Did he make you cum in his mouth?!' " I look over at Hannah.

"Yeah, that pretty much says it all."

The tears well again.

"I'm so sorry you had to go through that, Sweets," Hannah says, walking over to the bed and sitting down. "You didn't deserve that. Nobody deserves that."

"She was so beautiful, too, even wearing all that evil."

"It's the accent; it even makes asking for tampons sound chic."

"I still can't believe he's married to Mercedes fucking Gold; she's legendary." I light another cig.

"I know. I Googled her." Hannah stares at me blankly.

I close my eyes and picture Mercedes wearing fantastic couture at her wedding. I'm positive Hannah is picturing the same thing. We both exhale.

"Now I totally get why everyone on set was acting so weird last week, why Bliss kept warning me. They all let the new girl completely humiliate herself."

Hannah takes the Capri from me and puffs on it, then hands it back.

At first I prep to scoff at her, but then decide I haven't got the resolve.

"What's gonna happen when you go back to work next week?"

"I don't know; but I'm pretty sure he won't be bragging about his wife walking in on me taking a bubble bath with Prince."

" 'Darling Nicky'?"

" 'Little Red Corvette.' "

"Of course."

We stare off into the distance in silence.

"So what are you gonna do?" She takes my hand in hers.

"I was actually happy, Bug. I mean, *before* Supermodel ditched *Project Runway* and came home."

"That asshole is married!"

"And to a fucking supermodel! As if just being married isn't enough." I roll onto Hannah's lap and ball myself into a fetal position.

"But what's with the racism, the overt snark-fest . . . 'a thing for the minorities, hiring the darkies'? First Lady O would've bitch slapped her—at least back in her Chi-town days."

"I really liked him, Bug." I sigh.

"Bitch!"

"Even though we only met a couple weeks ago. We had a connection, you know. We connected."

"I know."

"I didn't imagine it; there really was something there."

"I know."

"And I know this is going to sound completely absurd, but I think I'm going to miss it."

"Oh. I know."

"Don't tell anyone."

"Oh. I won't."

"Promise?"

"Pinkie swear." She strokes my hair between wiping away each tear as it falls.

We suffer through that moment until it finally passes—then we rejoin it again.

"But who does that!? Who lures someone into their apartment and into their life with *a script*?"

"So you really don't think he's serious about producing it?"

"Not the way Mercedes was talking; apparently he baits actresses with that line of bullshit all the time." I catch a few more tears in my mouth. "I even made a joke about it. We laughed about it. We fucking laughed about it!" I force myself to take a deep breath. "He probably even uses that same script." I start to freak and laugh at the audacity of that reality.

"Fucking wow!" She continues to rub my hair with empathy. "You sure you don't wanna at least check your voice mails?"

I shake my head.

"Okay. How 'bout a shower then?"

"Do I smell?"

"Lil bit."

Chapter 46

"Go away!" I scream, a few hours later, as someone shakes me back to life. "I'm dead."

"Hey, pretty girl, wake up."

I hear Max's voice through the thickness of the two blankets and the comforter that are burying my head. "Bug!!!!!"

"You said Britt, you didn't say anything about Max!" Hannah yells from the living room.

"Max, what're you doing here? Don't you have a game tonight?"

"Yeah, but I had a little time to check on my favorite girl."

"What do you want?" I whine without much affect.

"Need to talk."

I don't say anything for a while. I feel tears singeing behind my lids. He doesn't move from the edge of the chair beside my bed. "Go away."

"I can't do that!"

I pull the covers from over my head and pry my eyes open. "What is it?"

His voice is solemn. "I'm sorry about what happened."

I snatch the covers back over my head. "Now. Go away!"

"And I want you to come to my game tonight."

"No."

"Okay, I *need* you to come to my game tonight."

"No."

Max doesn't budge. "So, I kind of got myself into a situation and I need your help. Actually, you're the *only* one who can help me."

"What is it?" I say after a few more minutes of distressing silence.

"I kind of made a bet with someone and lost—on a pickup game."

"And this has *what* to do with me?" I toss the covers back onto the bed, revealing my decades-old, extra snug, sixth grade Wonder Woman jammies with the feet cut out of them. "Look at me; I'm in no condition to help anyone right now."

Max concedes with a grin. "Okay, I hear you." He throws his hands in the air. "But actually, since I lost the bet, you're the only one who can help me."

"Seriously, Max!"

"You're kind of the prize for the winner, the other guy."

I scoff, pointing down at my DC Comics couture. "Seriously?!"

"Yeah." He rubs his hands together, still smiling.

Hannah pokes her head into the room. "Tell her who and what you bet."

"Just that I'd make an introduction."

"Introduction?!" I fuss. "To who?"

Max clears his throat. "Cole Winters."

Hannah surveys the landscape and tiptoes to my closet to fetch my liquid-latex leggings. "You'll totally have a crush on him," she sings, then pulls out a crisp wifebeater.

The smile that sneaks up on me is unwelcome and uninvited. "Why are you all putting me through this?" I yank the covers back over my head to hide any preliminary signs of interest.

"Apparently he saw you on one of your reality shows and he heard you were gonna be on ANS," she says, ripping the price tag from the tank. "I wasn't going to tell you about him with all the stuff you've got going on, but hell, now is as good a time as any—considering all the stuff you've got going on." Hannah plops down on Max's lap.

"But I hate athletes. No offense, Max."

"None taken, darlin'."

"But, Sweets, he's not a starfucker," Hannah clarifies, with a straight face.

"Or a man-whore."

"Or married."

No one utters a word.

I peek at each of them between the fibers of the covers. They are both dying for an answer. I glimpse the patent leather and velvet stiletto booties that are crying to be pampered. Finally I throw the covers onto the floor.

"Courtside?"

Chapter 47

"I can't effing believe Cole Winters is digging your bony ass," Britt yells at me from the other side of Hannah, as we get situated in our coveted seats a model's stride away from the announcers.

"He just wants to meet her," Hannah intercedes. "He's a fan."

"Modelizer."

Hannah points to one of the shooting guards flying over a legion of defenders for a dunk. "That's him right there, Sweets."

"A *sexy* modelizer," Britt cosigns.

"He's all right," I finally say solemnly.

"There is nothing just 'all right' about Cole Winters or his signing bonus," Brittany declares, popping open her binoculars. "That man will be raking in eighty million dollars over the next four years. Fourteen months ago he signed a bootylicious contract," she says, licking her lips. "And is that Beyoncé over there?" she asks, shoving a pickle into her mouth.

"Where?"

"Over there, with Mr. Ed glued to her head." Britt points across the court and scoots to the edge of her chair. "And is that little guy next to her Baby Daniel?"

Hannah snatches the binoculars from Britt and peers through them.

"That's Spike Lee!"

Hannah throws animated hand signals across the court at Max. "Here." Hannah forces the binoculars on me. "Get a good look at him. I dare you to tell me the man is not hot," Hannah challenges.

"Which one is he again?"

"Right there, standing next to Max—number thirty-nine."

I look past Cole and scan the fans in the fold-up chairs along the perimeter of the court. "Is that Paul Walker?" I gasp, lowering the goggles and squinting across the hardwood. "That *is* Paul Walker."

"Annie, please, leave the white men alone and come back home to the other side."

The stadium explodes with energy. On cue, all the fans fly to their feet and Hannah stomps onto my toe as she soars from her seat.

I wince in pain as my big toe throbs, but I don't dare take my eyes off Paul Walker. "What just happened? What'd I miss?" I ask.

"Max hit a three-pointer!"

"Oh, that's too bad," I say, completely ignoring her as I patrol Paul Walker's stroll across the sideline. "He's coming this way." I shake Hannah's shoulder. "Bug, here he comes! Bug!"

Hannah looks adoringly at the dancers as they slide across the floor in an abbreviated timeout routine. "Who?" Max looks up from his huddle and winks at his fiancée. *Gross.*

"Paul Walker!" I say, waving my hand in her face. "Aren't you listening to me?"

"Movie star, B-list," Britt proclaims, and dips her nacho chip into the processed cheese before sticking it into her hot dog bun beneath the shriveled sausage.

"Hannah, you have to introduce me to him."

"But I don't know him."

"But he knows Max, everybody knows Max. . . ." I shake her shoulder. "So . . ."

"What's the big deal?" Britt asks, chewing a fistful of Milk Duds.

"He's supposed to be reading Sam's script—allegedly."

Britt shoves popcorn into her mouth along with an oversized handful of Twizzlers. "So Paul's attached?"

"Sam may have mentioned that he was interested."

I focus all my attention on Paul Walker as he slows his stride to sign an autograph for a ballboy. "Okay, Bug, here he comes," I prompt, as Hannah stands up to intercept him. Within a few seconds, she's motioning for me to step into the aisle and join them.

A few minutes later, after a brief three-way convo, I plop back down into my seat. "His agent loved it? He's giving it a read right now?" I mull that over.

Hannah rubs my shoulder sympathetically.

"Looks like Sam *is* taking this script seriously."

"That just doesn't make sense; that's so not what his wife implied."

"Who, Mercedes?" Britt blurts out, blowing on her hot pizza.

Hannah and I lock eyes. "I swear I didn't tell her," Hannah mouths to me.

"Mercedes?!" I yell at Britt.

"We *are* talking about Mercedes Gold, Sam Cohen's wife, right?"

"You knew he was married?" Hannah puts her hands over her mouth.

"Everybody knows he's married; it's Mercedes Gold." Britt sprinkles five packages of salt onto her french fries.

"You knew Sam had a wife? All this time you knew he was married?" I rage.

"Yeah, and—" She tears open the ketchup packet with her teeth. "Do I have to Etch A Sketch it out for you two?"

"Well, why didn't you say something to us about it?" Hannah shrieks.

"Yeah, why didn't you tell *us* he was married?"

"Because you bitches never asked!"

Chapter 48

"Bug, I really don't wanna go to anybody's party; I don't care what basketballer it's for." I grip my clutch and clack my stilettos into the concrete, dodging the processed cheese and popcorn that's virtually glued to the stadium floor. "Don't you think it was enough for me to just come to the game tonight?" I protest as we hustle through the tunnel and onto the concourse toward the players' locker room. "And don't think for a minute that I didn't see Britt duck out; she's the one who should be slobbering on some player's balls anyway."

"She had something to do—Friday Fetish Fest or something."

"Me too!"

"Climbing back into bed with a couple cans of cupcake frosting and listening to Billie Holiday does not a freaky Friday make."

"Why do you care what I do?"

"Because I love you—" She stops. "And I don't want you to be alone." Hannah takes a deep breath and squares both hands on my shoulders. "And maybe I'm a little worried about you." Her smile vanishes as she punctuates her words with concern. "I don't want you to be alone. No sulking over Sam tonight." Hannah nods at the usher guarding the terminal. "Hey, Reggie."

"Evening, Hannah. Great game tonight; Max killed 'em."

"I know, he hates Miami," she coos, giggling and grabbing me by the hand. "Now put on that model face and come on, you still have to meet Cole. He's hot and, more important, he's *not* married!"

"Okay, you win. But just an introduction; I'm not going to any Groupies-Need-Love-Too party."

"Too late."

"I'm serious, Bug. I just wanna go home and—"

"Crawl back into bed? Not tonight, Chickie, we've got some boogying and, more important, some boozing to do." Hannah pulls out her cell as we approach the locker room door.

Boogying? "I'm not really up for *boogying,* and I'm not really prepped for any fabulous festivities." My anxiety is building. *Timeout for a bathroom break!* I look around.

"Why are you fighting this? It's just a meeting with a boy. So he's interested in you; what's the big deal?" She looks straight through me and without permission, a tear drops. "Hey," Hannah soothes, wiping it away, "what's this really about? Is it Sam?" She fumbles around in her purse for a tissue. "Of course it's Sam. But is there something else you wanna say about what happened? That it hurt?" She dabs my cheeks with the tissue. "That it really hurt."

I take the Kleenex from her. "No."

"Then what?"

"It's just that—it *really* hurt," I whisper, and let my head fall into her shoulder.

"I know, baby. I know." She slides both arms around me and squeezes tightly. I lean against the wall in the concourse next to the boys' locker room and try to pull myself together. "But tonight, we're gonna fight—fight the bullshit, fight the drama, fight the"—Hannah eyeballs a gorgeous notorious groupie who's recently been blowing up Max's cell—"bullshit and party like porn stars." The curvy Colombian eyes her back. "Now FIGHT!—I mean blow." Hannah turns back to me. "Who's my little Blasian porn star? Come on," she coaxes. "Who's my little Oriental whore?" She gives the girl one last look. I harden and join Hannah in her standoff until the *chiquita* looks away. My eyes are red from tearing but I immediately soften and straighten when Max exits the locker room with his guys.

"Looking for me?" He bends down to kiss Hannah on her forehead, without acknowledging the peripheral pussy.

"No, I was checking for my other man, the one who scored thirty-two points tonight and crushed Miami," she gushes.

"Thanks for all that cheerleading, darlin'!"

"Thanks for always giving me something to cheer about." She never mentions his fan club.

I clear my throat to interrupt the nauseating lovefest. "You're making me sick!"

Max grabs Hannah's hand and steps aside to let his teammate by. "Kennedy," he says, smiling down at me. "This is Cole Winters." He pounds him on the shoulder. "One of the best forwards out there."

"Nice to meet you," I say, extending my arm. "Max and Hannah have nothing but good things to say about you."

"You too." He shakes my hand with authority. "But I pay them to say all that stuff."

Okay, so Cole Winters *is* HOT! Tall, *muy* chocolaty, and devilishly handsome. Six foot six with magnificent dark bronze skin, his hypnotic eyes and enchanting smile catch me off guard. I glance at Hannah. She smiles back at me and her eyes taunt, *I told you so.*

"Congratulations on ANS," he says, taking a step closer. "That used to be one of my favorite shows." He lowers his voice. "The only soap I ever watched."

"I won't tell anyone."

He laughs and I stare at his lips. "My sister got me into it when she moved in—wouldn't let me eat dinner without it on."

"That's an interesting house rule."

"Used to be, till I put her up in her own spot. So, I'm all alone now," he says, melting another layer of ice from my anti-player position.

"Thanks, I'm excited—I mean about the show."

"So Hannah tells me you're gonna be Bliss's rival," he says comfortably, adjusting his duffel bag on his shoulder. "Man, was she a bitch."

"Still is—even worse in person," I sputter, not realizing I've said it aloud. "But you didn't hear that from me."

"It's okay; if it makes you feel any better, I'll point out a few of our team bitches when we get to Bungalow 8."

"Oh, I'm not going to the party."

Hannah grabs my elbow and squeezes it. "Yes, you are. I thought we discussed this already."

"No, I'm not. I'm going home so I can get back to work."

"What work?" she presses through clenched teeth.

"Work you don't know about—work."

"It's cool: I get you," Cole intercedes. "I'm not usually up for all the flash either. But since it's for our captain we all kind of have to be there. I was hoping you'd join us, at least for one drink."

I stare up at him and fidget with the ends of my hair.

"I really can't." My cell won't stop ringing in my clutch. I glimpse Cole lowering his eyebrows to sneak a peek. I fiddle around for the telly.

"That's too bad," he says, resting his hand on my shoulder.

"Maybe some other time; tonight just"—I stop and cringe when I peek down at my cell screen and eyeball Sam's number—"isn't good for me." I exhale, Hannah's expression showing sorrowful sentiments as she studies my eyes. We stand silently in the hallway outside the team's locker room. Max, Cole, and Hannah watch me patiently.

"You think you're the first little actress he's done this with while I was away on assignment? . . . Did he go down on you . . . make you cum in his mouth . . ."

I toss my cell back into my clutch and eye Cole. "Did you say Bungalow 8?"

Chapter 49

"OH HELLL NO!" I shriek, when we pull up to the club. "What kind of . . . ?!" I gawk through the tinted window at the schizophrenic celebrity scene. "You said small party for one of the players!" I sink into the car seat. "There are at least two hundred people out here fighting to get into this thing."

"Small party, biggest party of the year—same diff," Hannah jokes, giggling to Max as he curbs the Range Rover.

"NOOO! I'm not doing this!" I protest, eyeing the red carpet and the snaparazzi assembled outside. "The photographers are still at the top of my shit list. There's no way I can face them—not after my Page Six debut," I fume. "And why does that banner say MAXIM HOT 100?!"

"Evening, Mr. Knight." The valet greets us, taking the keys from Max. "I'll keep it right out front."

"Just one drink, Kennedy," Max reminds me. "Then you can leave. I'll drive you home myself. C'mon, do this for me."

"I can't face them. And aren't you the least bit concerned that they plastered your face all over my Page Six exposé? That was you, you know, carrying me in your arms!"

"It's just ink. And besides, you're gonna have to get used to it sooner or later. Put your game face on, darlin', and let's make it sooner."

"The best way to deal with the press is to face them. You know how to manage them, you're a pro at this, Newspaper Girl," Hannah snorts. "Smile and pretend they did you a favor," Hannah advises, as she touches up her lip gloss and re-fluffs her hair. Interlocking my arm in hers, she continues, "Now, come on. You're still the IT GIRL, remember, America's Next Sweetheart!"

"Kennedy Lee, over here."

"Kennedy Lee, America's Next Sweetheart . . . look this way!"

"Kennedy, Kennedy, is it true? Are you and Max Knight the new hot couple?"

"NO!" I yell out, unable to temper my temper.

"No comment," Cole barks at them, already at the door. He grabs my hand and hurriedly leads me inside. "Thought you could use a little help out there," he says, as Rafael Blanco, the sexiest celebrity publicist on the island, seats the four of us at a polka-dot banquette. From a private table in the center of the club, beside the potted palm trees, we inspect the perky and posh party that is already packed.

"Not my best moment."

"Yeah, well, you're gonna have to get used to it. Millions of people love that show."

Sam's words stalk my mind. *Soon all of America will love you, too.*

"What's your poison, Baby Girl?"

I look over at Hannah and Max, who are already engrossed in their own deep house groove that D-Nice is wrecking from the DJ booth. "See, I didn't really plan on staying long. I have to be up early in the morning."

"So do I—Boys and Girls Club in Harlem." He makes a vodka and cranberry cocktail and sips it without reservation. "Well?"

"Okay, maybe just one. I'll have what you're having," I concede, when I spy Max watching me.

"That's my girl," he says indulgently.

I sit back and take in the spastic energy around me, thinking that this is far more glam than my superhero Underoos and chocolate icing combo I'd had on reserve for tonight.

"So did you enjoy the game?" Cole asks.

"Of course, it was great." I take a sip of my drink and watch him relax into his seat. "You were great."

He laughs heartily, and then puts his glass on the small cylinder table in front of us.

"What?" I stop staring at the booth that's a couple of celebs over and tune back into Cole. "What's so funny?"

"You. You have absolutely no idea how I did tonight. You didn't watch me; you weren't paying attention to the court at all."

"Yes, I was." I try and hide my face behind my glass that I realize has far too many ice cubes for my taste.

"No, you weren't."

"How would you know?" I try and pick out two of the cubes.

"Because I watched you. You were preoccupied, to put it mildly."

Oh.

Cole perks up to play bartender. The second drink he pours is screaming at me to pick it up and put it out of its misery. I kindly oblige.

"You want another?"

"Yep," I admit, knowing this can only lead to trouble.

Chapter 50

Gang bangs of girls are positioning themselves in front of select tables, vying for face time with the athletes and celebs. One of the "professionals" who'd been hobbling around since we got there was beginning to grow impatient. Although it was a waiting game I know her feet have to be killing her. Hannah and I dance around a curvy brunette with über-skinny stilettos who'd managed to perfect the balancing act of oversized boobs, at least two Yaki horses, a coin purse, and a drink. Finally a studded-out Turtle in Shaq's entourage took mercy on her hustle and asked her to sit.

Finally done two-stepping, I smile at Cole as he slides over to make room for me. The three scantily clad wolves that had been swarming Max blatantly scoff at Hannah and me. They huff and puff, threatening to blow our booth down. We squeeze in anyway.

Without protest, Hannah gives Max "The Look." (That look that screams "You better handle this shit or else. . . .")

Max obeys. "Nice meeting you, ladies. Have a good night." He reaches around to rub Hannah's shoulder. She peels his fingers away. "What, darlin'? They just came over to tell us how much they enjoyed the game tonight." He attempts another shoulder play. But Hannah doesn't flinch. "Come on, darlin', now you know—" He stops kissing her ass and starts kissing her lips that she's puckered out into a predictable pout.

I scoot forward to grab my glass from the table. I take a lonnnggg gulp but stop to duck when I spot Bliss walking toward us. *Shit!* "Shhh, I'm not here. Hide!" I giggle, feeling the Grey Goose chasing me.

"So, Lacey Madison," Bliss says, sauntering up to our table.

"You made it all the way up to VIP on your own, I see. But that shouldn't surprise me; you do have a way of getting what you want."

"Bliss," I greet, without affect, looking around for her table. I catch my reflection in her Solid Gold sequined micro-mini.

"So, where's your boyfriend?" she asks, devouring Cole with her eyes.

"Hey, I'm Cole," he says, extending his hand. "I'm a fan."

"Thank you, Cole," Bliss responds, extending her knuckles for him to kiss. He does. *YUCK!*

"Care for a drink?" he asks Bliss, winking at me. My eyes bore hatred through Bobblehead, and when I channel Hannah and Max for sympathy, they shrug their shoulders in unison instead.

"I'd love to. I've got my own table over there with a few friends, you know, all A-List." She throws her head back. "But I guess I can be down and hang for a few." Bliss damn near sits on my lap as she attempts to squeeze in between Cole and me.

"So, Bliss, Kennedy tells me how much she loves working with you and how you've been such a great mentor to her since she's been at *America's Next Sweetheart*."

Bliss flips her blond hair into my lashes when she jerks her head around to look at me.

"Is that right, Lacey Madison?" She smirks.

I shrug. "Sure."

"Well, she's our little star over there now." She takes her drink and twirls the ice with her fingertip. "Lacey Madison's got us all in the palm of her hand."

"Yeah, she said you've been quite an inspiration to her."

"She did?"

I did?

"I think she's quite an inspiration herself. She's definitely got a way with getting what she wants. A real go-getter, this one." She clears her throat. "So, LAAAYYY-SSSEE MAD-I-SUN, I'll ask you again. Where *is* your boyfriend tonight?" She freezes me with her dilated pupils and I think I see a trickle of blood escaping from one of her Michael Jackson–narrow nostrils.

"Ohmygod!" I look over at Hannah.

"Ohmygod!" Hannah shrieks.

"What?!" Bliss blurts out, turning around to face Cole, who taps on his own nose to clue her in. He stops when the bloody droplets land on her upper thigh, just beneath where her Solid Gold frock stops. She looks down at the blood and up into the flashing lights from a flock of shutterbugs who are yelling out her name.

Bliss gasps, jumps up from her seat and switches to the loo on her five-inch heels, screaming at the stalkerazzi to shoo.

"OH-MY-GOD!" Hannah laughs. "She didn't even feel it."

"Her entire face must've been numb." Max wipes the laughter from his eyes. "Her eyes were about to pop out of her head."

"Wow! Up close she's a real buttaface."

"Then why the hell did you invite her to sit down?" I fuss, scooting over and settling back into my seat now that the few inches she'd squeezed herself into are free.

"Buttaface?" Hannah queries.

"Yeah, her body is tight, BUT HER FACE . . ." Max explains, pulling her close as he laughs.

"She said she's here with her people." Cole touches my thigh. "She wasn't gonna stay long, Baby Girl."

I throw him my best side-eye.

"C'mon, Lacey Madison," he teases.

"You don't know her." I look around the VIP section for her table, knowing that Jesse James is lurking about. "That girl is— she's so—I mean totally—UGH!" I shiver.

"But you can't tell me that wasn't entertaining."

I finish my drink and suck on a small piece of ice. "Well . . . I guess," I finally admit. "But I didn't enjoy the rubdown she gave me with her girly parts when she gyrated her way between us."

"Okay, well dig this, Baby Girl." He pours me another drink. "I won't let anyone else come between us."

"Whatever," I say, trying to play aloof.

"Whatever? That should get me at least a kiss on the cheek. Right here." Cole points to his cheek. I roll my eyes. "I'm serious! Right here. Right now." I don't budge. "You want to see a grown man cry?"

Despite my previous opposition, I reach out to quickly kiss him on his cheek. Just as fast, he turns his head and greets me with his lips. They are soft and commanding. I gasp and pull away.

"That's one reaction I'm not used to."

"I don't have a boyfriend," I hear myself say through the haze in my head.

"Good . . . neither do I."

Chapter 51

"Where the fuck is Jesse James?" I hear myself yell into Hannah's ear. "Two more Grey-Goose-'n'-You-Won't-Remember-Shit-Tomorrows. I know he's here and I can't be caught off guard. I don't see him anywhere." I sift through the crowded room. "I don't see Bliss either."

"When the boys come back we can take a walk around to scope. It shouldn't be that hard to find the Dynamic Duo."

"I bet you Bliss told him that I'm here—right here in this splace," I struggle to say.

"I bet you're right."

"C'mon, let's bet," I insist, shoving my pinkie finger in her face.

She flicks my baby finger with hers to seal the deal. "Good to see you're feeling no pain."

I steady myself against her baby biceps and work up the nerve to tell her the latest. "I need to tell you somethin', Bug." The room spins just a smidge. I dig into her arm. "Jesse wants you to sign him to Tru Records."

She screams over Lil Wayne. "NO FUCKING WAY!"

"Yup! Gave me his demo."

"Your ransom?!"

"He wants to hear from you this weekend, or else. HA!" I scream. "GTFOH! ROFL!" I nudge her shoulder. "Right?" The vice president of Tru Records and third in command starts laughing. "I mean, I didn't wanna bring you into this shit, Bug, but—"

She suddenly stops laughing. "Does it suck ass?"

"Worse," I snort. "Worse than greasy elephant balls."

She throws her hands in the air when Weezy rocks the dance floor. "You just let me handle Eminem."

I shuffle through my clutch. "His number is in here." I fumble for my cell. "He is so fine, Bug. DAY-UM!" My mind is as cluttered as my mini-purse.

"He can't do nothing for you—eva again!"

"Nooo, not Jesse." In my condition, I can't seem to focus long on one man.

"Ohhhh! Hate to say I told you so, but, 'told you so,' " she taunts over Lollipop. "Have I ever steered you wrong?"

"I just can't believe that cocksucker is married!"

"He's not married."

"Soooo married."

"Let me guess; we're not talking about Cole anymore."

I toss my purse on the floor and take another chug of my drink. *Screw that phone. Screw Eminem. Screw his whack-ass CD.* "And fuck Sam."

"We're so not gonna go there; we've been having a good time.

You danced—twice, and it was very sesssy!" She swivels her hips, eyeing her man and Cole as they approach us. "You goin' be his Bust It Baby tonight?"

"Like a porn star, right!"

"Sweets, are you sure?"

"I'm sooo sure." I roll my eyes into the back of my head and feel a wave of dizziness. Hannah raises her glass to mine and we take the last of the tonic to the throat.

"Shhh, here they come."

"I'm hungry," I confess.

"You're what?"

Chapter 52

Cole and Max are both wearing noticeably serious expressions when they return to the table.

"What's wrong?" Hannah asks Max.

"Nothing."

"You ready to go?" Cole asks me.

"Yup."

"Can you believe she said she's hungry? Have you ever heard her say she's hungry?" Hannah screams at Max, who is intent on wrapping things up at the booth.

"Oh, you're one of those," Cole states.

"Whose?"

"A bird."

"Yeah, sure, I'm a bird, whatever you say. I'll be your bird; I can definitely be a bird—if you like birds. I can be whatever you want me to be." I start to chirp until Hannah nudges me to stop.

"Let's ride," he offers, holding my coat for me to slip into.

"Hannah?" I look behind me and begin to fasten my coat.

"That's cool with me if you wanna roll with Cole. Just make sure she gets home safely."

"Yes, ma'am; I wouldn't have it any other way."

Max grabs Hannah by the hand and leads us all out. "Good, cuz I'm tired and I've been holding on to this last bit of energy just for you, darlin'." He smiles at her before nodding good-bye to a few of his teammates on our way out.

Cole grabs my hand as we approach the door. I slink away, aware that the photogs are still on work alert. Being the flavor of the month has gotten me into enough trouble already. We get to the door and I drag farther behind, stopping to count to ten. When I feel a tap on my shoulder I turn around into Jesse James and immediately my head starts to spin. Cole is outside rapping with Max. Hannah is handling the valet. *Breathe and be cool,* I coach myself from the sidelines. *You remember how to be cool, don't you?* "'Sup, Jesse." *This can't be good,* Coach says in my head.

"Hey. Saw you with Cole Winters, playing it kind of close."

"Sure." I look past him, in search of some relief.

"You fucking him, too?"

Where is everyone? In the sea of onlookers they've managed to disappear. I fidget with the buttons on my coat. "Look, I don't want to get into this with you."

"Me either. I'm sorry, I didn't mean that." He takes a step toward me. "That was your girl, Hannah Love, right?"

"Yup."

"Did you pass her my demo?"

"She's gonna call you."

"That's what I like to hear." He smiles indulgently. "Cuz my agent is talking to the producers at *Dancing with the Stars* and that cross promotion—"

"Uh. Yeah." I spin on my heels and hide my laughter but he immediately grabs my hand, pulling me into him. *Uh-oh.*

"Let's hug it out." He wraps his arms around me and squeezes me tightly. I begin a plot to throw a power punch to his penis. I look over his shoulder again. *WHERE IS EVERYONE?* Before I know it Jesse releases me into an awkward kiss. My eyes are saucered open. I'm frozen in place. Everything is happening so fast. *PULL AWAY!* A camera standing beside Bliss begins flashing so close to my lips that I think we're about to threesome. *Holy Snapperoni!* I try to push him off. I need to focus. I fixate on Bliss. She has three heads. All three are standing in my periphery, laughing hysterically, pointing at ME!

"You got knocked the fuck out!" a bouncer yells when Jesse James is forcibly flung from me.

"MAN DOWN! MAN DOWN!" Hannah shrills.

"You totally killed him!" I yell.

Jesse James's body is laid out on the concrete, sprawled outside the front door. "No, I didn't," Cole assures, stepping over him to make sure. When Jesse starts to squirm, Cole rushes me from the scene. "I told him to stay away from you."

"What?" I cover my mouth with both hands. "What're you talking about?"

"Let's roll, Baby Girl; this is gonna be all over TMZ." He grabs my hand as the paparazzi frenzy begins and they cash in on their flavor of the month—all over again.

Chapter 53

"So let me get this straight, you actually saw him talking to the pap in the bathroom?" I ask from in front of Cole's fireplace in his haughty Harlem brownstone. I'm going through the fuzzy sequence of events in my head for the zillionth time.

"No, I saw him *and* I heard him." Cole is putting the final touches on my breakfast binge.

I was trying to concentrate but that wasn't proving to be easy. Between Skinny Cow's screaming about the caloric content of the flapjack Cole was flipping into the air and the recurring flash-backs of Mercedes F'ING Gold gawking at my Brazilian, my life was turning into a nightmare.

"... So we step into the bathroom and ..."

But he has to be the sexiest man I've ever seen flip a pancake.

"... Bliss yelling something about London and what her agent ..."

I think a primo blow job is in order. Yes. Definitely a blow job.

"... And he said he would make sure he got him the money shot ..."

With humming balls and all.

Cole stacks my breakfast feast onto a tray. "... And that's when I told him to stay the fuck away from you!"

"I see."

He grabs the syrup and brings it over to the sofa. "Now you got your pancakes, scrambled eggs, OJ, and now ... me. Let me get you a bigger tray, Baby."

"Baby?" I mock, piecing together the bits and pieces of what he's just revealed while marveling at the urgency with which Bliss seems to make moves. Who was *her* agent?

"Oh, so I knock a nigga out and you're still not my baby? Fuck's up with that?"

"Maybe 'Baby' just for tonight."

"I told you, Baby Girl, I don't see something I want very often and when I do ..."

"And you think—"

"That I could've caught a case for you tonight. Good thing I knew the bouncers; they do security for the team sometimes."

"Thanks," I say when he sets up the tray. "Did you hear anything else?"

"That dude's an asshole." *And I had been his whore.*

"So what did you say to him in the bathroom?"

Cole covers my cakes with syrup. "That's grown man's business."

Five hundred twenty-five calories each.

"Him waiting till I was out the front door—a pussy move. Straight up bitch nigga shit."

"Maybe it won't make the papers."

"Don't be naïve—papers, blogs, maybe even Perez."

"He wants a record deal from Hannah. He's threatening me."

"With what?" Cole stares at me.

Shit! I walked right into that one and I'm two shots of tequila too drunk to think fast. So I don't say anything.

"You don't have to talk about it."

"I don't think I want to talk at all."

"Okay." Cole laughs, then licks his lips. "So what *do* you want to do?"

I push the tray away and lean into him. "This." I kiss him on the cheek, then on the lips. "You're syrupy sticky." I start to giggle.

"You gonna take care of that for me, right?"

"Uh-huh." I lick his lips clean.

His breathing is heavy. Cole pulls me onto his lap, shoving the food to the side. He grabs my hair and pulls my head back, sucking and licking my neck. I close my eyes and the room spins. "You think you can handle all that?" he says, when I reach to unbuckle his pants. "I mean, I'm a grown-ass man."

I pull the wifebeater over my head. He cups my breasts in his hands. His shirt is on the floor and his pants are next in line when his goddamn telly rings. He slides from my grasp and jumps up to get it, but the answering machine is already in full swing. I watch him struggle with the reality of there being someone on the other end of the call that will be leaving a message within seconds if he doesn't pick up the line.

"Cole! It's Sandra!" Too late. "I'm not sure why you won't return any of my calls or my texts. I hit you on MySpace every day this week. If I would've known how you get down, I never would've fucked with you in the first place! I shoulda listened to my mama; she warned me about you!"

"Well." I smile. "I guess she won't be coming over tonight."

Cole stands over me on the couch. "See, she, uh—"

"Can we just get back to what we were doing?"

He starts pacing around the room. "Listen, Baby Girl, I don't think that's such a good idea."

"Seriously?! Because your throwback called?" I reach out to him but he pulls away. "Now, what's the problem?"

"I just don't think this is how I want this to go down."

"Trust me; you're not gonna catch a case."

He laughs. "That's not it."

"Are you, you know, on the down low?!" I ask carefully.

"WHAT!?" He wipes his forehead. "Fuck outta here."

"Well?"

"Believe me, Baby Girl, I want you! I do. But"—he clears his throat—"first, you've been drinking—a lot. And I don't want you to do something you're gonna regret in a few hours when you start to sober up."

"And here I thought you were this—"

"This man who wants to be extra careful with you." He walks toward the French doors and studies the reflection of me on the couch.

"I can hold my own."

"Naw, I can see you," he says gently, then returns to the couch beside me. When he bends down to kiss me on the forehead, I pull him down onto the couch and crawl back on top of him.

"What does any of that have to do with right here, right now?"

I'm determined to get so sexed out that I can't even think about Sam's reaction to whatever the dish devils ink out in tomorrow's papers.

"Listen, Babe." Cole pulls me off his neck. "I'd be lying if I said I'm not into you, but this is not how this is going down."

Of all the asshole athletes in all the clubs . . .

"Look, I get it; you're running from whatever is in your head. And I'm not that dude to take advantage . . ."

Suddenly I'm wet all over, yearning to be his submissive. I rub my fingernails over Cole's chest as I lick the outline of the tattoo wrapped around his biceps.

"Stop it!" He moves away. "Look, I'm digging you and I ain't going nowhere. Now, put your clothes back on. And eat your food."

I fold my arms and pout. "Put your fucking clothes back on. Then maybe we can talk about it."

"No." I sulk deeper into the couch cushions.

"So you don't want to talk about it?"

I shake my head.

"You're fucking intense, Baby. Anybody ever told you that?" He grabs my tank and throws it over my throbbing breasts. "But I can dig it." I pull it over my head.

"Making progress over there. Now eat. I cooked, you eat, and that's how this is going down."

Mmmooo, the herd takes their mark. *MMMooo,* they get ready. *MMMOOOOO,* they get set—*MMMOOOOO—SHUT. THE. FUCK. UP!* And I start with a little nibble on a pancake and before I know it my plate is clean.

"You ate like nobody's fed you in years. That's a damn shame; somebody needs to step their game up."

Cole is clearing away our plates when my cell rings. I reach for it and answer.

"Hey, Bug, I know it's late but I'm still at Cole's."

"Hi, Gorgeous." He clears his throat. "It's Sam."

I toss the hot potato around in my hands as it slips and slides through my fingers. I'm instantly dizzy. I look around the room and all the furniture starts to run together. I put the phone back to my ear to listen to the staggered words running from the receiver.

". . . and I need to talk to you. Where are you?"

"I can't talk right now," is all I hear myself say. I kill the line and snap the phone shut. I feel clammy all over. My back is damp. I'm pretty sure I'm going to die.

"You okay?" Cole asks, rushing the sofa.

I shake my head until it begins to hurt. "I don't feel so good."

"You look pale. You need to lie down?"

"No, I think I should go." The room breaks out in a Beat Street Breakdown, poppin' and lockin' all around me.

I twist right off the sofa and into the head of the nearest waste-basket and lose my Cole Winters' Brownstone Breakfast Special.

"Yeah, that's hot."

"Sorry." I sigh, sprawling out on his floor, relieved that the room has hit its final pose. "I threw up."

"I can see that. Don't worry about it; I'll clean it up." He reaches under me and picks me up from the floor. "Stop talking for a while. You'll be fine after you rest."

"I really need to go."

"You can't go anywhere like this, and you're definitely not fucking up the interior in the Escalade. Not a good look, Baby Girl."

"Okay, fine," I say, as he cradles me in the muscle of his huge biceps and climbs the stairs. Echoes of my cell ringing follow me up to his master suite.

"You'll sleep it off and be fine. I'll be right here." He pulls the comforter back and lays me down on top of the sheets. The last thing I hear is Sam's voice rattling through my mind. "I need to talk to you." My stomach turns.

Chapter 54

"You okay?"

"Hey, Baby," I say to Sam.

"I need to make you pancakes all the time if it gets me directly to 'Baby.' "

I open my eyes. The sun is just beginning to kiss the day. I look up to see Cole, whose arms I've been lying in quite comfortably. I gather myself and flex out of the snuggle. "How long have I been asleep?"

"About two hours."

"Was I snoring?"

"Oh yeah, you were knocking 'em back." Cole places the back of his hand over my forehead. "You got real hot there for a while." He reaches for the towel that's beside the bed.

"Thank you; I haven't been taking good care of myself."

"Upgrade, Baby."

I close my eyes. "It's not that simple."

"Sure, it is." He rubs my frizzy hair, which I realize is damp. "You ready to go home?"

"I guess so."

"I got shit to do this morning with the kids. Cole Winters loves the kids."

"And I'm sure they love you, too," I say, sitting up in the bed amid a rush of dizziness. "How much did I have to drink last night?"

"You killed the Goose."

"I would never do that to PETA."

"Who the fuck is Peter?"

I laugh out loud. "No, PETA."

"I know, Baby Girl, I'm just fucking with you. PETA's cool with me."

"You drank a lot, too, you know."

"Yeah, but I keep telling you, I'm a grown-ass man and my liver can metabolize that poison a lot faster than yours. But what I wanna know is what's really good with you and the cancer sticks?"

"Huh?"

"You heard me; saw 'em in your purse. That shit is nasty. Damn near a dealbreaker."

"Who said I wanna make a deal with you?"

"I did. Now you need to leave that shit alone, just go cold turkey."

"Take me home."

"Shit'll kill you, know what I mean? You need to back away from the cancer—just say no, Baby Girl!"

"NO!"

"Good, now with a little practice we'll have you rolling with the Cole Winters Program in no time."

I stumble down the stairs and into the living room to grab my cell from the couch. Eleven missed calls.

"You're popular. Shit kept going off all night. He must've really fucked up. But I ain't worried 'bout him." Cole pours me a glass of tomato juice. "That man is lucky I didn't let you have your way with me last night." He laughs. "He'd really be an afterthought right about now."

Is that what it would take?

*   *   *

"The second building from the corner."

Cole pulls in front of my building and I damn near slide underneath the dashboard when I see Winston leaning against his car at the curb.

"Let me guess," Cole says, zipping his leather jacket. "Your man must be here."

"I told you last night. I don't have a man."

"You don't *wanna* have a man. Somebody's in your head, and it ain't me—not yet. But trust me when I say, I ain't worried 'bout the next man."

"I wanted it to be you last night."

"And I wanted you, too. But the deal is I gotta have you all to myself." Cole rubs the back of my neck gently. "Can you dig that?"

I watch Winston, wondering how long he's been standing there. "Thanks for the ride and for the food . . . and for the celebrity boxing at the club." I look down at my fingers that are twitching to hold a ciggie. I shake the thought from my head. It returns. Quickly.

"You good? You want me to walk you in?"

"No," I say hurriedly and slip my aviators over my eyes. "I'm good."

"That's what I thought, just wanted to make sure."

I reach over the seat and kiss him on the cheek, letting my lips linger there for a few extra seconds. "Bye, Cole."

"See you soon, Baby Girl. Now go handle your business and tell my man his days are numbered."

Chapter 55

"Ms. Lee, may I have a quick word?" Winston asks, rushing me as I beeline for my front door.

"Hi, Winston. It's good to see you, really it is, but now just isn't a good time." I look around for Sam.

"I know, Ms. Lee, but it's really important. Just a quick word." He grabs my arm gently. "It'll only take a second," he pleads.

"Go ahead." I stop in my tracks, just outside the revolving door.

"I know it's not my place and I don't want to step out of line here but, but there's something you should know," he stammers as he lowers his voice and looks around.

I pull my leather gloves out of my pocket and pull them on. "If this has anything to do with Sam's marital situation then I don't want to discuss it."

"But Ms. Lee, if you will—"

"I think I know everything I need to, Winston. His WIFE made it all perfectly clear."

Winston exhales. "That's what I wanted to talk to you about. I feel really bad about that."

"Winston, really, I don't mean to be rude, but this just isn't a conversation I intend to have with you."

When I hear Sam's voice behind me I turn on my heels. He bolts from the door of my building and I storm away.

"Kennedy, I need to talk to you. I've been waiting here all night."

"That's not my problem and I don't have anything to say to you either."

"Listen, if you'd just listen to me for a second," he yells after me as I push past him into the lobby. "Kennedy. Kennedy!" Sam commands from a few feet behind, determined to shove me further into embarrassment and shame.

"Okay." I stop and rage. "What can you possibly have to say to me that Mercedes Gold didn't already make crystal clear yesterday in your apartment in your bathtub in your—" I take a deep breath and stop myself when I realize my doorman is gaping at me from behind the desk. "I gotta go."

"I'm really sorry about that. I didn't know she was coming back into town so soon."

"So you really are married? I mean, you admit it—just like that."

"Well, yeah, but—"

"Asshole!" I seethe.

"I never meant for you to find out like this."

"Do you hear what you're saying? How is that supposed to make me feel better? Can you imagine how I felt when your WIFE walked in on me having a bath? I can't say that I've ever felt more exposed in my life." I ball my fists. "And do you actually think I care about her rearranged schedule or her surprise return home?" I burn into him. "What do you think this is? Who do you think I am?"

"No, that's not what I meant."

"I really gotta go." I do a one-eighty and head for the elevator. "And to think I actually bought all that bullshit about you wanting me to star in your movie," I throw over my shoulder.

"I did." Sam shakes his head. "I mean I do."

"You could've left it at just sex, you know," I say, trying to bring this conversation to a close. "You didn't have to create that whole seduction scene with the wine and the piano playing. You could've left it at just sex! I would've been okay with that." My heart flutters at that little white lie.

"Yeah, well I wouldn't."

The elevator doors open and an old wrinkly woman who's been frequenting God's waiting room exits in a red beret. She gazes at Sam and me and doesn't utter a word. Finally as she hobbles away she smiles, nodding into my personal space. "Give him another chance, dear. Life flies by and before you know it, you're old and alone."

"Morning, Mrs. Roosevelt," the doorman greets her, shuffling over to handle her.

"Lovers' quarrel," she coos. "Makes me miss my Henry."

Fuming inside, I peer into Sam's eyes. "Look, I don't want to be in your stupid movie and I don't want to work on your stupid show anymore either."

"What?!"

"You heard me. I don't want to be associated with Sam Cohen or any of your escapades—ever!"

"Kennedy, what are you saying? You have a contract."

Right. A PAYING gig, I think to myself. "Okay, so I do want to work on your show," I amend sheepishly. "But not your mooovie, that is if you're even making a movie." Now mute, Sam doesn't move. "Yeah, that's what I thought; there is no movie, is there? You're too chicken to make one anyway, even *if* there was one."

"Kennedy!"

"Save it, Sam. I'm so over your little gimmick. The irony is that you turned out to be the *biggest* cliché of all! You could've fucked me without throwing on all the bells and whistles," I scream. Mrs. Roosevelt spins out of her conversation with the doorman and glares at me, then shakes her head in disapproval.

"Kennedy, I'm not going to take too much more of this."

Feeling relatively stable for the first time in the last twenty-four hours, I challenge Sam. "And it's not just you; you're all crazy—you, Bliss, Jesse James. Now I *really* wish I would've been offered that role on *All My Children.*"

Sam's face hardens and his lips pinch together. He takes a step back. "You should really watch what you say."

"Why? Because you're my boss and you can fire me?"

Mrs. Roosevelt gasps then begins choking. As the rubberneck scowls at me, the doorman taps her back gently, sending me running back to a whisper.

"Because you know what's best for me, including how to seduce me into being another notch on your executive producing belt?"

"I'm serious, Kennedy. You don't know what you're saying right now."

"I know exactly what I'm saying." I can't be sure, but I think

Sam's eyes begin to well. He looks down at the floor. No tears fall. I watch him take another step away.

"So if there's anything else you need to say to me . . ."

"No, I think you've said it all. Although I am sorry about Mercedes."

"And that's it? That's all you got?"

"And not telling you—"

"What? That you're married? You can't even say it. I—I wish I never would have met you!"

"If that's how you feel," he says tightly, standing up straight and taking his final step away from me.

"I feel sorry for her, you know, having a husband like you. If I cared enough I think I would hate you! But I just don't care enough." A shock pulses through my body as the words thrash off my tongue. I turn away and push for the elevator, wondering how long before the pain will go away.

Chapter 56

"GO. AWAY!" I scream into my answering machine later that evening. Brittany simultaneously bangs on my door and leaves her fourth message on my telly. "I'M DEAD!" I profess from underneath the covers where I've been nestled comfortably all night in my makeshift cave far far away in a land of frolicking and frosting, hidden from the universe. The bottle of sleeping pills is within reach. I coach myself. *You can do it!*

"That's exactly why I keep a key, Annie! Cuz you're fucking borderline!" Britt says, storming into my room, snatching the pills from the nightstand before I can. "And it's worse than I thought; you've got Fiona Apple on repeat."

"What. Are. You. Doing. Here!?" I manage.

"How many of these have you already taken?"

"DUNNO! Now. Go. Away."

Britt looks around the room for any other contraband. When she doesn't find any she rolls me over on the Posturepedic. The covers follow. "Oh, no! It's worse than I thought. You've squeezed yourself into those dreadful Underoos." She removes her couture stilts and crawls into bed beside me. "Hey! Hey! Open your eyes." She shakes my shoulder until I have no choice but to tune back into the room. "How many of these did you take?" Britt rattles the bottle before opening it. "There are only two left. Work with me here . . . How many were in the bottle the last time you opened it?"

"I'm not stupid! I don't wanna die, just vacay for a while," I explain and roll back over, shoving the pillow over my head. The darkness is soothing, but her voice isn't. "What do you want?" My gums tingle.

"We need to have a lil heart-to-heart," she whispers calmly into my ear.

"You don't have a heart!" I scream, then roll over, attempting to prop myself up with a goose-down pillow. My arms are completely numb and I slink back into the sheets. Britt holds me in her arms and adjusts the pillow so I can gangsta-lean comfortably. My eyes roll into the back of my head and my lids begin to close. The dazed confusion feels good and I am happy to be numb—at least for now. But my heart still burns. I can't seem to figure out how to make that stop.

"Look, Annie, I can't go away until I show you this." Forcibly, she nudges me again.

"Will you go away after . . ."

"Pinkie swear."

I pry my eyes open and see that Britt is holding a newspaper in her hands and a tall glass of water. "Thought you might need this."

She wraps my fingers around the glass. "Now, today on our very special episode of *Blossom* . . ."

THE *POST*! *Where are my pills?!* I snatch the paper from her. She's already propped it open to Page 6 and I can see the headline over a short piece in the bottom right corner. AGAIN!

"B-LIST SOAP STAR AND BENCHWARMING BASKETBALLER DUKE IT OUT OVER AMERICA'S NEXT SLUT!"

The glass of water breaks when it slips from my hand and re-verberates against the floor.

"That's you." Britt points. "Kissing Slim Shady!" She rattles the paper. "And that's Cole Winters kicking his ass."

I snatch the sleeping pills from her and swallow the last two, hoping to find "The Light."

"You dirty whore!"

"It was sabotage, I tell you!"

"New York's newest C-List Celebu-Tart is up to her old tricks. She's already got a new man, or BEAST, as he's known on the b-ball court, and he's not a big fan of EX-MEN. The Beast de-livered a one-two punch when he caught Kennedy Lee slipping the tongue to her co-soapstar and reported ex-fling, Jesse James. A few weeks ago we caught up with America's Next Slut stumbling out of a club in the arms of Max Knight, the New York Knicks' super-guard and Cole Winters' teammate. Hey Cole, sloppy seconds much? Note to Jesse James: Come out of the closet, already. We'll still love you."

"DIE! DIE! DIE!" I beat my head against the headboard. *This shit never happened on* Blossom.

I put my head in my hands and peek through my fingers, looking down at the picture of Jesse James with his tongue shoved into my mouth. My thoughts are suspended in time. *SAM!*

"And don't worry about Sam. He didn't see the piece about you two weeks ago and he probably won't see this one. Bet he only reads the trades anyway—and maybe *Soap Opera Digest*. He's got no time for D-list Scandal."

"C-list!"

"Uh-huh, okay."

"I was only trying to have a good time—and maybe escape for a little while," I whisper. "It's been ten years—ten fucking years! Do you even remember?"

Britt won't look at me. She doesn't respond. She never does.

"All I wanted was to forget about—" I stop myself. "But"—I point to the pic of Jesse's tongue down my throat—"he kissed *me!*"

She shrugs. "Your hair is to die for. Look," she oozes, "I love what it's doing in that shot."

"DIE! DIE! DIE!" I bang my brains against the headboard again.

"Stop it! You're going to give yourself a concussion." She takes the paper from me and stares at it. "I can't pay for this kind of publicity, and let's face it, you're not doing anything out of my ordinary. They've got you sexing Max, Jesse James, *and* Cole—with hot hair!"

"Get out!"

I snatch the paper from her, throw it on the floor, and roll over. "And Cole was a no-go."

"I call Bullshit!"

"Total! Wasn't feeling me."

"That's not what I heard. Bug said that Max said that Cole said that—"

"I threw up on his floor."

"Ew!"

"Beat it, Brittany!"

"Sorry; I'm being totally supportive now."

"You don't know how," I huff before I drift off.

"Look, Annie, I know you're dealing with a lot right now but I really need to say this. I'm totally here for you—even if I haven't exactly . . . Look, I've been doing some thinking and, well, I want to say I'm sorry for not saying anything about Sam being married."

I cringe.

"I know that's what this is all about." She shakes the empty bottle of pills. "I know you have a thing for him."

"No, I— What're you talking— Did Hannah—"

"Seriously, Annie?! Stop it! Nobody had to tell me." She shakes her head. "You think I didn't know? That I couldn't figure it out?"

"I didn't—"

"Kill it! I know you fucked him the other night, too."

"How did you know that?"

She pauses. "You just told me."

I kick my feet against the mattress and growl.

"Get over yourself, Annie. I know you better than you do. You're my other half. Shit, we once shared a rib."

"That was Adam and Eve, idiot. And even Eve would've told him about Mercedes Fucking Gold." I spit the words off my thick tongue.

"Look, you were the one who wanted to keep it from *me*, so I let you and Bug have your little secret. You thought you knew what you were doing."

"You're a bitch! MAY-JUH! I wish I was an only child."

"I was going to tell you, really," she says, frustrated.

"When? Before or after she walked in on my bubble bath?"

"You weren't supposed to fuck him! You were supposed to be telling him about Jesse that night. That was the plan, remember?"

"And you told me not to. You said I should 'Deny. Deny. Deny'!"

"Right." Britt furrows her brows. "I forgot about that." She twirls her hair and looks for split ends. "Well, if you're gonna go around acting like me and playing my games—"

"So you were trying to teach me a lesson?!"

"Yes . . . well, no."

"Get out!"

"Would you have believed me if I told you he was married to some supermodel? Would you have acted any differently?"

"YES!!!"

"Oh."

I pull the covers over my head and force my eyes shut.

"Okay, well I guess *I* wouldn't have acted any differently so I figured— See, you're confusing me now. So it's not really my fault."

I kick my feet out from under the cover. "It never is."

"I guess what I'm trying to say is that I liked you better the other way, the old way. And I forced Hannah to tell me what happened. She spilled about what Mercedes said to you and I'm sorry—"

"She's a bitch," I growl.

"I kind of like her," Britt says under her breath.

"You would."

"Sweets, I'm so sorry. Really I am." She fumbles around trying to pull me into her arms. I flop into them. *I should punch her,* I think. I don't. We settle and stay still in that moment for a while. It's been a long time. It feels nice.

"I really didn't want Cole. I just wanted to forget about Sam. I mean I wanted him cuz he's hot—and I was tipsy—"

"Tipsy?"

"Drunk."

"Carry on."

"But even he knew my mind was somewhere else."

"Have you talked to Sam yet?" She strokes my hair awkwardly at first, then finds a soothing flow.

"He was in the lobby when I got home at six this morning. Said he'd been there all night."

"Shit! If you weren't humping, then what were you doing with Cole till six in the morning?"

"Eating and sleeping."

"YOU ATE?"

Chapter 57

An hour later my pills have kicked in and my mind has turned to mush. I want to cry. *I can't feel my face.* "I think I hate Sam Cohen," I declare to Britt, who's still snuggled beside me. I close my eyes. *Is that the white Light?*

"Is that code for 'you think you love Sam Cohen'?" she whispers into my hair.

"NO!"

"Are you sure?"

No.

"Because it's okay if you do."

"Do you think you can love someone that you don't even know?" I ask tepidly.

"No."

"Then why did you ask?"

"Because I think *you* can love someone that you don't really know."

I tune her out and walk toward the Light.

"I'm just way too jaded to get swept up like that. But that's one of the things I admire about you."

I tune back in. "You admire something about me?"

"Of course." She slips my hair behind my ear. "A lot of things."
I don't recognize the vulnerability in her voice. "You know, I
never told you this before but I was so jealous when you were engaged to Ryan. I always wanted that." She tightens her grip on me.
"Well, not with *him;* he's a pompous ass. But I wanted someone to
want to spend their life with me, too." Her breath is sweet. Her
words are warm. "I never wanted you to turn out like me. I still
don't." I lie still. I don't want her to stop. "I'll never admit that I
said this, but it can get lonely over here." Britt exhales. "That's
all."

She doesn't say any more. I don't expect her to.

We stay quiet for a while.

"So you love him."

I turn away from her. "I don't even know him."

"Sometimes love happens and you don't even see it coming.
Sometimes—if you're lucky. At least that's what I hear."

"We just met. We just went out. We just—"

"Happened to stumble into love?"

"Have you *seen* Mercedes Gold? She's brilliant. And I'm no
homewrecker."

"Who said it was a home?"

"It is what it is," I concede.

"And what is that exactly?"

"Married!"

"Interesting." Britt gets lost in her thoughts, twirling the ends
of her hair again.

I close my eyes and enjoy the smell of my sister so close to me.
She massages my shoulder gently and I hold on to her tighter.
"No, work is all that matters. Sam is right; I have a contract with
ANS and a job to do." I fight the flashback of his stunning wife.
"Maybe one day I'll be a big star," I say dreamily.

"Maybe."

"I have to believe in something, even if it can't be love right now." I turn to face her again. "Don't you ever want to believe in something?"

"I already told you; I'm way too jaded."

"I always wondered why that is."

"Life."

"But we shared the same life."

"But we're two different people, despite what I said about the rib."

"By what, then?"

"By experiences, things I've seen, been through, things that have hurt." Britt's voice grows soft. "Things that were done to me."

"By Racquel? By Papa? It's been ten years—on our birthday." I whisper into the headboard. "I know you remembered."

Britt holds me in her arms in the bed beneath a tear-soaked comforter. She inches closer and squeezes me. I take refuge in the fact that she knows I'll always be here—not like Racquel. Without a single whimper, she cries quiet tears into my hair. I cry with her.

"She shouldn't have left us."

"I miss her, too," I admit.

"I don't," Britt says harshly.

"Then I'll miss her for you."

Chapter 58

"So is it en vogue for you to answer your phone this morning?" Britt nags, as the telly shrills into our ears. Her arms are still wrapped securely around me. We slept the distant nightmares of last night away.

"Sorry. I'm sure you had something sexy planned last night and here you were taking care of me." I roll over. "You haven't held me like that since I caught Ryan cheating on me with that candy striper."

"You said you needed me that night."

"I needed you last night, too."

"Then there wasn't anywhere else I was supposed to be."

"Hello," I say into the cordless that she's already snatched up.

"Baby Girl."

"Hi Cole." I smile into the phone. I don't know why. Britt eases out of the bed, picking up shards of glass still scattered across the hardwood.

"So, I'm in your neck of the woods and I was thinking I could come scoop you up and we could grab some breakfast."

"Breakfast?" I look at Britt.

"Yes," Britt encourages, nodding her head. "You'll absolutely go to breakfast. But tell him to make it brunch—showers for everyone!"

"Sure, sounds good, but can we do brunch instead?"

"I don't see why not. I can lose myself for a few hours."

"Okay."

"Pick you up at twelve."

I glance at the clock. 9:45. "I'll be downstairs."

"So . . . brunch with the Beast, huh?" Britt grabs the newspaper off the floor and crumbles it in her hands.

"Looks that way. But Brittany, it's just a meal. No big deal."

"Well I'm a fan; you could do much worse for yourself."

"According to my track record, I have."

"New beginnings, Annie."

"I don't want to lead him on, though; we're just friends. That's all I can handle these days anyway. I'm officially retiring myself from the fast-lane game. You can run it dolo."

"Just a meal, right?" Britt vanishes from my room. I hear my apartment door close behind her.

Right, just a meal.

Chapter 59

"Good morning, Baby Girl!" Cole greets, as he opens the passenger door for me.

"Afternoon, Mr. Winters."

"You're right; it is. Feels like I just left you yesterday. Wait, that's right, I did." Smiling, Cole helps me into his giant truck and leans in to kiss me on the cheek. "You look good. But you could really hurt somebody with those cowboy boots. I better stay on your good side today, try and watch what I say."

I check out what I'm wearing like someone else dressed me. Pulling down on my brand-new Double Stitch crochet T-neck halter top, I wonder again why I turned my room upside down searching for this hot top the twin designers sent over themselves. I watch Cole smile at me before he closes my door. *Maybe that's why.*

"Thanks. You look nice, too," I say, when he slides into the car, admiring the jeans and argyle V-neck sweater combo he's rocking on this brisk sunny day. "So where're we off to?"

"Well I was thinking we'd go somewhere with good hangover helpers."

"Purrrfect!"

"I figured I'd leave brunch up to the experts today. So I was thinking Cafeteria. They've got the best baked mac and cheese, unless you wanna roll back up to Harlem and hit Amy Ruth's?"

"No, you did good; I like it there. I don't know if they can compete with your culinary skills, though."

"You remember?"

"Of course I remember. I cleaned my plate."

"I wasn't sure, it's not like you were able to keep it down."

I reach over and slap him against his hard thigh. "And it only took you two point five minutes to go there—longer than I thought, I'll admit."

"It's all good, Baby Girl; *mi baño es tu baño.*"

"And in exactly how many other languages can you say 'It's cool if I puke around you'?"

"You're funny." He laughs aloud. "But just for the record, I speak Spanish, French, Italian, and Latin."

The buttwarmers in the seat are overheating my cheeks. I shift in my favorite pair of Blues. "But Latin is a dead language."

"You ain't know? I bring shit back to life."

I sit silent, wishing he'd been around ten years ago.

We ride to the restaurant making small talk along the way about the little things that have already comprised his day. Cole fusses to me about some of the kids at the Boys and Girls Club who got into a vicious turf war this morning. "It's not like I've been a good example, at least not Friday night," he says, when we're immediately seated in the crowded restaurant. "So I don't really know if I had any right to be upset with them. Well, more like disappointed."

"Did you have a talk with them?"

"I tried, but one of the kids had already seen the paper. So there wasn't very much I could say." He looks down at the menu. "I take it you saw the paper?"

I nod.

"So . . . how you holding up?"

"Is that why you wanted to hang out with me today, to make sure I was okay?"

"No, of course not." He puts his menu down. "Well, maybe a little," he says, reaching across the table for my hand. "Is that such a bad thing? I mean they were pretty hard on you, almost like it was personal or something."

"I don't know what to say."

"Well look, if I had anything to do with that, anything at all, I'm sorry, Babe. Matter of fact, that's exactly what I told the kids at the center."

"What's that?"

"That it's not okay to fight. And there's nothing cool or hard or sexy about punching white boys in the face. Unless you're defending the honor of a beautiful, sweet, intelligent superstar who you can't stop thinking about."

"No, you didn't say that." I blush.

"Of course I did. That's what happened and I'd never lie to the kids. Cole Winters loves the kids!"

"Well that's sweet of you, but I don't need anyone defending my honor, especially if it lands me in the paper with a headline charging me with being the latest 'celebu-tart' to hit the tri-state area." I exhale. "Let's just say I'd rather have my honor attacked and killed if it means—"

"I hear you, but you would've made the paper anyway."

"I know, but at least you would've been spared the embarrassment."

"Don't you know it's good for my rep? I'm already fucking up cats on the court. Now they'll think twice before running up on me out there when I'm in my zone."

"Oh, so you're saying that I helped your cause?"

"Among other things."

"I see."

"So," he says, after our waiter takes our order. "You wanna tell me about that dude you work with?"

My heart smashes into my chest. "What dude?"

"That dude I defended your honor against? The one I knocked the fuck out."

Oh.

"You were really fucking with him?"

"You just get right to it, don't you?"

"Well, I figure if you're going to eventually be my girl, I need to know what I'm dealing with."

"Your girl?"

"Look, I'm not going through that speech with you again." He smiles at me until I finally smile back. "When I think you're ready, we're doing this and that's all there is to it."

"I don't even know you."

"That's why I'm courtin' you, Baby."

"Oh." I laugh. "Is that what you're doing?" I fold my arms over my chest.

"You can't tell? I pulled out the Gucci cashmere for you and everything . . ."

I shake my head at him, thinking that his humor is refreshing. "Are you really brushing your shoulders off?"

"And you know this, ma-an!"

Chapter 60

When our food finally arrives, a round middle-aged man with slicked back hair who'd been seated at a table full of young busty blondes passes us, then doubles back.

"Hey, you're the Beast!" He points at Cole. "Great game yesterday, brother." He extends his hand. "You've been my favorite player for like, forever. I'm a total superfan," Superfan gushes, then looks over at me. "Hey, and you're, from the papers, you're America's Next—"

"Watch it, man," Cole warns.

"No, yeah, no," he stammers. "Of course, brother; it's all good." He turns to go back to his table.

Without taking his eyes off Superfan, Cole puts his napkin in his lap. "Yeah, it's all good till somebody steps out of line."

"No, brother, I definitely don't want you thrashing on me like you did that gay dude the other night."

Cole and I look at each other. "Hey, Slickback, our food is here. Thanks for the love—but do you mind?"

"Yeah, not at all." Superfan starts to walk away, and then changes his mind. "But would you mind signing today's paper for me, brother?" He looks over his shoulder again, motioning for Blond Girl #2 to pass him the *Post.*

Cole nods at the manager to assist in handling the situation and Superfan and his clan are escorted out the door before my tomato basil soup gets peppered.

I acknowledge the nagging butterflies in my belly. "Well I guess everyone has seen it by now."

"Don't worry about that. Tomorrow it'll be yesterday's news." Cole digs into his southern fried chicken and buttermilk waffles. He catches me watching him as I'm really wondering about Cole Winters for the first time since we met. "It ain't Roscoe's, but for a New York spot in Chelsea . . ."

When the waiter clears our plates, Cole wipes his mouth and stretches. "That was great."

"I liked it, too."

"You barely ate."

Not again. I toss my napkin on the table. "I can't have this convo with you, too. I ate. It was good. That's all I got."

"Why you girls put yourselves through that shit I'll never understand."

"Whatevs! You know you wouldn't be digging on me if I was walking around with three chins and four rolls hanging off my back."

"What?!"

"If I was a chubby!"

"To tell you the truth, I like a woman with a little meat on her bones."

"Until we get preggers and gain a few, then you're off hitting the skinny nanny or gettin' it in with the candy striper."

"The candy—"

"Yeah, uh-huh."

"Look, all I know is you could stand to eat a lil mac and cheese once in a while cuz no man wants a—"

I lean back in my chair and whisper under my breath, "I call Bullshit!"

"Language, Baby." Cole shakes his finger at me and winks. "Use your words."

"Whatevs! You're lying through those pretty teeth."

"Four years of braces, Ma. Four years."

"Nice." I study him. "So looks *are* important to you. My spidey senses are telling me that if I packed on the pudge, you'd be out that door so fast."

"I didn't say get fat. . . . What I'm saying is curvy is hot, it's in right now. Look at J-Lo, look at J-Hud, look at Jay-'n'-B . . . and I'ma leave it at that." He wipes his mouth with his napkin and throws his hands in the air. "I know when to say 'when' and shut the fuck up—and that's probably right about . . . NOW."

"Good call."

Cole leans into the table and licks his lips. "Baby Girl, don't get me wrong; I still think you're sexy as hell."

"Thank you, Mr. Winters."

"But a biscuit every now and again—" he starts under his breath.

I throw my napkin at him.

"Hey, hey, hey! Easy, killa! Don't hurt me before I even have a chance to give you your present."

"My what?"

"You heard me." He reaches into his pocket. "I got you a little something something."

"Cole, you didn't have to do that."

"Oh, but I did. I really wanted you to have this," he says, sitting a little square box with pink-and-red-striped wrapping and a red shoestring bow on the table between us.

"What is it?"

"Open it." Cole pushes the box toward me.

I grab it and delicately scoot the bow off the box before yanking the wrapping away. I look at Cole from across the table and burst into a girlish grin. "I can't believe you got me something." I open the box slowly and peek in. "THE PATCH!?!"

"Yeah, the PATCH."

"You got me a nicotine patch—in a jewelry box?!"

"Oh, come on, it's a joke—sort of."

"Waaay over my head."

"Okay, so maybe it's not a joke." Cole pulls out a small bag from his jacket pocket. "These are the rest of them. You're supposed to change it every day."

"Nuh uh; you can't be serious."

"Well, yeah, I sort of am." He reaches across the table. "Here, gimme your arm." He takes the patch from me and slaps it right above my elbow, onto my inner arm. "There. Nobody will ever know."

"Oh. My. God. You're serious."

"Yeah, you gotta quit that shit, Baby Girl. It's not sexy."

I watch him put a few bills on the table and stand up. "Now," he says, as he walks around to pull out my chair, stopping to kiss me on the forehead. "Let's ride."

Chapter 61

"I don't know why you insist on being so secretive. Just tell me where we're going already," I say to Cole as he steers into a garage on 50th Street, between Fifth and Sixth Ave, dodging a pretzel stand.

"Who says I'm being secretive, just because I want to surprise you with something a little unexpected." Cole hops out and hands a parking valet his keys.

"Cole Winters. My man!" he screams, flashing a set of crooked pearlies. "The BEAST, right here in the flesh," the valet says in awe, and throws him a high five. "I'll keep it right here, keep an up close and personal on it myself." He tosses the keys in the air as we walk away. "My man, Cole Winters! Hey, great game the other—"

"And it doesn't matter to you that I have to get home. I told you at brunch that I've gotta go over my lines. I can't go in there unprepared. I'm already a freakazoid."

He laughs at me. "And why is that?"

"Well, let's see—" Cole reaches out for my hand and I hesitate. I observe the giddy passersby who recognize the athlete and before I can ponder my privacy he interlocks my fingers in his, escorting me down the street. "There's the little matter of my costar being punched out by YOU in front of the entire country, maybe even the world. Do they get the *Post* in Asia? What about in Africa?"

"Do you really think they care about who you're locking lips with in Uganda?"

"Not the point," I explain, and walk through the doors of 30 Rockefeller Plaza. "And where are you taking me?"

"My God, woman, just be easy and go with the flow."

"That's against my nature," I say, staring at the gorge chandelier in the atrium of the building. "Wow." I read the sign. "Joie" crystal chandelier. I feel absolutely lovesick. "That's beautiful."

Cole looks down at me. "Yeah it is."

Stopping in my tracks to gaze at the brilliant light fixture, I can't help but remember my enchanting night with Sam when French wine, carriage rides, and bedazzling chandeliers had been all the rage.

"You okay?"

"Yep," I lie, attempting to shake off the empty feeling that's starting to strangle me.

"Come on, let's make this elevator."

"We're going to the top?"

"Top of the Rock, Baby." Cole sucks in all the air around him, letting it out slowly.

With each passing second his face bleeds color. I study him closely. "Are you okay?"

"Of course," he says. "Why wouldn't I be?" When he hands the ticketing agent our printouts I think I see his fingers tremble.

"Have you done this before?"

"Not exactly," he admits once we've been escorted onto the Sky Shuttle, which shoots us into the Manhattan stratosphere in fifty seconds flat. "But I was feeling a little adventurous. Plus the guys said this was an inspired first-date spot."

"Meant to inspire what?"

"I'll leave that up to you."

"I guess you forgot to tell them that you're obviously freaked out by heights."

"Don't confuse me with the next man, Baby Girl; I'm not afraid of anything."

When I step onto the terrace I throw my arms into the air. "Wow! Such a rock-star city from up here." I turn to Cole who is taking his time easing out of the lift. "You sure you're okay?"

"I said I can hold my own." He walks to the railing to join me and peeks over. "Seventy stories, huh?"

I try not to laugh at his sad display of machismo. "That's what they say," I soothe, rubbing his muscular arm. "Don't worry; I won't let anything happen to you."

"I got this," he convinces himself.

As Cole relaxes we watch the tiny dots moving about below us. The crisp wind blows through my hair.

Cole tightens his scarf. "You okay? You cold?"

"No," I say and take a deep breath, huffing out gusts of frosty air. "This is amazing. Everything seems so peaceful from up here."

"Almost makes you forget there are one point five million people on the island with you."

I watch the tourists around us as they marvel through bolted-down telescopes at the wraparound views.

Cole looks out toward the Statue of Liberty. "That's crazy, right Baby? One point five milli."

"I take it you didn't grow up around a lot of people?"

He laughs and takes a minute before answering. "Connecticut—the 'burbs."

"Really? You?"

I didn't know very much about Cole Winters but never would've guessed the 'burbs. He seemed every bit the sophisticated man, with a distinct urban flair. At thirty-one, his braggadocio and sex appeal denoted big city living. It was evident that he was comfortable in his star status.

"Yeah, me. And it was typical. Boring. Nothing like Chicago."

Magnificent memories of North Michigan Avenue initiate my mind's run down Lake Shore Drive, the summer volleyball tourneys and concert series in Grant Park. "Chicago was good to me. Lincoln Park was a perfect place to grow up, a good mix of city and suburbia." My voice lulls into quiet. "Do you like the city?"

"I love the city, *every* city. But I've lived so many different places I could never pick just one."

"How could you not have a favorite?" I ask, sneaking a peek at the cluster of teenyboppers snapping his picture with their cameraphones.

"Maybe Milan—when I played for them." He acknowledges his fans and shrugs his shoulders before looking back out over the world. "Maybe Barcelona."

"Beautiful women."

Cole laughs. "Yes, very." He doesn't hesitate to put his arm around my waist and pull me near. I am admittedly comfortable there. Somehow he makes me feel safe. There is no question that he is in control. "But there are beautiful women everywhere, Baby Girl. And besides the culture, the food, the languages . . . Well, when my number was called I was ready to come home—to play in the States."

"And your family?"

"They prefer me here. I studied abroad in college and played overseas, so when they found out I was flying home for good . . ."

"Where are they now?"

"Where I left them—in Connecticut. Mom's retired and Dad keeps threatening to join her."

"Sounds like you all are close." I shove my hands into my coat pockets.

"Typical. They were high school sweethearts. Dad's a doctor and mom was a schoolteacher. House on the Vineyard; house in Aspen." He smiles warmly. "They love me and my sister—only wanted the best for us." It's obvious that Cole is content discussing his family, happy even. My eyes fixate on the exact spot where the Twin Towers once stood and I quickly try to think of ways to diverge the conversation before Cole starts digging about exactly what went down in my neighborhood. "What about your folks?" He kisses me on my forehead.

"Hmmm, well . . . they met when my father was stationed in Korea. I don't know if Racquel ever really loved him." I scan the blurred street below. "They're dead now." The wind is gusting against my cheeks. *That's all I got.*

"I'm sorry, Baby Girl." Cole wraps both arms around me now. "I didn't know." He breathes into me. "My mom would dig you."

An icy ball of air shocks through me. "So, the rink?" I strongly suggest, suddenly feeling alone among *one and a half million people.*

We step into the elevator, and I tighten my scarf. I grab Cole's hand this time.

Chapter 62

"I'm following your lead," Cole surprisingly surrenders, zipping his jacket and fidgeting with gloves.

We walk in stride toward the rink where it seems almost all of New York is enjoying their Sunday. They gush over the city's "rock star," the Christmas tree at Rockefeller Center. With the holiday now on everyone's radar, the season is revving into full gear. Christmas tunes chime from gigantic speakers, and tourists capture quintessential moments on film. Cole and I stroll leisurely while some folks feast on their afternoon meals, and skaters whiz by at full throttle, flying around and around the ice without fear. We both lean into the rail and marvel at this, the magical spirit that famously reunites Manhattan each year.

"So, you're over thirty, you're completely single, and you've never been married . . ." I fish for more.

"Engaged. Once."

"And?"

He assesses the nature of my query. I'm not so sure he'll answer. "Does it matter?"

"It probably did to you at some point."

He grabs my hand again. "Ashley," he says, squeezing my fingers. "We were in different places. She was on her way up."

"Ambitious?"

"You know the type. Real corporate climber, fast tracking her way to the top."

America's Next Sour Tart. I flinch. "And that was a deal breaker for you?"

He looks down at me. "I want what I saw growing up."

"What you saw?" I ask, even though I know exactly what he means.

"I want my wife to be home when I get there. I want her to eat dinner with me, help the kids with their homework, be at all my games . . ."

Isn't that supposed to be what every woman wants—to trade in their cubicle and Bally's membership to have a life with this man. He was cultured, educated, a protector, and a provider. *Wasn't I supposed to want that?*

"I want a wife, not a husband. That's all I'm saying. Not out all night brokering a business deal with clients."

Sounds a little Stepford to me. "So Ashley was a doctor, a lawyer, an Indian chief?"

"Attorney." He laughs. "And a pretty good one. She's a partner now at Dewey Ballantine." He digs into his pocket for a few bills. "Two cups of hot chocolate," he orders from the street vendor working the world famous rink.

"Marshmallows?" the vendor asks, all too eager to fill an order from The Beast.

"Of course. What's hot chocolate without the little marshmallows?" Cole answers for me. *Twenty-three calories per spongy ball of sugar.*

"So, Ms. Lee," he begins, handing me the cup of steaming cocoa.

"Yes, Mr. Winters?"

"Now that we've gotten to know each other better, don't you wanna share some of your secrets with me?" He blows into the steam rising from his paper cup.

"I don't have any secrets."

"Tell that to the next man who punches out some model frat boy you may or may not be sleeping with."

"I'm not sleeping with him," I say reticently, and begin to stroll away.

Cole follows. "But you *were* sleeping with him?"

"Why are you so insistent? I just told you I'm not shagging him; isn't that all that matters?"

"Come on, Baby Girl, I need you to look at it from where I'm standing. I've been dodging calls from my publicist, my agent, and reporters since this thing hit the other night. And I still have to deal with all my guys. I don't even know what to say to them except I got this all under control. And that's kind of hard when they're talking about it on ESPN." He lowers his brows. "John Salley hit me up and asked if I wanted to come in and do a guest spot on the show. This thing is bigger than you and me and some frat boy named Brad."

"Jesse James."

Cole laughs facetiously. "Even worse."

I look down at the ground. "I'm sorry about that."

He reaches out for my elbow and slows my stroll. "It's cool; I just wanna know the deal."

"There is no deal."

"Baby Girl, there's always a deal."

I slow our pace to a complete standstill. "I never told you to hit him."

"And you didn't tell his lawyer to call my people and threaten me this morning either."

I gulp. "What?"

"Dude wants to sue."

"For what? He can't sue you for hitting him, can he?"

"Defamation of character and damages to his face," he says, matter-of-factly.

I struggle to curb the laughter that has already begun to creep out. "I'm sorry, it's not funny. But what does his face look like?"

"Can't be that serious; I didn't hit him that hard."

"Well yeah, you kind of did. I heard it echo down the block."

He shoves his guilty hand into his pocket.

"So what did your lawyer say?" I squint into the sun that is beginning to set behind him.

"Said he would do some digging." Cole smirks and his voice lightens. "Why would Brad get his panties all in a bunch about being called gay? I mean the dude works on a soap is all I'm saying." He eyes me in an afterthought. "No offense."

Flashbacks of Jesse James penetrating me into multiple orgasms crescendo through my mind. A chill causes my cocoa to spill.

"So now you can see with all that going on, I just need to know what's really good."

"No."

"Come again?" Cole challenges.

"No. You want to know just because YOU want to know."

He looks around like someone should be in his ear helping him figure out what to say next. I don't budge. He slowly surrenders. "Okay, look, maybe you're right. I just thought that I could somehow make you understand how I feel."

"I know you're this big basketball star, Cole, and believe me I don't want your rep tarnished either." My eyes dart away. "I know how that feels."

"I can take care of myself. That's why I got people."

I suck on my straw, wondering how this will ultimately affect *my* career, considering I don't have "people" besides Roxy, and well, she doesn't run in circles with your typical William Morris skirt fueled with Gloria Allred dirt on random celebrity folks. But hell, she'd dutifully called to check in, and for now that would just have to do.

Cole grabs my hand. "I didn't mean to push."

"And I didn't mean to pull."

He puts his arm around my back and lures me into him for a loose hug. "You hear that?"

"Yeah," I say, honing in on the voices behind us whispering our names. "We've been officially spotted."

"Baby Gi—"

"I know, I know." I toss my hot chocolate. "Let's ride."

Chapter 63

"So?" Hannah stops running lines with me and tosses my ANS script aside. "Spill!"

"I already told you three times." I roll my eyes at her, desperately attempting to stay on task. "Brunch. Observatory. Ice rink. Home."

"I love it. I absolutely love it!"

"Just a typical afternoon," I say breezily, before finally breaking down. "He's definitely an interesting guy, to say the least. And I had a really good time." My face blushes as I rattle off his hotness. "Did you know that he's lived in five different countries, he can speak Latin, he knows his way around the kitchen, and the man likes Bach?!"

"And you didn't even fuck him. Oh the power of the pussy."
Hannah winks at me. "Someone very smart once told me that the
cure to a broken heart involves some sand, a tan, and a brand-
new man! And one out of three—"

"He's not my man."

She cuts me a sneaky side-eye.

"But, Bug, there's no room."

"Make room; he's a great dick-straction. And something tells
me that a dick date with him would probably make Sam a thing of
the past."

I scratch at the nicotine patch on my arm, wondering if it will
eventually give me a rash.

Hannah eyes me suspiciously. "Are you really gonna stop
smoking?"

"Doesn't hurt to try." I scratch harder. "Now, can we get back to
running these effing lines?"

"I can't believe you're really gonna toss the sticks!"

"Well, it *is* a nasty habit, and I *do* get tired of sneaking off to
blow smoke. Who would've thought that ciggies would be so taboo
in New York City? That's just wrong on so many levels; I mean it
goes against the city's gritty tradition."

"Looks like Cole is having a fabulous influence on you already,"
she says excitedly.

"This has nothing to do with him. I'd actually been thinking
about giving up death-in-a-box for a while now."

"Liar!"

"Pinkie swear."

Hannah slides the rubber band from the ponytail in my head.
Ow!

She pulls back her thick hair and secures it into a bun with the
rubber band. I get up and fiddle through my junk drawer for another one, fighting the thought of the next eleven weeks with Sam

and the cast of *The Young and the Crazy.* "But I couldn't *completely* shake him," I finally blurt out.

"No worries. Britt said you really got it bad."

I hop back on the bed. "Yeah, well, what does she know?"

"She's worried about you, you know."

"Honestly, I didn't even know she cared before last night."

"She's always cared, and so have I." Hannah smirks and shrugs her shoulders up to her earlobes. "Britt just has her own special way of showing it."

Humph.

"So," she wades delicately, "since you're on the illustrious Cole Winters program now, what are you going to do about your, uh, appetite?" She treads a little further. "I mean, since you won't have the smokes to kill it."

"I don't know." I sneak a peek at the bathroom door.

"I'm proud of you, Sweets. I know this can't be easy. You've been smoking for fucking ever."

I look her in the eye. "And I only threw up at his place cuz of all that liquor you shoved down my throat." My voice quivers. "You know I didn't do that myself, right?" I look down at my fidgeting fingertips.

"I know." Hannah makes tiny circles in the lumpy comforter where my eyes are fixed. "But you've been doing that for so long, too. . . ."

My eyeballs sting. "I don't wanna get fat, Bug. You don't understand."

Hannah looks up from the blanket and grabs my hand. "I understand more than you know. And this is sooooo much bigger than you not wanting to get fat, Sweets. It's about so much more than that." She rubs my hand and soothes me with her words. "And *you're* the one who's been talking about being hungry and actually digesting something more than chocolate frosting and alfalfa sprouts lately!" She rattles my arm. "I know it can't be easy, believe me, I do."

I smash my head into my hands and fight through the craving for a cig.

"You have to know that I'm really proud of you." Gently, she pulls my hands away from my head and holds them firmly in hers. She doesn't speak again until I have relaxed back into our conversation. "You think you might want to see somebody?"

"See somebody?" I choke on that reality and fall back onto the duvet. "I'm NOT ready to *see somebody*."

"I think you are." My Best Friend Forever stares through me. "It's time."

"It's the only thing I've been able to control for so long now," I confess, and scratch at my arm.

"Believe it or not, always being in control can be so overrated." Hannah shakes her head and turns her nose up. "And if we're being honest here, you've been rebelling against that control since your birthday." She rubs my cheek and smiles. "You've been completely *out* of control. And that's okay," she recovers. "Even dancing on the bar in your demi-bra!" Hannah sucks in a deep breath for both of us. "For the last ten years you've been holding on to things that you never had control of in the first place. It's time you start letting some of that stuff go. You might really enjoy the freedom."

I exhale slowly, terrified of the truth. My secret restroom rendezvous were the only thing that had kept me centered, balanced. Normal. But I'd become addicted to the teeth whitening strips and my raw throat was starting to really scare me. What had started as a slippery slope had evolved into a mudslide.

"I'm here to catch you if you fall; I'm not going anywhere." She slings her purse between us and begins to rifle through it. "Now, I've got a number for you; one of the best shrinks in the city. Got it from Kimber but I didn't tell her who it was for. Not that she asked or anything, she already knows *I'm* certifiable. She says you're not anybody in this city unless you've got a head shrink and a standing weekly appointment."

I sit back up and stare past her, fixated on the bathroom door. "I just don't know if I'm ready to talk," I whisper, "if I'm even ready for help."

"I think you've *been* ready for help; you've been asking for it the only way you knew how." She hands me a business card.

"New York City's Metropolitan Hospital—the chief of psychiatry?!" My fingers flinch.

"Yep, black woman."

"Kimber doesn't play, huh?"

"And I got you the name of a top nutritionist in the city, too."

Oh boy! I surrender when I can't stop the tears from freefalling. "But really, seriously, what if I'm not ready?"

"Have I ever pushed?"

I shake my head.

"Sweets, it's past time for you to let go. Let go of all of it! You're not responsible for anyone's actions other than your own. The only person you're accountable for is YOU." She wipes one of my tears away. "Not me, not Brittany, and certainly not Racquel!" Hannah hugs me with warmth and unrelenting support. "You didn't pull that trigger, Sweets," she whispers into my ear. "Racquel did."

Chapter 64

"Did I wake you, Baby Girl?" Cole oozes through the phone when I finally answer, realizing that it's ringing outside my dream.

"Cole?" I grog.

"Sorry about calling so late. I know you gotta get up and be on set but I just got word and wanted to leave you with a little ammo."

"What time is it?" I peel the satiny sleep mask from over my left eye and squint at the clock. 1:57.

"Two"—he pauses—"Sorry."

I turn over in the bed. "It's okay, I'm up. I was, uhm, watching TV," I say, fumbling around for the remote.

"First, I, uh, want you to know that I had a really good time with you today. Most fun I've had in the city on a Sunday in a while."

"Me too."

"That's what's up."

"So . . . ?"

"Right." I can hear him breathing nervously through the telly. "I wanted to let you know I just got off a call with my lawyer."

I bolt up in the bed and yank the mask off, tossing it into the darkness. "Uh-huh."

"Well, my guy did some digging. He checked with some staff at the club about the other night."

"Yeah, and . . ."

"Turns out Bliss and Brad spent most of their time discussing you—you being top choice for some role in some big movie that's being done. At least that's all according to the waitress and the VIP hostess."

I tense when a shock surges through me and I collapse into the bed—headfirst.

"So, I guess congratulations are in order. I didn't know you were gonna be doing some big movie," he says, without very much affect.

No, not anymore, I sulk to myself through disappointment and pain.

"The thing is, Kennedy—" He stops himself. The line is quiet for a while. I dread his next words. "The thing is that you're supposedly getting the part because you've been fucking one of the producers."

I squash my head in my hands, sealing my eyes shut. My pulse picks up speed and I desperately wish I hadn't answered the phone. "Cole, I'm sorry," I say flatly.

"It is what it is." He exhales and his voice thickens. "Apparently your people felt that since it didn't bother you that your man is *married* they had to raise the stakes and stage that whole kissing scene for the papers." He inhales a deep breath and continues, again without affect. "That was so your boyfriend would be the one to walk away from *you* and maybe give your part to Bliss. Seems her agent is lobbying—"

"Cole, I—"

"Am I getting this right so far?" he presses, anger tainting his tone. "Cuz this shit is heavy, especially for someone who claims to not like drama."

"Cole, I told you, I don't have a man."

"Just let me get this out while I still can."

"B-but—" I stammer.

"Brad, who it turns out you *did* sleep with, is playing for both teams. He's been known to frequent the rainbow-flag scene in Alphabet City for the past year and a half—some hole called 'RIM'!"

"Ohmygod!" *OHMYFUCKINGGOD! OHMYFU—*

"And although he tells people his name is Jesse James and that he hails from the Upper East Side, he's originally from Flint—as in Michigan. My guy called his crib the 'Armpit of America.' "

"Cole, really, I—"

"And he didn't go to Juilliard." I can hear the papers he's reading from rustling through the line. "Dude only got through tenth grade and his last job in Flint was at the Denny's on West Pierson Road."

"But Jesse said—"

"His name isn't Jesse James, it's Arnold Seltzer."

NOOOO! I cover my mouth in shock.

"So, there it is," he relents.

Neither of us speaks. I try not to breathe.

"Now, I think I'm good on this end."

"What does that mean?" I ask warily.

"His lawyer said Arnold will back the fuck up off me now is what it means."

"Oh." I bite down on my nails. "That's good."

The line is silent. Again.

"And you should be okay, too, no matter how he decides to come at you. I'm sure he'll want to keep this under wraps although I don't see how he plans on doing that much longer. If my guy could find out—" Cole stops and clears his throat. "But you might wanna think about getting tested."

"I was safe," I murmur, clutching my knees to my chest.

"Yeah. Okay."

"Cole, please believe me when I tell you that's not who I am. Things just got a little out of control these past few weeks and I did some things that are sort of . . . out of character for me." The thudding between my temples is louder than the beating in my chest. "And I really am sorry you had to find out this way."

"Yeah, well it's not like I didn't give you a chance to tell me your own way, however you wanted me to hear it. You still don't get it do you? None of that shit mattered to me."

"But that's still my personal stuff and I didn't *want* to tell you— any of it. That's my right. I have that right." My voice quivers.

"Yeah, and when my guy asked me, 'Who is this girl?' I felt like I honestly didn't fucking know."

But you don't. You don't know me.

The line is muted.

"I'm sorry but I can't take back any of what's already happened."

"I'm sorry, too." His voice softens. "I gotta go, just wanted you to know—everything."

"Okay. But—"

"But what, Kennedy?" he demands.

"He's not my boyfriend."

"Which one? Your boss or the down-low dude?"

Ouch!

"I'm not tryna punish you, Baby; you should feel like shit all on your own. I'm just a little disappointed. I just wish you would've told me."

"And maybe I would have—in my own time and on my own terms."

"Okay."

"And that's really not who I am, before you walk away I just want you to—"

"Good night, Kennedy." He deads the line.

Good-bye, Cole.

Holding the phone to my chest, I slide under the covers and shudder, craving a cig. I feel like an irritable cat as I scratch neurotically at the nic patch. When I can't take the hot bubbling in my belly anymore, I reach under the bed for the spare carton of cancer. I grab the lighter. The flame sizzles in the quiet room. I inhale, sucking back relief. Empty, I stare at the shadowed ceiling with only the flickering of ash for light.

*   *   *

"Hello?" I answer the telly straightaway when it rings again thirty minutes later.

"Who said I was walking away?"

I toss both the I LOVE NEW YORK ashtray and the ripped carton of cigs back underneath the bed.

"I never said I was walking away."

Oh.

Cole's voice is raspy and his breathing heavy. Instinctively I slide my hand between my legs. My eyes pop open when I hear horns blare into the receiver. "Where are you?"

"Downstairs."

Chapter 65

I leap from the Posturepedic.

"You're where?"

"You sounded like you needed a little reassurance. And I wanted you—to see you."

I fluff out my hair and smooth down my frizzy edges and run for the door before realizing that I'd crawled back into my Wonder Woman Underoos. I peel myself out of the jammies and fling open my Victoria Secretions pleasure chest.

"Do you want me to come up?"

And dickmatize me. "Uh, well, I wasn't expecting—" I mumble, running out of breath as I motor from the bedroom to the bathroom and double back to the bathroom, prepping for my big game. Simultaneously, I step into the bath for an abbreviated soap down and swallow the entire bottle of Scope. I shove the dry towel under my arms and between my legs before slipping into a silky lacy thingy and dabbing a little Boucheron behind my lobes. I shake out my hair and my nerves.

"You there?"

"Uh-huh."

"Well? Can I come up?"

Five minutes later there's a knock at my door. I torch a candle and swing open the door. Cole is confidently wearing a sly grin with sex brooding in his eyes. I suspect he has something to prove, some manly-man bull. While I'm wildly vulnerable, half-naked, yearning for the comfort of his forgiveness.

Pheromones encircle us, and I immediately want to claw his clothes off. He seduces me with his eyes and I know it's time to let him in. He bends down and kisses me on the forehead, then on the cheek, then softly on my lips. They tingle—both pair. I close my eyes and kiss him back. My arms find their way around his neck and I squeeze my body into him, my breasts press against his hard chest. It's beating quickly. I fight the temptation to unbuckle his pants right there in the doorway and drop to my knees. He slides his hands around my ass cheeks and picks me up into his grasp, assuring me that I'm not the only one with late-night cravings. I kiss him back, harder this time, and feel his tongue slide into my mouth. My breasts are throbbing, my nipples at attention, and my lacy thong growing wetter by the second. No words are ever spoken. We understand each other well.

With my legs still wrapped around his waist, I let out a sigh of angst and lose myself in his mouth. *Delicious.* Our passion speaks for us both. I want him desperately, more than I knew. He grabs the back of my neck and I kick the door shut while he manages to find my bedroom without any direction or hesitation.

Cole throws me down on the bed and I rip off his jacket. His hands are wrapped around my breasts and as he sucks my nipples through the silk, all I can think about is how badly I want to take this ride. Impulsively, I grab his head and push it down between my legs. The candle lights his way. He tosses my legs over his shoulders. My back arches. He tongue-fucks me, masterfully licking and sucking me dry until my body begins to quiver, wet all over again. I pound my fist into the pillow and twist between the damp sheets. And when I slink away from him, barely able to take any more, he forces my hips back to his lips. I glance at the wall; I am his shadow puppet. Forcibly, I yank his T-shirt over his head and dig my fingernails into his skin, huffing with anticipation. He stretches me out with his fingers, fucking me, ensuring that I'm ready. I tense. But before I can cry out in ecstasy he stops, letting his tongue lick a trail up to my mouth. His muscles ripple over me and I exhale in pain when he lowers his body into me, thrusting inside me, opening me up to grip him tightly. The man is wild, unbridled. I'd been warned. My eyes are pinched shut and with each stroke, each push, each pull, my thighs tighten around him. I dig my nails deeper into his skin until I feel blood. My entire body blisters, every nerve ending alive with desire and as he fucks me with savage emotion, I understand why they call him The Beast.

Chapter 66

"Baby Girl?"

"Yes," I answer weakly, still out of breath, collapsed on top of Cole. He had held out until I came, making sure I screamed loud enough for my neighbors to hear.

"Was that reassurance enough?"

"Uh-huh," I say, still dazed and hazy. "I heard you loud and clear."

"Good." He wipes the sweat from my forehead. "And I'm impressed; you held your own. I wasn't sure if you could handle it." His deep voice is hot against my skin.

I moan, listening to his heart pound. My body is sticky and tingly, and although I did my best with The Beast I knew I wasn't equipped to go another round.

He lifts my chin and kisses my lips. "Now, I need something from you."

I shake my head, my eyes now closed.

"I need you—all of you. I'm not cool with sharing you with any-one else. That's not how I get down."

I open my eyes.

"You said you don't have a man. And I believe that. But if you need to tie up some loose ends—"

Share me? A late-night dick date was one thing, but I wasn't ready to jump into a relationship with him.

"I don't know if I'm ready for a re—"

"We can take this as slow as you want." He wraps his other arm around my waist. "But I've never been good at sharing my toys." Then he rolls me over on the bed and kisses my earlobe, breath-ing heavily into my neck.

Enraptured, I purr.

Chapter 67

I was stirred by the mating calls of chirping birds this morning. For a brief moment when I'd opened my eyes I wondered if it had all been a wicked wet dream. But when I turned over, both my stiff hips and the note left on the pillow said otherwise.

Good morning, Baby Girl. I had to roll and didn't want to wake you. Keep your chin up today. You shouldn't have any problems with Brad. Call you after practice. Dinner tonight.
And you were incredible last night.

I hobble to the bathroom and brush my teeth, examining last night's sequence of late-night events. *How did I end up in a rela-tionship?* Even though Cole had said that we could move slowly, I wasn't even sure if I liked him. Yes, he was smart, with ridiculous swagger, and he had a penis that deserved to be bronzed . . . but he was an athlete. I HATE athletes! And besides, I never learned to speak Stepford.

My head starts to throb and I feel clammy. I peel back the nicotine patch and toss it in the trash. I pull out a fresh one for today, craving a tiny taste of the cake I'd ordered from the bodega yesterday. *Maybe just a sliver.* I speedball to get dressed and grab my tote from the couch. *Okay, maybe just a slice.*

I reach around the asparagus spears and mixed greens and pull out what's left of the chocolate almond cake with strawberries and vanilla buttercream. Today's clusterfuck of bullshit had fully tyrannized my thoughts by the time the third giant slice of cake was melting in my mouth. *Maybe you should see somebody,* Hannah had said. *You didn't pull that trigger. . . .*

I cross my legs on the floor, the refrigerator door ajar and a buzzing in my ear. Suddenly, I can't shake the thought of Sam either, his supermodeling wife, and the inked reports from last Friday night. *Celebu-slut!* I shovel another piece into my mouth and wash it down with water. Cole's stern voice is on repeat in my head. *"You said you don't have a man. But if you need to tie up some loose ends—"*

I look down at my hands, covered in chocolate and now shaking uncontrollably. The cake platter sits motionless on my lap with just enough crumbs to attest to the dessert that once was. I close my eyes and lick gobs of frosting from my fingertips and around my lips. If only time would stand still, just for this one happy gluttonous moment . . . before the inevitable guilt sets in.

I slam the bathroom door behind me.

Chapter 68

"Morning, Ernie." I toss the greeting over my shoulder as I sweep through the lobby, past all of security, imperviously dodging the possibility of small talk. I count to ten but when I speed past thirteen I politely turn around and see that Ernie is ignoring me. He's completely engrossed in studying the weekend paper.

"Seriously, Ernie, what do you want from me?" It's obvious that he's stuck on Page 6 and I'm stuck right here, in the lobby of perennial shame.

"You know, Ms. Lee, we haven't had this kind of attention in our building since Ms. Donatella was here. I took care of the paps for you this morning. Didn't think you'd be open to a photo shoot considering how this last one turned out," he says, slapping the paper with his other hand just inches from the buzzer.

"Thank you, Ernie." I proffer a half-ass geisha-girl curtsy. "Thank you very much."

"Sure thing, Ms. Kennedy."

I smile away the embarrassment and the weight on my shoulders, already heavy enough from my tote alone. Finally he relents and buzzes me into my workday.

"Kennedy Lee to Wardrobe, Kennedy Lee to Wardrobe," God orders, a hint of disappointment in his voice, too. I rush from the elevator, past Bert, who barely nods at me.

"Morning, Bert."

With his mouth crinkled disapprovingly, he nods again—*barely*. I've got no time to either pacify his personal annoyance with me or acknowledge the power to my pissed off people. So I blaze down the hall, past several more antagonistic stares and glares until I stumble into the Wardrobe lair.

"Morning, Marge," I greet, relieved to finally see a friendly face among the barrage of blurred scowls I'd passed on the way in. I stop in my Underground Railroad tracks when I see Marge listening intently to Bliss, who is cuddled beside Jesse James, watching him beat the newspaper against his hands.

"And I positively can't believe those goons didn't publish my picture," Bliss blisters. "I stood there for fifteen minutes posing and voguing for them." She looks up from her hissy huddle. "Well, if it isn't our studio celebu-tart," Bliss bashes.

"Don't you mean our *C-list* Celebu-tart," Jesse James slithers into my ear. Trinity's makeup job has completely covered his weekend battle wounds, but the concealer and rouge don't hide the humiliation still scribbled beneath the cosmetics pancake. "You really think you can get away with this? Your boyfriend, The Beast, making me look like an ass?!" Jesse holds up the paper and points to his beatdown, courtesy of Cole's fist. "This better not fuck up my shot at *Dancing with the Stars* or my music career."

"Tell her, Jesse Baby," Bliss cluelessly blurts out from behind his shoulder. She nudges him in the back and wriggles her finger. "That little bitch doesn't know who she's fucking with, does she?" Neurotically, Bliss taps her foot against the floor, sniffling through her narrow nostrils.

Marge is anxiously watching me, awaiting my defense. I take a deep breath and unleash the wrath of a woman scorned by a double-crossing, double-dipping man-whore. "You should really be mortified, ARNOLD! Those reporters would sell their souls to hear all about that switch-hitting boy from Flint who took time off from his routine RIM job for that beatdown." (I'd practiced that in the cab ride over.)

Jack pops his head into the door. "Oh my, what's this I hear?"

Arnold's eyes immediately saucer. He takes a giant step backward, almost knocking Bliss into a rack of couture. "What?!" His voice trembles right along with his hand, which drops the newspaper to the floor. His mouth drops, too, and is gaping open when he nervously looks over his shoulder at Bliss. Without another word, he storms out the door with Jack on his heels.

"Oh Jessseee . . ." Jack stalks after him.

"I never knew Denny's was an acronym for Juilliard!" I shout, my words lingering in the halls, way over the heads of our other castmates.

"What? What's she talking about?" Bliss follows on Arnold's arches, glancing back at me. "Who's Arnold?!"

"Morning, dear." Marge smiles approvingly. "And how are we doing on this dark day?" She motions for me to undress.

"Dark? Not for you, too?" I stop removing my leggings and look her in the eyes.

"No, dear, I'm referring to this," she says, turning on her pink Crocs and pointing to the paper that's lying open to my weekend nightmare.

"Oh, Marge, c'mon, not you, too."

"Everyone else around here has already been caught up to speed as well." She relaxes her fingers into my shoulders.

"You can't believe everything you read," I huff. "It really didn't happen that way—not this time, at least." I crumble.

"Okay, let me guess," she says, shutting her door abruptly—something I've never seen her do so forcibly before. "Jesse James staged the entire thing."

"Whoa, Marge!" I cock my head to the side and acknowledge her Miss Cleo moment. "That's just weird."

"You're not the first lass who's been bitten by him."

I plop down in the chair behind a rack of tagged clothes. "He bites hard."

The edges of her eyes slip into a smile. She brushes her silky white hair over her shoulder. "Let's just say that I've been around for quite a long time. That boy is a soap star but he could be so much more. He knows it, too. Such a waste." Marge lowers her voice and takes the clothes from me. "I once heard that he broke off an engagement because he didn't like the way his fiancée looked without makeup."

"Who does that?!"

"The same person who tries to blackmail a fellow castmate even though they're living their own double life. How do you kids put it? Pitching for both leagues?"

I giggle. "Batting for both teams."

"That's right, dear."

"Then you know about—"

"Of course I know. I know everything that goes on around here," she says matronly, handing me a tailored pin-striped suit with a whimsical yellow Tracy Reese blouse that pranced the runway during Fashion Week. "This should look stunning on you. I pulled it especially for today." I slip into the costume and listen attentively to Marge while she nips and tucks. "He was never right for you, dear."

"Ow!"

"Oh, I'm so sorry; my fingers are getting clumsy in their old age," she mutters through the stick pins that are smashed between her lips. "I like to think that I've lived long enough to know that there's someone for each of us. But sometimes getting to love can be, oh, quite *challenging*."

"You believe in soul mates, Marge?"

"I believe in love, dear," she sings, and swings me around. "Now, you've got a rather *challenging* day ahead of you." She fusses with the understated ruffles on the lemony blouse. "And this power suit should be the perfect accessory to get you through it all."

"What's so special about today, besides the obvious?" I roll my eyes at my enemy that is Saturday's newspaper.

"Kennedy, are you in there?" Izzie yells from outside the locked door. "I need to talk to you."

Marge exhales. "And so it begins."

"What?"

"Let's just say you'll need something that screams confident and powerful, but still reads 'soft and pink.' "

"But it's yellow."

"Kennedy!" Izzie screams again, this time with more angst in her voice than before.

Marge yanks the door open and turns to look at me. "You're the only one who can make this right and I think you're up for the challenge." Marge winks at me. "And I'm not talking about Arnold, dear."

Izzie grabs me by the elbow and pulls me out the door while I'm still choking on Marge's words. "Who's Arnold?" Izzie asks, as we hightail it through the halls.

Chapter 69

"What's wrong?" I question Izzie. "And where're we going?"

"I've got my orders."

When we surf the stairs, taking two at a time into the yellow-brick hall, Izzie walks me up to a dressing room and hands me the key. "This one's yours."

"Izzie, not again," I mope, leaning against the door. "A new dressing room?!"

She curdles her lips and shrugs. "I've got my orders."

"And I wouldn't suppose that those orders came directly from Jack, did they? He's the only one that would happily put me in a four-by-four with Bliss right next door. I mean, really!" I push the door open and pull Izzie inside. "You've got to fess up this time. What's going on? You're the only one around here who'll give it to me straight."

"Straight, no chaser." Izzie sighs, before poking her head into the hall to check for spywitnesses. She closes the dressing room door and secures her headset in place. "Okay, but I don't have long. I've got to get to a briefing, and now you've got to report to Mr. Cohen's office."

"What!?" I think of all the embarrassing tabloid fodder Sam could lasso me with and instantly feel sick to my stomach. I was positive that he'd seen the paper and suddenly feared for my fledgling career. "I think I'm gonna be ill!"

"I know you don't want to hear this, but I've got my—"

"Orders."

Frazzled, Izzie nudges her glasses farther up onto the bridge of her nose. "Must be a full moon around here; we haven't had this kind of uproar in the ANS halls since Donna—"

"Tella was here. Yes, yes, I heard. Just get to the good stuff. Please!"

"Kennedy, you *are* the good stuff," she purrs. "I saw the paper." Izzie looks around the room, acknowledging imaginary onlookers. "Everybody's seen the paper. Didn't *you* see the paper?" She reaches into her black corduroy pants pocket and pulls out a folded newspaper clipping with Jesse James's tongue squeezed into my mouth. She shoves it at me reverently, unable to make eye contact. "In case you haven't already seen what they wrote about you."

"Of course I saw it, Izzie," I whine. "I get the feeling that even Bert the toy cop has seen it."

Izzie nods in agreement. "Jack made his morning rounds."

Jack the Rat!

I slide onto the dingy hard couch that's been hoisted against the muted walls of my new nondescript dressing room and shove my head into my hands. "I can't worry about why Jack has it out for me right now. I really, *really* need to know why Sam—I mean Mr. Cohen"—I clear my throat—"wants to see me in his office." I plead to Izzie for clarity. "I'm being ordered up to his office?!"

"Well, all I can tell you," she whispers, "is that he came in with newspapers shoved under his arms and an exasperated look on his face."

"Exasperated?"

"Yeah, you know, 'greatly annoyed, out of patience.' "

Raking my fingers over the nicotine patch adhered to my arm, I force a smile and collect my thoughts. "Okay, Izzie. Thanks."

"There's one more thing."

Say it ain't so!

"I'm so sorry, Kennedy, but the script has been revised."

I shriek. "What do you mean, 'It's been revised'?"

"Well, revised, as in 'amended' or 'altered,' " Izzie elaborates.

"I know what it—" I stop myself, realizing the futility of the words set to follow. I take the new script from her and begin to flip through it frantically before she stops me.

"Uh, Kennedy," she says delicately, as she taps on her Timex. "Mr. Cohen."

"Right." I exhale. *Mr. Cohen.*

Chapter 70

I follow Izzie through the soundstage maze and out into the main thoroughfare toward the elevator banks. By now all the bit actors are rushing past me on their way to Makeup or Wardrobe and each of them makes a point to snuff me on their way. It feels like my first day of work is being replayed and somebody just needs to shoot the goddamn groundhog already!

"Do you have any idea what he wants to talk to me about?" I whisper to Izzie while we wait for the lift, trying to ensure Bert doesn't overhear.

"No," she whispers back.

"Was he pissed?"

"I've never seen him so emotional, not since . . . well not since you started working here. I have to admit, it's been really nice seeing him kind of awake again. And I'm not the only one who's noticed."

The tiny hairs on my arm burn when I realize that I've been peeling at the edges of the nic patch that's just barely still stuck to my arm. *One drag off a cig would solve all my problems.* Reinforcements, I remember. I rumble through my tote and pull out a stick of nicotine gum and tear away at the wrapper. I can't suck the potent drug from the gum fast enough and when I don't feel any relief, I reach in my bag for another piece. I try to relax but my heart does the Riverdance against my chest. *EW! This gum is gross!* The elevator doors open and I swear I hear Bert laugh. I glance over to him and note that his charcoal chocolate lips had been permanently tar-stained long ago. I chew into the gum that much harder.

Izzie raps on the door. "Mr. Cohen," she squeaks.

"Come in, please."

I accidentally swallow the wad of gum when my eyes lock with Sam's.

"Thank you, Izzie," he says, walking around his desk. "Good morning, Kennedy. Please, have a seat."

I stand frozen in place.

"Izzie, I mean for *everything*," he says, matter-of-factly, then looks over to me. "Please, have a seat," he instructs again. Izzie lowers her head and closes the door behind her.

Sam's office is sprawling, though in an expected minimalist mod sort of way. Shelves of plaques, awards, and numerous trophies are encased along the long wall and several rows of books and show scripts are aligned in the adjacent built-ins. Beautiful candid portraits of the distinguished men in his family look like they belong in the study in his East Hampton manse, and a few more autographed shots of undisputable jazz greats keep watch nearby. I wonder momentarily what they see when they're the only ones here with him.

"So, how are you?" he asks awkwardly, removing his suit jacket and hanging it in his closet. I take a deep breath and desperately try not to think about his hard chest resting against my breasts between his soft sheets. The outline of his muscles through his crisp collared shirt doesn't make it any easier. "Kennedy?"

"Yeah," I mumble, watching him intently study me. "Oh, you wanted me to answer that?"

"Yes. Please," he confirms, as he walks back to his oversized mahogany desk and takes a seat behind it. "How are you?"

"Fine."

Sam bites down on his bottom lip and is noticeably uncomfortable. "I'm very aware that this is awkward for both of us—"

"You think?!" I blurt out before he can finish.

"Yes." He rubs his hand over his chin.

"Yes," I agree, again.

"I just feel like we need to have a quick meeting or a talk to discuss ANS, the staff, and the latest developments that seem to all be centered around you," Sam offers, not once looking directly at me.

"I see." I stop looking at him, too.

He leans back in his chair and folds his hands over his chest. "I think it's important to talk about what happened this weekend."

"I don't," I say, surprising myself.

"You don't . . . what?"

I cross my legs tightly and flick the sparkly Dior stiletto back and forth.

"I, uh, don't agree that we need to discuss what happened between us this weekend."

"I see."

My pressure is rising and I'm getting heated. Screw Jack the Rat, Bliss the Bitch, *and* Arnold Seltzer, let them sit in the effing dean's office and rehash what they've all done wrong to Father Forgive-Me-Then-Fuck-Me-Please!

"I really do think we need to talk about this," Sam forges, picking up the weekend paper. He opens it to Page Oops I Did It Again! But then I take a closer look at the headlines and realize that the newspaper is from *two weeks ago*. SHIT! Saturday's paper is on his desk beneath today's script. *Oh the horror!*

"I just need to know that you're okay, first." Sam's eyes are sincere.

"I'm fine," I lie, fighting back tears, desperate to keep them from making a scene.

"Fine." He shrugs. "You're fine. Everything's fine. Well, since you're 'fine' do you think you can talk to me about some of this—*any of this*?" He taps the paper against his desk. "I mean, what happened here? I'm getting quizzed by my ad guys and I'm hearing all kinds of stories on the floor, but the truth is that I'd really like to hear it from you—if you don't mind."

I look into the eyes of Sam's father and grandfather, who stare back at me from their pedestals on the wall. "I'd rather not discuss this with you," I admit sheepishly. "Isn't there anyone else I can talk to? You know, someone I haven't slept with?"

"Well, you're building out that list kind of fast," he quips, before he can catch himself.

A tear falls quicker than I can reclaim it. "Don't, Sam!" The tone in my voice slowly creeps into scary territory. "Just don't!"

"I didn't mean that." When I jump from the chair he hustles around his desk and reaches out for me. My chair tumbles over. "I'm sorry."

"Just don't!" I warn and run for the door. Sam runs after me, grabbing my elbow. I lean my head into the door and watch as the tears fall to the floor. "You have no right."

"I know, Gorgeous," he says, turning me into his arms. He grabs my neck and inhales my scent before he kisses me gently on the lips. I kiss him back and fold into his body like I've always belonged there. When I feel his tongue against mine I wrap my arms around him and hold on tight.

"I didn't mean to say that," he admits, inches away from my lips. "You're killing me here. I thought I could handle you and Jesse. I thought I could manage it all," he says into my skin, his arms still holding me.

"You mean you already knew about that? Before today?" My eyes sweep the floor, searching for my dignity.

"Yeah," he answers quietly.

"But you never said anything."

"I know."

"But—"

"Listen"—Sam moves a few millimeters away—"despite what you might think, I had no intention of anything happening between you and me." He rubs his hand against his stubble. "I looked up and there we were—together. It wasn't like I planned any of it." His voice is textured, filled with depth. "But there we were."

I ease out of his space and walk across the room to the window, frantically wiping tears away. The Hudson River is glistening back at me peacefully, mocking me. I turn around and eye the newspaper in his hands. "You never said a word about it."

"It never mattered. Right away you told me at the diner that you'd made a huge mistake. You were so embarrassed, so ashamed that night," he says, walking over to the window to stand beside me. "There was no need for me to bring it up. You were punishing yourself enough for me, for Smith, and for the entire network. I didn't want to make you feel worse; I didn't need to." He leans against the wall and runs his finger through his wavy hair, all the while watching me. "I thought you'd learned the lesson so I told everyone I had it under control."

"I'm sorry." I cover my face with my hands.

"Me too," he says easily.

"I slept with him," I confess, wanting to finally clear the air.

Sam laughs uncomfortably, and then sighs. "I know."

My stomach tightens. "How did you know?"

"Do you really think he would keep something like that under wraps? And it's my job to know everything that goes on around here, Kennedy."

Where had I heard that before?

"I know you might forget that from time to time; it's not like I've been rigorous about keeping the boundaries clear," he admits. "Hey"—he tugs on my arm—"but I've never slept with one of my actresses before—ever."

Ever?

"This is the first time this has happened to me. And I can't remember ever even feeling this way."

I allow myself to blush.

"Arnold Seltzer, on the other hand, is a different kind of guy. He doesn't do things without motive."

My eyebrows fly into my forehead. "You know about him— about his past?" Sam grins knowingly, but doesn't respond.

"Jesse James is typical, not surprising; he conspires to get ahead the classic Hollywood way."

"I, uh—I wanted to tell you when we were at dinner at Tavern. I struggled with it all night long." *Me and a big fat elephant.*

"I kind of figured you were trying to get that out, but I didn't want to hear it. I wanted to leave it where it was."

"I didn't know who he was when we got together, Sam. And I

definitely didn't know I'd be working with him. I'd had way too much to drink that night and things just—one bad decision after another."

"Well"—he drops the paper and intertwines his fingers with mine—"you're not the only one who's made some bad decisions." His voice is deep and warm against my ear. "I'm sorry for what I put you through." He kisses my neck and my lids close.

"I don't know what to say." He turns me around and my eyes stare into his lips, watching as they move closer to mine. I close my eyes and he kisses me again, this time with more intensity and warmth than before. I shiver when glamorous images of Mercedes Gold pop up behind my lids. Instinctively, I pull away from him. "NO!" I force out the command. "I can't! You should've told me you were married. You should've told me you had a wife—a wife, Sam!" I step away from him. "I don't care what the circumstances were."

"I know. And like I said before, I'm sorry for that." Sam wipes away my tears, comforting me when I start to cry, but overpowering feelings of resentment and anger seethe through me anyway.

"I can't do this with you. I won't do this with you." I pull farther away. "You're married!" The phone rings and I head for the door.

"Please, Kennedy. Wait."

"I have to go. I have to learn new sides."

"Please!"

I stop at the door and lean against it while he answers the phone and tugs at my heart. "Yes, Libby. Yes, I'll need to take the later flight." He pauses and looks at me. "No, Lib, it looks like I'll be traveling alone."

I feel a flush when I think of Sam leaving town without me. I shake it off and remember that I have dinner plans with Cole. That thought doesn't ignite a rushing flush or a lover's blush, but in that moment I am keenly aware that what I feel is safe.

"What is it? I have to go. I can't do this with you anymore." I sob softly.

"Don't cry, Gorgeous," he begs, walking back into my heart. I try to turn away but he grabs me, forcing me to connect with him.

"You're married to Mercedes Gold." I fight his grip.

"No, I'm not—not for much longer." He wrestles with my fingers. "I'm leaving her."

"What?!" Wide-eyed, I study him.

"It's over." He exhales slowly. "It's been over for a long time. That's what I wanted to tell you at dinner Friday night. And we don't live together." He holds my chin up to him. "Despite what she may have said, she doesn't live there with me—or anywhere else with me for that matter."

"At the apartment?"

"Or the penthouse on the Upper East Side or my house in the Hamptons or the villa in St. Bart's—"

"But—"

"She's got the apartment in Paris. And that's fine by me. I'll take Manhattan any day, especially if that's where you'll be."

"How did she get into the apartment when—"

"Winston," he relents. "She threatened him and he told her everything."

"Blackmail?"

"We all have a past. And she holds on tightly to his. He said he just freaked. He feels so bad; he wants to make it right," Sam says, looking away. "So do I. The truth is, after all these years I understand her. She doesn't want me, Kennedy, but she doesn't want anyone else to have me either. She's ruthless, I know. Everyone knows. I just didn't figure she'd find out so soon that I was finally moving on." Sam exhales. "It's never mattered to me before because there's never been anyone else. No one has ever made me feel so good, like I mattered, like what I wanted mattered—and yes, I know it happened so fast. But again, here we are."

"You're still married, Sam. Nothing has changed. Just forget about me."

"Forget you? I can barely remember life before you."

"But it's Mercedes Fucking Gold!"

"And you're Kennedy Fucking Lee!" He kisses my forehead. "And I only want to be with you."

"But, we don't have anything to build on; we ruined it all. How can I trust you? Or you trust me, for that matter." I quiet.

"We can start over. And take our time the second time around."

"No. We can't go back."

"Then let's go forward, Gorgeous." He squeezes my arms. "I don't want to do this without you. It's because of you that I'm even here right now, starting what should've been my life a long time ago."

I move away from him. "It's too late."

He searches my eyes. "Don't run away again—not unless you plan on taking me with you."

"Sam, I can't—"

"Kennedy, what are you *really* saying?"

My eyes dart away. "Just tell me one thing, just one thing."

"Anything. I'll never keep anything from you again."

"Does she know you're leaving? Does she know you're divorcing her?" I close my eyes and hold on tight. "Have you told her you're leaving her?"

Sam doesn't answer. Instead, he massages the back of his neck nervously and shoves his other hand into his suit pocket.

"So, I guess what I'm *really* saying is that I *won't* do this with you." I swallow hard and curl the tips of my toes, pulling strength from everywhere. I reach for the doorknob that's pressing into my back and turn it. "You're married, Sam!" I kiss his cheek, lingering for an extra beat. "And I'm so sorry," I whisper into him before turning to run, casting the final stone that I know will push him away for good. "But I've been seeing someone else."

Chapter 71

Once I'm safely in my dressing room, surrounded by dusty dingy silence, I shudder at my truth: Somehow I'd fallen in love with Sam Cohen.

"Kennedy, open the door!" Jack screeches.

"One second," I answer, cleaning my face, scrambling. "Yes?"

Jack switches into my space, partially closing the door behind him. He folds his arms across his chest and huffs, the weekend paper dangling from his manicured hands. "I told you that you weren't my first choice around here and now you've shown everyone else why." He looks around the depressing room. The paint is peeling off the wall around the tiny vanity where only two of the five lightbulbs still burn. "Yes, this is more appropriate for you; you simply don't deserve top of the line. YOU are not a star! Mr. Cohen should've never tried to treat you like one, you're nothing but the C-list Celebu-tart they said you are." He throws the paper at me and sniffs his upper lip. "Learn the new script, honey, although something tells me you won't have any trouble with *these* sides. The words should ring quite true for you!" He sneers, lurking in the doorway. "Okay then." He composes himself. "Good talk!"

I glance down at the revised script.

"Oh, and you can forget about running to Mr. Cohen about this script; he's on his way out."

What?!

"Yep, that's it!" Jack screeches. "Just the look I walked up here to see!" He rolls his eyes into his head. "Priceless."

Immediately, I flip through the pages, scraping my neon orange highlighter over every line of dialogue with Lacey's name above it. I slow down when I really begin to process the words on the page.

Lacey Madison is sloppy drunk at Blake Blass's launch party for *SuperBoy Magazine*. After passionately kissing Blake in front of a flurry of photographers, she clumsily hops onto the bar and strips down to her bra and panties. She is hoisted from the bar before she can continue her drunken striptease for industry onlookers.

The script is shaking in my hands and I can't remember the last time I took a breath. The script falls to the floor, and the walls of the crummy dressing room begin to close in on me.

"Kennedy, it's me," Izzie whispers. "Please, open the door." She knocks harder. "Kennedy!"

The words in the script mock my entire career from the floor. The knob turns and Izzie pokes her head around the door.

"Are you okay?" She runs over to the couch, scooping up the script.

Tragically, I shake my head.

"This is what I wanted to talk to you about," she says, shaking the script in her hand. "I know this looks really bad."

Wide-eyed, I watch Izzie, still unable to speak. Surely she can't explain this away. I get it, I totally get it. Art imitating life. No further explanation necessary.

"I don't agree with this. I think it's mean and rude." She rubs my hand.

"Sam."

"Mr. Cohen?"

I slouch back into the couch.

"He didn't have anything to do with this." She presses her headset into her ear. "He fought this every step of the way."

"But Sam—"

"He didn't tell you?" Izzie reaches for the door.

I raise my eyebrows.

"He's gone." She sticks her head back into the room. "He told me to pack up his things and have Libby pick them up. He's not going to be with ANS anymore."

"What?!"

"He's moving to L.A. . . . to make *London's Love.*"

Chapter 72

I plop down into Trinity's chair.

"Well hello there, Newspaper Girl!"

"Hi," I dryly reply.

"Not your day, huh?" she says, in bland understatement.

I don't respond. Instead, I reluctantly quiz myself repeatedly until I've got most of my lines committed to memory.

"What's wrong?" she asks rhetorically, pulling my face into distortion. "Cat got your tongue? Cat named Jesse?"

I blink twice as she applies mounds of midnight blue shadow to my naked eye.

"Well." Trinity sighs. "At least your hair looked fierce in that shot. I told everybody it was my creation." She plucks the barely there hairs from my brow.

OW!

I look at the call sheet that's taped to the vanity and glance at my watch. I've got twenty minutes before I'm scheduled to be on set to reenact one of the most embarrassing nights of my life with a cast of crazies who are sure to devour every demeaning second of it. Each and every line in the script reads like fragments of that fated eve I'd never been able to piece together. The scene seems to fall perfectly into place, like somebody spoon-fed the crew of writers the forgotten moments of my night.

Trinity continues babbling on about a cat, my tongue, and scattered ingrown brow hairs.

"Trinity, I'm sorry but I'm trying to get these sides down."

"I don't know why; it's YOU all over the page. The way I hear it, that's your entire night verbatim. Don't you recognize it—at least what you remember of it?"

I sink into the chair, my dignity shriveling.

"Yeah, that's you all up and through. I think I'm gonna pray for you," she snarks under her breath. "Uh-huh, you, boo boo . . . YOU!"

"What are you talking about?" I fish for more info, sure that she's dying to see me sweat through the thick foundation she's caked all over my worry lines.

"Don't try and act all brand-new like you ain't know. Jesse James came with the dirt and gave the writers everything they needed. Talk about sweeps; it's 'bout to be the best storyline in Daytime. And with all the media attention, somebody's sure to notice all this fierce hair and makeup poppin' off around here."

I jump up from the chair before she has a chance to secure the Diana Ross lash strip to my other eye.

"Oh, I see how you do; should've known from the start when you walked up in here that first day all jizzed up on hangover fumes." She pokes the faux hawk on top of her tiny head into the hallway, her foundation brush twirling in the air. "God don't like ugly."

Chapter 73

"Roxy, I can't do this anymore," I wail into my cell and rip the nicotine patch from my arm. "I've gotta get out of here."

"^^##*#***#!"

"No, Roxy, you don't understand; it really *is* that bad. There's got to be some sort of human resources clause that prohibits them from dishing out this level of abuse to me. And even if there isn't—"

"^^##*#***#!"

"Yeah, you heard right; I did sleep with him."

"^^##*#***#!"

"Yes, I slept with him, too!"

"^^##*#***#!"

"I don't care anymore; I'll go back to the fucking insurance adjuster's before I let them—" My Diana lash is now dangling from my lid and dipping into my eyeball. "They can't bring my personal life into this! They just can't!"

"^^##*#***#!"

"Yes, I quit!" I shiver when the words roll off my tongue. "Weren't you the one who told me to walk off the set of Pooky's 'Pissin' On 'Em' video shoot, when they wanted to pour warm Sprite all over me. You said if I don't stand for something then I'll fall for anything! And damnit, Roxy, I'm freefalling!"

Outfitted in my one lash and *Knots Landing* eye shadow, I toss the script onto the piss-poor excuse of a couch and take one last look around the lifeless room. I glance up, channeling God, seeking validation.

"Kennedy Lee to set. Kennedy Lee to set."

I mean, c'mon! You forgave Mary Magdalene!

When I step into the hallway, I exhale and toss my hair over my shoulder. The mean munchkins watch me with disdain from below but I clutch my courage and grip my tote as I make my final exit from this godforsaken horror show! I pick my left foot up and my right one down . . . My head is held high as I nervously ease on down the yellow-brick hall, past Smith who is hovering over monitors in the control booth. *You can do this!*

"Kennedy, exactly where do you think you're going?!" Jack screams from the center of the room.

There's no place like home, there's no place like home, there's no place . . .

"You'll regret this! And don't think you'll work in this town again if you—"

The thick heavy doors to Studio 26 slam behind me.

"Marge," I say, hastily poking my head into Wardrobe. "I don't have much time before the toy cops come for me, but I wanted to return this to you personally." I hand over the power suit and the gushingly gorge sparkly red shoes.

She smiles, letting her fingers rest over mine for an extended moment. "I'm proud of you, dear."

"And you don't think I'm a quitter?"

"Only a winner is strong enough to know when it's her time to move on."

"I have no idea what I'm going to do. But doing that scene would've made me a joke, robbed me of what little dignity I have left."

She pats the top of my hands. "You've got much more than you know, dear. You've had it all along. This is a cutthroat business, that's for sure. And most of the time it's not even personal."

"Then why do I feel like this is very personal, because I brought all this bad publicity?"

"Please! Do you know how many people are TiVo'ing ANS to check out—"

"America's Next Slut?"

"No! They all want to check out the beautiful exotic model-turned-soap-star who's turning New York upside down." She rubs my hands again and I can't help but note the buttery soft feel of hers. "And I have a strange feeling that you're gonna do just fine. Your agent is bound to have her hands full as soon as the world finds out that you're available and free."

Free. *I'm free! I'M FREE!*

An afterthought of Sam flashes through my mind. *I hope you're right.* I reach out and finally give her the hug I'd wanted to give her the first day we'd met when I was sprawled out next to the urinal.

"It's been nice knowing you, Kennedy Lee."

"Yes. Nice," I wholly agree, and touch the ends of Marge's silky hair.

"Oh, before I forget—" She turns around and picks up a thick envelope from the vanity with my name scribbled across it. "This is for you."

"What's this?"

"You'll know exactly what to do with it, dear. Of that I'm sure."

Once downstairs, I toss the package into my tote and walk through security. Ernie tips his hat and I nervously smile back, now terrified that I have no place to go.

Anxiously, I fumble around for the king-size Snickers I'd stashed in my bag, in case of emergencies. Instead, I pull out the head shrink's business card and hold it tightly between my fingers. I stare at it until the card begins to shake. The doors of the network building swing open and I exit, never looking back, hoping to hell I won't ever need to.

Chapter 74

"So that's it? You just quit!?" Cole asks indignantly over dinner at Tao, Manhattan's hipster pan-Asian hotspot. Although a few weeks had gone by since my abrupt departure from ANS, Cole's basketball schedule hadn't allowed him an adequate chance to re-hash his feelings, but I was well aware of how he felt about my scandalous soap opera suicide.

"I had to; you don't understand. There was no way I could take it," I whine. "They were so mean to me." I push the veggie rolls around my plate and mash into my sake-braised shiitake mush-rooms with dismay. They were beginning to look as lifeless as I'd felt since I'd secretly started seeing the head shrink and had to trudge back to the temp agency with my tail between my legs.

"Okay, so let me get this straight: You're saying that you quit your job because they were being *mean* to you?" Cole bites into his wasabi-crusted filet mignon, letting the ginger scallion sauce spew from his lips. "I just don't understand that. Who does that, Baby Girl? No backup plan, no job waiting in the wings?"

"Well, there's always the insurance adjuster claims gig through the temp agency." I stare into the giant sixteen-foot-tall Buddha bolted to the floor.

"Is that supposed to be a joke?"

I shrug. "No, they're getting me reassigned to the Chinaman."

"So that's it? You left *America's Next Sweetheart*? To temp?" he asks pompously. "What about your agent? Is she working on get-ting you seen for another show?"

"I'm waiting for Roxy to line up some more auditions now. This afternoon I went out for a PSA, though."

"A public service announcement?" He contorts his face, and then laughs scornfully. "You shouldn't have left ANS, that's all there is to it."

"They didn't leave me much choice."

"You always have a choice. You can't just walk out on a job; nobody does that. You've got people who are depending on you: you've got an agent, there are writers and producers and even advertisers." He looks away. "And most important, you've got a reputation to protect. And I don't mean the one that's gaining popularity in the tabloids, either. If people find out you walked out on your job, no one else will want to hire you. You could get blackballed and it's still relatively early in your career to battle something like that." He stares sternly into my eyes. "And we don't want that, do we?"

"Cole." I slouch in my chair. "One of the producers called me a fuck-up. He reminded me that he didn't want me there in the first place. He lit into me, cursing me and calling me a slut. What part of 'hostile work environment' don't you understand?!"

Cole sops up some black bean sauce with his Chinese broccoli. "My coach calls me a pussy every other practice, and I can't even count the number of captains and teammates that have yelled at me, trashed me, put me down, and made me do some pretty embarrassing, albeit character-building, things when I was a rookie."

"I understand that, but I'm not a rookie, I'm an actress—a professional actress on a professional set."

"No, you're being a self-indulgent brat."

Too pissed to verbally respond and downright afraid of what will come out of my mouth, I choose instead to say nothing. Britt was the only one who ever called me that, when I'd lock myself in our closet after Racquel satisfied her rage-induced urges to whale on me. "Don't call me that! Ever!"

"I'm sorry, I'm just saying that—"

"Just because you can let people treat you like shit and demean you in the name of basketball doesn't mean . . ." My voice creeps up an octave over the electric house music pumping through the bustling twelve-thousand-square-foot dome. "It's—it's . . . mean!"

"Lower your voice. You're overreacting."

"No! You're still punishing me for something that happened before I even met you!" It was becoming apparent that no amount of back-breaking sex was going to change that.

"What? Of course I'm over it, but—"

"But what?"

"Well, since you went there . . . *did* your leaving have anything to do with Sam Cohen going on hiatus to film that flick, the one you wanted to be in so badly?"

"Why would you say that?" I ask, somewhat shaken.

"Why do you think?" He doesn't blink.

"No!" I shake my head. "This has nothing to do with Sam. This has everything to do with the fact that they were writing my life into the storylines of my show and there was nothing I could do about it! They were mocking me!"

"Well maybe if you'd been a little more discreet with your sex life then they wouldn't know enough about it to ridicule you."

"Are you serious!?" I screech.

"Lower your voice!"

"NO!"

"Look, Kennedy, I'm just saying—"

"You were right there—right next to me that night." I pound my fist on the table. "You know I had nothing to do with Jesse James or with Bliss or with the photographers or with—"

"I know, Baby Girl, but what I'm trying to get you to understand is that you can't go around prancing all over town with the paparazzi preying on you like they've been. You just shouldn't be out, especially while I'm on the road. It's just not a good look."

"I'm not prancing, Cole; I'm hanging out with my girls."

"And that usually leads to only one thing."

"Wait a minute! What happened with ANS has nothing to do with me going out with my girlfriends to have a good time."

"Apparently it does! Look around; you don't have a job! You need to lay low for a while, that's all I'm saying. If you're not out in the streets then fucked-up shit can't happen to you."

"You mean if I'm home alone you don't have to worry about—"

"No, what I'm saying is I can't protect you when you're not with me. So, yes, the best place for you to be is home—where I know you're safe." He looks around and smiles at his admiring fans. "Running the streets is no place for my girl anyway. And maybe this is a good thing, you getting fired."

"I didn't get fired. I quit!"

"Whatever. Maybe it's time for you to start thinking about settling down, to start thinking about not working so much. You're with me now, it's not like you *need* the money."

"But I love my work. I love acting and modeling and—are you seriously saying I should give up my dreams?"

"No, I'm just saying that maybe you should start thinking about other dreams, like running a household or maybe starting a foundation and running that."

"Oh, I get it; anything not to be running the streets."

"No, that's not it at all—well, not all of it."

"I'm not *running* the streets! And you're on the road in every major city and I have no idea what you're doing. And I don't get all postal about it."

"That's cuz you know I can handle mine."

WTF?

Brashly, he leans into the table. "What I'm saying is that I'm a man, and it's different."

"What!?" I finally force over the music.

Cole narrows his eyes, growing increasingly frustrated by the power of my pitch. "Kennedy, lower your voice; you're embarrassing yourself." He takes his final bite of cow and sips his sake before dabbing his mouth with his napkin.

"Excuse me," I say, suddenly feeling constricted. I push out my chair and gather myself before storming outside for air.

The night is cold and the wind unforgiving. But the corner of 58th and Madison Ave is bustling with all sorts of late-night noshers clacking down the block to crowd into Tao's revolving door. A flashy Euro-trashy guy stands nearby in a tailored zoot suit and watches me long for his Marlboro. I flash him my nic patch. He offers me a stick anyway.

"Kennedy, come back inside," Cole commands from the doorway of the restaurant. He cocks his head to the side. "Are you smoking?!"

I look over at Zoot and smile.

"Yes," I admit, and blow smoke into the air. "I've had a bad day and if I want a cigarette then damnit I'm going to have a FUCKING cigarette," I bellow belligerently.

"Your language!"

Fuck off!

"I thought you were quitting that disgusting habit." He looks around. "That's *really* not a good look. Just put the cigarette out and come inside. Right now!" he demands, motioning for me to follow him. When I don't move, he walks beneath the heat lamp and bears over me. I shiver. "I need you to be civilized and come back into the restaurant where it's warm so we can talk about your next move."

I puff away on the butt.

"I'm sure we can come up with something and maybe we can agree that this might've worked out for the best. I want you to start thinking about taking some time off."

I puff even harder. But when I don't budge and the ciggie doesn't get snubbed, Cole forces it from my fingers and tosses it.

"Look," he says, steadying my shoulders as my eyes dart into the street directly behind the smoke trail. "I know you've had a bad day." Annoyed, I roll my eyes and pout. "Okay, so it was a *very* bad day. But everything is workable. I'm sure we can figure out a way to make both of us happy."

Cole follows my gaze to the stretch Hummer sitting at the stoplight. "I want to be with you. I want you in my life." He shakes my shoulders. "Hey, look at me."

I don't.

"Baby Girl, I really dig you."

But will you ever accept me?

Chapter 75

" 'I postpone death by living, by suffering, by risking, by giving, by losing.' "

"Let me hear it—this time with CUN-*VICK*-SHUN!"

" 'I POSTPONE DEATH BY LIVING, BY SUFFERING, BY RISKING, BY GIVING, *BY LOSING.*' "

"Brilliant." My shrink applauds rambunctiously, crossing her hands over her heart. "And to think, I could barely get you to say it with a semblance of sincerity before." My noted psychiatrist, a regal middle-age woman with a brainiac vibe, let me know the first time I'd discreetly met with her four weeks ago that she was definitely some sort of smarty-pants. "You've selected a magical affirmation. I've always held Anaïs Nin in high regard." She smiles, her ageless freckled honeywheat skin glowing.

The Doc is of the Toni Morrison and Maya Angelou ilk, with subtle nuances of my kindergarten teacher. The Doc, however, is due to discuss "The Epic Ramifications of Obsolete Mental Health

Care in Impoverished American Communities" next month with *Oprah*. My kindergarten teacher—not so much.

"Have you been reciting your affirmation twice a day?"

"Sometimes more," I answer honestly, knowing this will delight her. It scared the heebie-jeebies out of me.

She sparks a Master Sanna healing candle in the corner of the room just below an Ansel Adams photograph of thunderclouds in Yosemite. In deep thought, she turns back to me and rests her hand on the nape of her neck, just below her salt-and-pepper 'fro.

"Like when you feel . . . how?"

"Like a fail—"

"Not the F word again?!" She pounds her fist on her knee. "Words have power, Dr. Lee. POW-WAR!"

She'd taken to calling me Dr. Lee when she found out I'd finished medical school. She'd felt it should be a source of pride, not failure, for me. She also knows I still need a bit more convincing.

"Yes, and I felt like 'the F word' pretty much every day this past week."

"All righty then, let's explore that."

"Well—" I glance out the window, trying to shake off thoughts of Cole and Sam—denial is way more than that river in Egypt. "No callbacks except the Olive Garden spot and another one for Wal-Mart."

"Commercials? Congratulations, that's—"

"No, no, no! This is NOT how it's supposed to go. Roxy's not even sending me out for the good roles."

"Hmmm, excuse me but . . . did she tell you that? Or are we making assumptions again? We talked about this last week, remember? When we were digesting your relationship with your sister?"

"I, uh, just think that—"

"The paranoia—not good, Dr. Lee! It only distracts us."

"Okay, but I *still* think she blames me for Racquel's *and* my father's deaths," I mumble under my breath. *No matter what you might think.*

"Well, what about you? Do *you* blame yourself?"

I dig my cowgirl heels into her Aztec throw rug and play with the seams of my acid-washed jeans.

"Ken-ne-dy?" she prods slowly, always knocking before entering. She somehow knows when to stop pushing me. I know she's trying to teach me the same.

"All righty then." She places her notepad and pen on the table beside her and leans back into the eggshell leather chair. "Let's stay on task. What about doing commercial work has you undervaluing yourself?"

"It's a spot for a singing hostess and a checkout girl at the Annual Super-Saver Sale!"

"But it's work!" she sings.

"But I'm working backward. I'm *back* at the Chinaman's office and *back* doing pickup work on weekends when I was just STAR-RING in a soap opera!"

"It's a few weeks of seasonal work—actors in the city do it all the time."

"I'm a dancing elf in Santa's Entourage at the Manhattan Mall!"

I haul myself back from the verge of tears that I'm aware stem directly from this heavy fear and disappointment I feel—both of which I've been learning are triggers for my bad behavior.

"Sometimes we have to take a few steps backward to see where we need to go. Sometimes, Dr. Lee, it's the only way for us to get ahead. It's a process. And these are the steps."

"And I'm okay with following your 'Steps to Success,' no matter how backward they may feel. But Saturday, when Bliss popped up at the mall and camped out next to the Cinnabon, I sure as hell felt like a *BIG FAT FAILURE!* I had to hide out in Wet Seal; they thought I was trying to steal something." I throw my hands in the air.

"After an hour, the salesgirl finally just kicked me and my red-and-white-striped tights out."

"Then why are you doing it?"

"I need the money," I say, dejected.

"No, you *want* the money; you don't need it. Your friends and your boyfriend have offered to help you out financially. They've done it before. This is a definitive choice *you've* made—all on your own. You have to start acknowledging when you exercise control over more than just your diet and your exercise regimen."

Although I'm getting the lesson today, *she* didn't spy Bliss lurking, sneaking around the Sunglass Hut gamely waiting to pounce.

"And that made you feel like a failure?"

UH, YEAH!

"So, Dr. Lee, what did you do when that happened?"

I didn't need to use my MD to see where she was going.

"Did you binge? Did you purge?" I sink into the leather cushions, wishing I was invisible. "Did you cut yourself or indulge in some other form of self-mutilation?"

I watch the Doc watch me. She studies me quizzically, like I am an endangered species.

"All righty then," she relents.

I glance at the clock and scratch at my throat that's been burning. I'm fresh out of lozenges. I'd already gone through two packs today. Last week she'd stressed that it would only get worse, then she rattled off my truth like a grocery checklist. "Your hair will become brittle, your eyes will not shine, your knuckles will scar, your period will disappear, your teeth will erode, your cheeks will swell, your fingers and toes will bloat, and your throat—your poor throat will be seared like char if you don't begin to protect yourself," she'd warned. "We'll work on those demons," she'd promised, "whenever you're ready, Dr. Lee."

After watching the second hand crawl around in circles I begrudge her an answer. "Yes."

"Which was it?"

"I may have . . . gone to the bathroom." I slide my hands underneath me.

"And did you feel better after you purged?"

"Yes." And then I realize— "But just for a second."

"And then?"

I stare at the chunky heels on her pumps. "And then I felt like a failure—all over again."

"Because?"

"Because I couldn't face her, because I was working at the mall, because I was wearing a green-and-red pointy elf hat with black horned pleather boots and an itchy pair of polyester-blend culottes." I feel a tear drop. *Shit!*

"What you do to make a buck on your Saturday morning is in no way a reflection of who you are, Dr. Lee."

"Then why do you insist on calling me Dr. Lee?!"

She narrows her eyes and leans onto her knees, smiling knowingly. "Because you have achieved many extraordinary things in your young life and those things, *Dr. Lee*, are a testament to your strength, your talent, and your innate power. You must harness it, protect it, honor it. That, which is your essence, will always be there to validate who you are and why you are here. When you begin to realize and accept the sum total of your worth, no one will ever be able to steal it away. Then, and only then, will you effectively silence your demons—and set yourself free." She crosses her arms and leans back in her chair comfortably. *"DR. LEE."*

Chapter 76

I swig back the last drops of the Dom Perignon that Cole had specially delivered to me. Inside the gift box, an engraved diamond pendant necklace accompanied it. "LOVE" was all it said. It was his way of saying he was sorry. He did that a lot. A trinket here, a bauble there, and an incessant amount of phone calls peppered with "Where *are* you?" and "where *were* you?" and "why didn't you answer my call?"

"Yeah, whatever, S-S-Seacrest," I slur at the TV as the repackaged Dick Clark spouts on about the fabulous New Year's Eve outfits the celebs had donned for their platinum-encrusted festivities. I hadn't been invited to a single one. Instead, I'd ushered in the New Year nestled inside this lonely apartment during the rest of the world's countdown. It didn't matter much, I was in a bit of a huff and with Hannah away with Max on vacay and Britt nowhere to be found, the forced sabbatical had given me time to reflect on my totally dismal lifestyle. And I preferred to reflect with the remote. It was past time for me to unwind and find out if Meredith and McDreamy were still keeping it steamy.

My TiVo had been working overtime, and was probably starting to feel a little underappreciated. I understood. Roxy still wasn't sending me out for substantial roles, although I'd booked a few more national spots. Valtrex and Massengill. Yum! It wasn't regular work, but when I considered the alternative (an extended stint at the mall) I was happy to suit up and oblige. So I twirled and monologued my way in and out of auditions, but nothing revived me from the blahs. Things with the Chinaman were working my nerves and I was on the verge of spiking his chi. His incessant

"B-baby" and "H-honey" were like nails on a chalkboard and "there are just no other gigs," said the agency.

Visits to the head shrink had taken priority and each revealing session was a constant reminder that I needed to up the fab factor in my shriveling luxe life. My shrink nodded in agreement when I told her "My pathos has officially eclipsed the four-season-long tragedy that is Meredith Grey!" And after jotting down a few choice words on her legal pad she'd responded simply by saying, "I'm glad Shonda finally sent her to a shrink." *Touché.*

Cole, on the other hand, captivated me in bed. The sex was totally transcendent. I mean, his mantra was "Go Hard or Go Home." (And not to brag but . . . nuff said.) The barbaric, unrestrained, damn near primitive fuckfests were epic. And his endurance was borderline heroic. To be so refined in public but behind closed doors an animal, a monster, a nine-inch BEAST.

So I've tolerated the constant questioning and put up with the never-ending nagging, and maybe I turned my head the other way when "Diamond's" digits fell out of the glove box. Somehow it never seemed like the right time to bring her or her Lucite heels up. He's Cole Winters so "what did you expect?" Britt had tagged. I expected more—just more. And between the award-winning sex and the Cole Winters Program, I didn't dare mention the Doc and our sessions either. Cole was convinced that all I needed was the CWP. And every time he mentioned it, I'd wanted to light up a Capri and blow secondhand smoke in his face—something I'd decided to address with the Doc at a later date.

I scratch at the nicotine patch that had begun to burn off my arm hairs, the craving for a cigarette overwhelming me. I reach underneath the couch for my earthquake stash. Instead, I feel around and pull out the hatbox I'd given Britt three months prior with instructions to strategically hide somewhere. *Racquel used to keep her pills in here.*

I remove the lid and attempt to remain in control, the cigs on the other side of the room (in the middle drawer, hidden beneath the stacked packs of printing paper) calling my name. My hurricane stash (in case anything happens to my earthquake stash).

Resting comfortably in the middle of the hatbox is the package from Marge—still unopened. I fight the thought of Sam. I'd gotten pretty good at keeping memories of him at bay, stored far away in my mind. Cole had made that easier. I situate myself with my cigs (yes, I fetched them out of the witness protection program. So sue me!) and tear the package apart.

LONDON'S LOVE—REVISED

I drop the script in my lap. Sam's screenplay. I pick up the pages and fan them from front to back. I inhale the smell of Sam's future in my hands along with the faint hint of his cologne. Marge's words play in my mind: "You'll know what to do with it, dear."

I'd heard all the brilliant buzz about the film he was prepping to produce out in Hollyweird. Hell, everyone had heard about it. An all-star team had been assembled but no one was allowed to talk about casting—supposedly all A-list. I'd heard rumblings that Megan Fox was attached along with Alicia Keys. I turn the first page and sigh past the brief intro straight into the opening scene. . . .

FIN

A muted paid program on E! is silently watching me as I turn the last page of the script, now wet from my tears that have randomly blurred a few finishing words. A quick glance at the clock on the wall tells me that I've been frozen for the last hour, five minutes, and twenty-three seconds. I've been completely engrossed in this romantic espionage reminiscent of Jason Bourne shopping with the Bodyguard. I squeeze the script in my arms, leave the pile of dirty Kleenex on the sofa, and sniffle my way to the bedroom.

Good night, Sam. Sleep tight. And don't let the bedbugs bite.

Chapter 77

" '*Life shrinks or expands in proportion to one's courage.*' "

"Let me hear it . . . with CON—"

"Viction. Yes, I know," I assert, standing in front of her for my weekly recital. " 'LIFE SHRINKS OR EXPANDS IN PROPORTION TO ONE'S COURAGE.' "

"Ah, yes! Another brilliant one you've chosen." The Doc applauds, and stands with me. "That French author really suits you."

"I get her."

"How many times per day?"

"I'm up to five, sometimes more. But never less," I confess, no longer afraid that drawing on my affirmations will signal weakness. I have, on the other hand, grown terribly afraid of my own mind over the last few sessions. Two weeks ago, when I'd sat in her office on this very couch, I'd had an aha moment—one so powerful I had to sleep with the lights on, so pure that its clarity sent me toppling over. I HAVE THE POWER. Simple. True. *Terrifying.*

"All righty then," the Doc says with pep, penciling onto her pad. "And your week, Dr. Lee?"

"Not so bad," I profess, loosening my woolly scarf and situating myself onto the couch. "I'm slowly moving away from the vagina and her issues; I booked a Lubriderm spot. Roxy's even talking about sending me out for a reality show."

"And your thoughts about that?"

"I'm just happy to be working." I blush. "The money is nice. I'm thinking about joining a community theater in Harlem, maybe helping out with their performing arts program for the teenagers."

"That sounds inspired."

"Well, since I started taking my acting classes I've never felt so, uh, connected to my work." I process her words. "Yes, inspired even."

"And you're at Lee Strasberg's school?"

I nod my head.

"Ah yes, 'The Method.' " She beams. "You're finding *CON-NEC-TION,*" she enunciates.

"I'd forgotten."

"And what, exactly, have you been connecting to?"

"To my voice. Even though I'm still really discovering it."

"Very good!" she says, thrilled. "And it only took you until the middle of February to actualize Stage Four."

I appreciate her enthusiasm, psyched that someone else would be so joyous about *my* voice. "Are you ever going to tell me how many stages there are before 'Success'?"

"This is not a twelve-step program, Dr. Lee," she teases. "Let's focus on where we are today, shall we?"

"All righty then," I tease her right back.

"And you were supposed to start with group therapy last week?"

I nod my head, glad to be on task.

"And how was that? All a bunch of 'freaks,' as you put it?"

"No, you were right," I exhale. "I liked group."

"Uh-huh," she says sardonically.

"I admit it: You know a thing or two about all this healing jazz." I smile. "I've been twice and both times I related to them. We had stuff in common."

"You connected," she asserts approvingly.

Yes. Connected.

"And did you share?"

I shake my head. I wasn't ready to put my scary past out there—for all the world to see. But right now it was nice just being part of the circle.

"Are you starting to realize that you're not alone in this? That you're not drowning in your own abyss?"

"I guess." I shrug, afraid to completely surrender.

"And your bingeing, your purging, your restricting, your exercising?"

"You make it sound so—so—"

"Real?"

"Scary."

I'd been fighting my bad behavior. Struggling. Some days were better than others. I was saying my affirmations and doing the visuals the Doc had been teaching me for times when I couldn't manage the anxiety. I'd found a happy place. My childhood bedroom. I was nine. I had a window facing south and I could see the Chicago skyline. I can still hear the birds chirp if I listen long enough. The air is crisp. The leaves are green. The promise of tomorrow is solid. It was the only day my mother told me she loved me.

"Don't be afraid of the weight of it. You're closer to the other side than you think."

"And what's on the other side? Success?"

"Yes." She looks up from her notepad. "But not the way you think. It's in the form of knowledge, of acceptance, and arguably most important, forgiveness."

Arrrggghhhh! I lower my head into my hands.

"It's supposed to be hard!" she avows. "You're battling behavior that's been with you since you were ten. Since your mother told you she hated you, since she said you'd never be good enough, thin enough, smart enough. Since the first of many times she knocked you to the floor."

I cringe.

"And you've never developed the appropriate coping skills to deal. Three out of four people will suffer from this disease in their lifetime. But this is *your* truth. *Your* struggle. And it's going to be hard." She hands me a tissue. "But I'm here. And I'm not going anywhere. I promised you we'd defeat those demons—together."

· · ·

I leave her office and walk down the hallway, passing the bathroom on my way to the elevator bank. *Mmmooo.* I stop in midstep and double back. My hand is pressed against the bathroom door. I don't have to go. WOMEN, it says.

I walk in anyway.

Chapter 78

Nearly naked, the Brats and I sit around the amethyst crystal steam room on the thirty-fifth floor of the Mandarin Oriental hotel's luxury spa. Wrapped tightly in our towels we exhale the city's grind. Although Hannah and Britt had decided to treat me to a pre–Valentine's Day of posh holistic pampering, they seemed to be enjoying the urban oasis overlooking Central Park far more than me.

Syncing our schedules had been harder to do than scoring front row at the Marc Jacobs show squished tightly between Posh and Becks. Although Hannah had developed a dysfunctional attachment to her CrackBerry, today she was going cold turkey. And

Britt had dutifully canceled a series of exclusive showings and priority meetings with the Darling family and all their dirty sexy money. Both intent on refreshing my chi and reconnecting my chakras, they'd bunkered down in typical BFF style when I'd told them about Sam's script that I'd found.

Hannah refused to believe that Cole was due a pink slip, while Britt was in denial about Sam's marital bliss. And me? Well, I'd given up on convincing either of them that no amount of facialing, exfoliating, massaging, or mani-/pediing was going to change any of it. But, alas, here we are.

Hannah coughs through the humid thickness around her. "I honestly don't think you should give up on Cole just yet. I understand what you're saying about him being controlling, but he can work on that."

"Fuck that!" Britt belts through the misty fog. "First of all, you know damn well you can't change a man! Have I not taught you bitches anything?" She shifts around. "And second, you don't have to take that shit. Now while I do respect his nine inches of hard dick, I don't appreciate his manic attempts at locking you down."

"Well, not lock me down—exactly," I amend sheepishly.

"Well what the fuck do you call it? Him not 'letting' you go to Beyoncé's release party, not 'letting' you go to Denzel's premiere, not 'letting' you—" She neck rolls her way through the vapor. "Do you know what I had to do to get those passes? I'm still looking over my shoulder for Pauletta, cuz she *will* cut a bitch—ask Sanaa."

"Weren't you the one who told her to suck on Cole's contract and hum on his basketballs?"

"Yes, I was all for her coming back to the dark side. She'd been indulging her blond-boy fetish for far too long. I can admit that. But now that she's completely clear on why chocolate is in such high demand"—Britt bolsters—"I am in no way gonna support her being under the thumb of a controlling, borderline abusive ass-hole. Now that's *my* truth so go suck on that!"

"Oh, so now you're the only one who can abuse her?" Hannah challenges.

"Normally it's every bitch for herself around these parts; you know how I do. But lately I've been watching our little flower blossom and. . . ." Britt's voice trails off. "Let's just say . . . I'm working on my demons, too."

"If I wasn't sitting here myself, I wouldn't believe you just admitted to having some problems of your own."

"I don't have problems. I have *issues*," she clarifies indignantly.

"While I appreciate the in-fighting," I interrupt, "I don't think Cole is abusive. I just think he has his own way of dealing with his women."

"Women?!" they both challenge.

"Diamond." I look away.

"See, that's the shit I'm talking about. He can swag around like he's the man, but she can't take a shit without him blowing up her cell, Googling her cross streets. What kind of backwoods, red-state, country-ass chauvinistic shit is that?"

"Brittany, you don't understand," Hannah explains. "They have all kinds of pressures on them and sometimes they—"

"Don't you fucking get me started on you and your 'turn the other tit' approach to your 'relationship.' You haven't even set a date!"

"This has nothing to do with me and Max. We'll get married when we're ready."

"When *he's* ready," Britt bashes.

"You have no idea what you're talking—"

"Cut!" She turns to me. "I'm with the Doc on this one, Annie. You need to keep finding that inner voice of yours. I'm quite sure it's going to tell your lil ass to kick him and his nine-inch cock to the curb." She crosses her arms, rolling her eyes at Hannah. "You wouldn't know anything about riding dolo; you haven't been single since sophomore year at Prep."

My heart flutters as I listen to my sister put her forceful foot down—for me—revisiting the same argument with Hannah for the fourth time this month. Though this isn't the first time she's defended me, it's definitely not a routine.

"I don't love him," I admit aloud, but mostly to myself.

"You just like to fuck him," Britt acknowledges favorably.

I nod. "He's a beast in bed." I chuckle, feeling a weight lifted.

"And he keeps your mind off Sam," Hannah recounts, reasoning again why I shouldn't break ties with my baller BF.

"Just *try* not to think about Sam," Hannah urges. "He's married, remember."

"Of course I remember; since I read that script it's all I can remember." I tighten the towel around my chest. "I can't seem to think about anything *but* him—how much I love the simple things, like the way he calls me 'Gorgeous.' " I hush the words into reality. "I'm useless."

"See, that's why she shouldn't dismiss Cole." Hannah throws her arms in the air, contradicting Britt's logic. "He serves a purpose."

"Misery loves company." She forcibly pokes Hannah in the arm.

"OW!"

"You should be ashamed of yourself. You just wanna have your wing chick with you when you go up against the Candys and the Diamonds and the Lexuses of the league."

"Max isn't cheating on me!"

"From your lips to God's—"

"HE'S NOT!"

"Then why won't you set a fucking date?!"

Hannah fidgets with a hang nail.

"You know I love you," she says soothingly to Hannah. "But it is what it is, bitches. And everything ain't for everybody!"

I eye my cell again, hopelessly wishing it to ring Sam back into my life.

"Have you heard from him since you two had your heart-to-heart the day he left—anything at all?" Hannah asks, ignoring her own truth.

"No. Just word from Izzie when his stuff was shipped to L.A. a few months ago. She sent me a text; said she'd slide me the address if I wanted."

"Do you think he'll be back in town this week for the Soap Opera Awards?"

"Dunno." I shrug. "They're up for seven Soapies; Smith Jensen took over as EP so technically he'd accept if they won. I guess."

"Who's gonna accept Bliss's award if she wins? Are they doing a live feed from Promises this year?"

They both giggle at Bliss's recently reported rides through recovery. I slink down the tile and pout. "If Sam does decide to show, I'm sure he'll have his wife by his side. Supermodel ain't letting him out of her sight these days."

"You really don't think he's gonna leave her?" Hannah asks tepidly.

"Nobody leaves their wife, especially not for the other woman!" I say, as if I've been living "in the know."

"WRONG! Eventually, they all leave the FIRST wife. It's the SECOND wife you have to worry about," Britt recounts matter-of-factly. "And you've never heard of a THIRD wives club, have you?"

"Well, now that I think about it—"

"That's because they're just called widows; the THIRD wife'll quietly kill his ass before she'll ever let him leave."

Rue the day!

"Well, if you do decide to get the addy from Izzie, does this mean a trip to L.A. could be on the horizon?"

"Why wait?" Britt asks.

Hannah and I eye Britt suspiciously. "What's that supposed to mean?"

"Stay in your own lane, bitches!"

I shake the ridiculous, albeit fantastic, thought of seeing Sam from my mind. "L.A. is thousands of miles away but how about a trip to Sixty-first Street to Philippe? I'm starving."

Britt licks her lips. "You know I love me some Peking duck, but Sylvia's is calling my name—right along with two stacks of buttermilk cornbread and a side order of candied yams."

"Starving?" Hannah rustles her brows. "For food? Not cigs and frosting?" Her eyes brighten. "The sessions with your shrink must really be paying off."

I smile at the comforting thought of the Doc. "I like group, too. A lot. And I shared last week. *A little.*"

"Baby steps," Hannah says, eyes gleaming. "Glad my money is being put to good use; Supershrink ain't cheap." She throws her arm around me. "But I'd go to bat for you any day; you're worth every penny."

"Looks like I might have to find a new name for you, Baby Sis. Sounds like Annie might be due for a burial."

"That might be the nicest thing you've ever said to me."

Chapter 79

The evening temp was settling in at an outrageously evil two degrees, but you wouldn't have known it from the heat generated by every kissy-faced couple dining with Cole and me at Butter, another fabbie chic downtown restaurant with an insatiable celeb fetish. The downstairs famer-fueled after-party might as well have been on fire; couples were freaking on the banquettes like hotel rooms had long gone out of style. I was glad to finally escape.

I slide into the limo pulling down on my platinum corseted Hervé Léger bandage dress. Cole slips in beside me and I undo the top button on my vintage cashmere coat. I'd gone through the trouble of getting it dry-cleaned when Cole told me that he'd made Valentine's Day reservations for us. And after seeing the decked-out limo and the curbside valet, I was glad I'd gone through the aggravation. I was freezing my couture off as it was.

"Did you enjoy your dinner?" he asks, reaching over me for the bottle of champagne.

"Uh-huh; the house-made fettuccine and the trumpet mushrooms are always a favorite." I plaster on a smile, secretly loathing the lover's holiday. But dinner with the BF was the requisite trend of the night. So who was I to fight it?

"Good, I'm glad," he says, pouring into two flutes. "You looked beautiful tonight, Baby Girl. I knew you would kill 'em in that dress as soon as I saw it."

"I love it; thank you. But I wasn't the only one who looked hot tonight," I say truthfully. The man was a black stallion. He knew it, too. Three-button Versace suit, Eton shirt adorned with colored diamond studs, and white diamond cuff links. Some of my old friends had walked in one of Eton's shows and let's just say that bodyguards were involved—and not for the models.

"Did you have a good time?" He eyes me adoringly. "All VIP, for my Very Important Princess."

"I did." Admittedly, I'd grown accustomed to the pampering and preening. That was one of the numerous perks of being Cole's girl, and as long as I abided by the CWP, I was guaranteed to be treated to the ride's thrills, complete with custom twenty-two-inch wheels. I scratch at my nic patch.

"You make *me* look good. I mean that."

"With all your adoring fans, sometimes it's hard to tell," I say sullenly. I'd come to realize a while ago that Cole subsisted on the fame and glory that came with being The Beast. Despite what he'd said when we met, it was his air. I look out the window as the car races through SoHo, wishing I were home with my cat (mental note: Buy cat). But we weren't going to my place. We never did. And truth be told, tonight I just didn't wanna be bothered with any more of Cupid's crap. I was officially on overload.

"Don't even start with that bullshit. You know I love having you by my side. That's where you'd always be if it were up to me. That's one of the things I wanted to talk to you about tonight." He rests his hand over mine.

"What's that?" I turn to face him.

"About us spending more time together."

"But we're together all the time," I say acerbically. "I mean when you're not on the road or shooting spots for your endorsements or doing your charity thing or at practice or—"

"Okay, okay, I get it. I'm busy." He laughs.

"I'm not complaining." I knew better than that. Besides when he was off leading his very full life it gave me time to unwind. And I definitely needed that. I take a big sip of the bubbly.

"Well, I am complaining. See, when I come up for air after putting in time with all those other things, I wanna be able to come home to you."

I spit the bubbly back out. *Come again.*

"Baby Girl, I want us to move in together." He clinks his glass with mine and swallows. "Well, what I really mean is I want you to move in with *me.*"

Of course.

"Don't you think it's a little too soon for that? I mean we've only been dating for—"

"Four months!"

"But Cole—"

"Listen, Babe, you don't have to give me an answer right away. Take some time and think about it—but not too long. You really don't wanna make me wait too long, do you?"

The car turns off Fifth Avenue onto 124th Street and my stomach is wrought with knots. The driver shuts off the ignition and Cole pulls me into him, bestowing upon me the fabled "forehead kiss." "I think I love you," he says.

I jump out of the car and run inside, abruptly excusing myself to head to the loo.

Chapter 80

"Baby Girl." I hear the front door slam behind him. "Baby Girl, you okay?"

"Up here," I yell, flushing the toilet and washing my hands like a maniac. I drop the Visine into my watery eyes and dab the face towel against my chipmunk cheeks. *I've got to do better,* I think, closing the bathroom door behind me as I leave.

"Was it the champagne?" he asks, jogging up the steep flight of stairs.

I nod my head, flipping on the TV as Cole walks into the master bedroom and stands over me. He places his hand over my head, gauging my temp before coolly removing his suit jacket. "You sure you okay?"

"Positive." I suck on the lozenge I'd grabbed from my overnight bag.

He flips off his D&G shoes, disappearing into one of the walk-in closets. After a few seconds, Cole emerges, wearing a sly grin and holding a small box with shiny metallic gold wrapping. "This is for you."

My heart sinks. The box was definitely of the jewelry family. "What is it?"

"Happy Valentine's Day," he rasps sexily, sitting on the bed beside me. "Open it." Cole kisses me on my neck, just below my earlobe, as he unbuttons his shirt.

I hold the box in my hand, my fingers tightening around it. "I don't know what to say. The dress was more than enough. I, uh—"

"Just open it, Baby. I went through a lot for that."

"But I didn't get you anything."

He kisses my neck. "Move in with me."

The wrapping paper is floating to the floor and the box sits idly in my hands. A RING BOX, I quickly discover.

"Keep going."

I flip it open. "Uh, uhm—" I hesitate, looking down at the eighteen-karat white-gold three-stone diamond ring.

"Cole, what is—"

"Be easy, Baby. Now before you jump to any conclusions, I'm not asking you for forever. I just wanted to give you a little something to show you that I'm serious about doing this thing we got going."

"Serious?"

"It's a promise ring," he says with pride.

How tenth-grade of you!

I hold the ring in my hand. He takes it from me and slips it onto my *right* ring finger. It trembles. "It's perfect, just like you." But before I can respond, Cole pulls me into him and hugs me tightly. His biceps squeeze around my shoulders. I look around his arms and stare into the TV, suddenly stunned into focusing my eyes on what I see. Giuliana DePandi, blond bobblehead in charge at E!, is mumbling something about red carpet fashions at the Soapies.

The awards show had ended just a few hours ago and as I stare at the remote control, telepathically blowing up the volume on the tube, I struggle to make out what she's saying. I watch closely anyway. Just as Cole is loosening his grip on me, Marge walks into her light for her mini-interview. My body stiffens when I spy Sam walk up beside her.

"What is it?" Cole questions, turning around to focus his attention.

I don't say a word.

"I should've known." He stands up. "Did you know he was in town?" Cole raises his voice. "Kennedy!"

I shake my head.

"Turn it off!"

I don't move.

"Kennedy, I'm fucking serious! Turn it off!"

I still don't move. The room is thick. Cole's breathing is heavy.

"Yeah, my mother deserves to win tonight." I watch Sam's lips say.

His mother?

"She deserves to win her category just as much as any of us." Sam smiles, his dimples light up the screen. I try not to smile back.

The reporter asks about *London's Love* and I think Sam says, "No, I haven't signed the lead yet. But I know she's out there."

Darkness.

It takes me a second to realize that Cole has powered off the tube.

"You'll never look at me that way, will you?"

I can't bring myself to answer. But it's obvious I can't hide what I feel.

"You love him."

Cole paces the floor, shoving his hands in his suit pants pockets. "I guess there's nothing left for me to say." He drops the remote. It echoes when it hits the hardwood. "He won."

I manage my voice. "Cole, this wasn't about winning; this wasn't a game," I say, flustered. "I didn't mean for this . . . I didn't expect . . . I didn't—" I interrupt myself and stare down at the ring. I slide it off and attempt to hand it to Cole. He turns his back on me. I place it on the nightstand beside the bed just as my cell rings. I don't answer.

"We could've been good together. I really could've loved you." He rubs his fingers into his forehead.

"And you'll never know how much I appreciate that." I sigh. "But, Cole, I'm just not *in love* with you." I plead for understanding as my telly erupts into ringing again. I scan the room for my keys and my coat and bolt into the hallway behind distant, left-over hope. I shoulder my overnight bag and turn to look back at him. My heart is on fire, my thoughts scattered, my pulse racing—my life somewhere waiting. "Thank you, Cole—for everything," I whisper.

"Get out."

Dutifully, I oblige when I hear my inner voice—my better half—tell me to head straight down the stairs and out the front door.

Excited to finally meet her, I listen.

Chapter 81

I turn the key in my front door, relieved to finally be home. The ride back to SoHo in the gypsy cab was *très* liberating, despite having to haggle over the fare. That had been the least of my worries. Cole didn't run after me, didn't rush to save me, never came out to hail me a cab. "What did you expect?" Hannah had yelled through my cell. "Home! Do. Not. Pass. Go," she'd said. Hell, I'd been in New York almost a year, so I did what any urban-chic chick would have done—I muzzled my ears and flipped up my collar and walked against the wind alone. When I got to the corner at 125th Street, it was officially the middle of the night, but in spite of the wicked windchill all I could really feel was warm and fuzzy inside. I'd tried to see if the tagged town cars that passed in my periphery were certified cabs or express rides to decapitation (I know, way too much *Law & Order*). But after twenty minutes in the blistering cold, I gave up, trusted my gut, and just jumped in. I decided in that cab ride that I'd only miss one major thing about Cole: the safety that came from being His Girl. With him, I didn't have to think about being alone, about standing on my own, and I didn't have to think about Sam. But now I had the Doc, I had group, and I had this new inner voice. And I fancied she needed a name. I'm thinking of calling her Free. Free Lee. She'd finally spoken and I was awfully glad to meet her. And though soft, she was there—confident, encouraging, and forgiving of me (at least for now).

Surprisingly, the lights in my apartment are bright. I'd flipped them off before I left earlier. I was sure of it. I stop in my tracks when I look up to see Britt sitting anxiously on my sofa.

"What're you doing here?"

"I have something—"

I stop her. "I'm so glad you're here. You'll never believe what just happened to me. Never. I just left Cole's, well actually he put me out—"

"Sweets—"

"But I was leaving anyway. Really, I was." I pull my suede booties off but don't come up for air. "I had an epiphany tonight and my voice just started talking to me, you know, like she'd been bottled up for all this time, living inside me on mute." I throw my bag down in the foyer. "And OMG! Britt, he gave me this ring—a *promise* ring. Who does that anymore?! No, really, who *does* that?" I unwrap the scarf from my neck. "He asked me to move in with

him, can you believe that? He's all 'I want you to move in with me!'
We've only been going out for like . . . a day. I mean I didn't give
him an answer or anything, not that it really matters now, but seriously, why would I wanna give up all this—"

"Sweets, there's something—"

"But wait, it totally gets better. Right before he kicked me out,
but after he gave me the ring, he hugged me really tight and I
looked up at the TV screen and Sam—" I gasp! "SAM!!!"

Sam is standing in the bathroom doorway.

"Hi, Gorgeous."

My bathroom.

"What are you doing here?" I ask breathlessly. I don't take my
eyes off him. He's still sexily dressed in his tux, casually missing
his tie, with both his French cuffs and the first two buttons of his
shirt undone. "What is he doing here?" I stare at him, in disbelief
that he's in my hallway, inches away from my bedroom.

"That's what I was trying to tell you," Britt says, rising up from
the couch. "Look, I know I've made my share of mistakes with
you, but this was something I had to make right," she amends,
walking over to me and opening my front door. She leans in to
kiss me on the cheek and discreetly purrs in my ear, "And I can't
be mad at the second wives' club."

Chapter 82

"Hi, again," Sam says, slowly approaching me. We are all alone;
750 square feet of apartment, Sam Cohen, and me.

"Wh-what are you doing here?" I look around. "In my apartment?"

"That was your sister's call—waiting up here. She insisted. I didn't need much convincing, though."

"But how—"

"She found me at Tenjune. I was getting ready to leave the after-party. I knew who she was right away." He chuckles. "She's very determined, that one."

"Yeah, that's one way to describe her." I eye the sofa. "Do you wanna sit down?"

"Yes. Thank you." He walks through the miniature living room. "I wasn't sure if you were gonna be pissed that I—"

"Can I get you something to drink? I don't have very much," I say, flustered, interrupting him, once it dawns on me that Sam Cohen is in my matchbox apartment, sitting on my Jennifer convertible. I toss the dirty dishes in the dishwasher and kick some stray crumbs under the oven.

"No, I'm good." He rubs his hands together. "Why don't you come sit with me."

"I uh, uh—"

"Come sit down, Gorgeous."

Free Lee tells me to do the same. Again, I listen.

"I need to tell you something." He wipes his forehead. "Do you mind if I take off my jacket?"

"No, not at all." I stand and reach for his tux. "I'll hang it up in the—"

He grabs my hands instead and holds them firmly in his. His palms are damp, his pulse fast. "Damn, I've missed you."

I fall back into the couch.

"I'm going to tell you some things, Gorgeous, and you're just going to have to listen."

I nod my head but don't blink.

"First, it's really good to see you." He squeezes my hands in his. "You're even more beautiful than I remember."

My cheeks burn.

"Second, I really just want to say thank you. I owe you so much, Kennedy. You have no idea." He exhales. "I wouldn't be in L.A. launching Dreamweaver 2.0 Films and working on my life if it weren't for you. You made me really examine what I was, or really what I wasn't doing with it. And for that I can't thank you enough."

I look down at my fingers intertwined in his. He pulls away and brushes my cheek with his fingers, forcing me to look at him again.

"But Sam I didn't—"

"I thought I was clear about you listening—hopefully with your heart this time."

Okay.

"I left Mercedes. For good, Gorgeous. Filed for divorce, the whole thing."

My face flushes.

"I meant what I said to you before. We were done—me and her. We'd been over for a long time. I just didn't have any reason to leave. I mean officially." He licks his lips. "And baby, I'm so sorry for what happened to you that day at my place when she . . ."

I am keenly aware that I am here—right here in this moment. I study his sincerity, inspecting his truth. My heart races and aches all at the same time. The physical pain of wanting him hurts. Self-control and composure are dead to me!

"And I'll never hurt you again if—"

I throw my arms around Sam, burying my face in his neck. I can feel shock shoot through him. I squeeze him tighter. I shut my eyes and take it all in, carving him into the fibers of my mind. His cologne dances between us. I inhale him. Intoxicating. I can't believe he's here—with me, no longer a stalked memory. "I'm not going anywhere, Gorgeous," he whispers in my ear.

My fingernails grip into his back. My breasts press against him, swollen. When I feel his lips against my moist skin, the tears sting behind my lashes. *I am here.*

His soft kisses crawl up my neck, stopping at my earlobe. "I missed your sweet skin; the way you taste, smell."

My back arches. I curve into him.

"Did you—"

I nod.

He disentangles me from his embrace. *I traveled so far just to get here, so long just to be here.* He holds my chin between his fingers and leads me to his lips. He brushes them gently at first, then wets each of my lips with his. My back bends into submission and a soft moan escapes my control. *And I am rightfully here.* Sam slips his hand around me, pulling me into his mouth with power, parting my lips with his tongue. I mold my body into him. His invite is warm, welcoming. He wants me here. *Right here.* I kiss him back, with dominance this time. Our tongues dance and layers of doubt and fear and complication melt. I fall for him, getting lost in his promise, safely trapped in his arms. *I AM PRESENT. ACCOUNTABLE. AFRAID . . . but here.* The world stands still. We don't come up for air and I willingly let go, losing track of time.

* * *

Several cow jumps later, the moon is still beaming through my window as Sam carries me in his arms to my bedroom. With my legs dangling over his arms, I realize that I am comfortable in his control, willingly under his spell. His power is hypnotic. I like being here. He leans over me on the bed and my pulse is pumping with excitement to the rhythm of my hungry hips. His shirt is on the floor and his pants not far behind; nothing about this night is forbidden. My craving for him had shot past insatiable months ago. My appetite for him is now out of control.

After retreating from inside my thighs he lifts himself up to me and with his intense eyes, Sam thanks me. "You're welcome," I rapaciously reply. I'd missed him, too. It was evident in my ride. I gripped him tightly, rode him passionately, and pleasured him abundantly.

"I need you, Gorgeous," Sam whispers into my wet neck after my second climax.

"I'm right here," I reassure him, relaxing my thighs above his waist. Making love to him had moved me. He'd reignited *my* need to be needed so direly. I snuggle deeper into the nook.

"I need you to star in my movie."

I lift my head. Our eyes meet. This time he doesn't blink.

"But I heard Megan Fox and Rachel Bilson were reading—"

"I've seen over twelve hundred actresses and I keep coming back to the same thing." He wipes my moist cheek.

"What's that?" My voice is coy.

"It's you, Gorgeous. It's always been you."

Tears begin to well behind my eyes.

"You're the epitome of London—strong, vulnerable . . ."

"Sam."

"Beautiful."

"Well." Finally one tear drops and my mouth trembles. "I'll have to check with the Chinaman on Monday and see if—"

He kisses my lips. "But that's not all. I need you to star in my life, too. I need you to make sure the bedbugs don't bite *me* this time." He brushes the damp hair from my eyes. "I can't do this without you."

I kiss him back sweetly and answer him honestly. "And I promise, you'll never have to."

Finale

I look around my empty apartment and marvel at how lonely it seems. I, on the other hand, felt anything but. Although I was being a scaredy-cat just thinking of starting a new life against the backdrop of a different ocean, I'd never been so equally filled with fear and hope. Okay, maybe more fear than hope. But my bags were stuffed, my boxes taped, and my BFF staring back at me from on top of the kitchen countertop. Her legs dangled above the marble floor.

"Did you remember your Wonder Woman Underoos?" Hannah asks seriously. She picks up another one of the decadent treats that Sam sent over yesterday—a vanilla-bean cupcake baked with brown sugar, chocolate chips, and walnuts, and on top, vanilla buttercream with chocolate chip cookie dough folded in. *MAS-SIVE!* Between bites, Hannah dabs her wet eyes with even wetter tissues.

I nod, tearing up, too. I'd packed the jammies first.

"Did you remember your—"

"I packed everything except you. Come on, just go with me. Zip yourself into one of the suitcases; no one will ever know you're in there."

"Even though you're flying out on his private plane, Sweets, you still have to go through security."

"I know, but—" I flop down on top of one of the boxes.

"You don't need me for this trip." She hops down and walks over to me. "It's only six months, then you get a short break and I can jet out there or you can fly back here, or we can meet some-where in the middle."

"We can't meet *here*." I look around. "The new girl is moving in next week—the sublet from Craigslist."

"The dancer?" She sits down beside me.

"Uh-huh. Sydney."

"Well, that's even better." Hannah says, wrapping her arm around me, shoving the rest of the cupcake in her mouth. "If you decide to come back here for your mini vacay, you'll just stay with me. It'll be just like old times back in Chicago." She picks crumbs from her baby Tee.

I flash back to our time together in that penthouse on top of the world. My best friend's life had changed that year. She'd loved, lost, and fought for her dreams. She'd found love again before it was all said and done. Now, almost a year later, it was my turn.

"But, Bug, I'm totally terrified."

"You better be; I'd be worried about you if you weren't. I mean you're jumping out there, you're totally going for it." She hops up and twirls around the room. "And following your passions—literally."

"But I'm passionate about you, too, and we haven't been apart in the last two years. Who am I going to turn to when my life spazzes out of control?"

Even though Hannah had slept over last night and celebrated with me through an assortment of truffle cupcakes and champagne, when she'd finally nodded off in a twisted stupor, old voices of vice and sabotage took over. They threw their own soiree in my mind. I'd struggled to fight through the "Who do you think you are?" and the "What makes you think you're so special?" and my favorite, the "You'll never be good enough or thin enough to pull this off." I'd talked myself through a flurry of affirmations and had even come close to calling my sponsor, a skinny blond girl named Rebecca. I'd just wanted to purge the voices away. But it had been too late to call and I was too drunk to use my tools, so

I retreated to bad behavior and hit the loo. They call it a relapse. I call it Racquel's Revenge. Even from the grave, she wasn't gonna let me be happy, at least not as far as I could see. It was evident that it was gonna be a super-slow process shaking myself free from the dark depths of my own stinkin' thinkin'. I'd just need to be patient. Free Lee had agreed. And also forgiven me. Again. I called Rebecca first thing this morning.

"Well, you'll have your new shrink and your new support group that you're gonna join as soon as you unpack," she says firmly. "And you'll have Sam." When she walks over to me, I look up and see that she's on the verge of tears.

"You can't cry, too; then we'll both be pathetic."

"No worries, Sweets, I'm flying out as soon as I get a chance. I'm even pushing to shoot Rain's next video, *'Fire and Ice,'* in one of the mansions in The Hills."

"Very LC and Brody?"

"Think Audrina v. Lo."

"Ohhh."

"See, so I'll be out there before you know it and then you can show me your bungalow at The Beverly Hills Hotel, and you can introduce me to your fabulous all-star cast, and you can even take me to Disneyland." She laughs. "Or the Valley where they film all the good porn."

"It looks like I'll only have about a month to get my feet wet while they're still in preproduction. Sam wants me to meet the director, meet the writers, meet the other producers, and the cast. It's all about the chemistry, he keeps saying. After that, I'll be working sixteen-hour days without a break in sight." I sigh. "Then it's off to London."

"You see that?" She rubs her thumb and index finger together in the air. "That's the smallest violin in the world playing a song just for you."

I grab a cupcake and throw it at her. It sticks to the wall instead (red velvet with cream cheese frosting and raspberry sprinkles). Indulgently, I suck the sugar from my nail beds.

I knew I was lucky. Nobody needed to tell me that. But that didn't stop Britt from dipping in yesterday, her triple-Ds squished into a T-shirt that read "SAVE A DRUM, BANG A DRUMMER!" She'd come to drop her two cents in, sitting me down to quotes and warnings. She'd said I better not apologize to anyone for the life I was seizing, the one I was gradually growing into. She'd casually quoted, " 'And the day came when the risk to remain tight in a bud was more painful than the risk it took to blossom.' " She'd cleared her voice over Veuve and continued, "Now go bloom, bitch! Bloom!"

Last week, I left *The Diary of Anaïs Nin* outside her door. It was my soulful way of thanking my sister for Sam.

He was in L.A., meeting with a few French investors, but he'd made all the arrangements and covered all the bases. He even reserved a limo and driver to escort me anywhere in L.A. I wanted to go. I made my first appointment with my new head shrink and had gotten the meeting schedule for the new group the Doc had suggested. "Word is they're young and they're fun," she'd professed. "I did some checking and of course I remembered, no freaks allowed." Admittedly, I just started getting used to my group here in Chelsea, but she said the change would be organic and that I shouldn't force it. "Take your time, work your program, and listen to Free Lee; she's growing up to be a special little voice, I must say, Dr. Lee." Sam had already offered to drive me on those days when I didn't want to go alone.

"Hello," I say into the telly on its second ring. "Sure, send it up."

"Who's that?"

"Dunno. Delivery."

"Are you expecting something? Who doesn't know you're on your way out?"

"Dunno; I told everyone."

After Sam faxed Roxy my contract two weeks ago the only people that had been left to tell had been the temp agency and the Chinaman. I think deep down the Chinaman was sad to see me go. He'd reminded me that he'd already taken me back once, and that his door would always be open. I was mildly touched, until he punctuated that statement with a creepy "B-b-baby" and an even creepier ass slap. *EW!*

"Coming," I yell, swinging the front door open.

"Ms. Lee?"

"Yes."

"Sign here, please."

Hannah knifed the big boxes open as soon as she realized all seven of them were emblazoned with Louis Vuitton logos. She couldn't help herself. I couldn't blame her.

I look quizzically at the delivery guy. "And this is for you." He smiles, handing me a note. Even he seemed to be impressed.

"From Soaps to the Silver Screen. See you in Hollywood, Gorgeous" Sam's note read. It was his handwriting, his personal attention to detail. The man was meticulous when it came to making me feel wanted and deserved. He'd promised to make my first movie-making experience one I'd never forget. "I'll never stop reminding you how much you've changed my life and just how much I'm ready to change yours."

"What are you going to do with him?" Hannah asks, sitting on the floor drowning in a sea of LV.

"The luggage is beautiful. I've never had a complete set."

"I don't even think Kimora has this piece," Hannah brags, holding up a ginormous monogrammed overnighter.

"But I don't have time to repack my bags. I've gotta hop in a cab, like, five minutes ago." I panic, studying my watch. My flight was scheduled to leave in nearly two hours, and traffic through the tunnel to Teterboro was going to be a nauseating game of hit-and-miss.

The delivery guy sticks his foot in the door as it's closing on him. "Sorry, Ms. Lee?"

"Yes?"

"I think there's been some sort of misunderstanding. I'm from the concierge service; your personal assistant is on her way up. She's handling all your packing, rearranging, and shipping. But your car is downstairs waiting to take you to the plane whenever you're ready. Mr. Cohen has instructed us to see to it that you bring only your overnight bag with you. The rest will be handled."

"Oooh, handled," Hannah gushes.

"But I need my stuff."

"Mr. Cohen has seen to it that everything you'll need, you'll have."

Hannah and I stare at each other. As I run to change into the sleek Giambattista Valli jumpsuit gifted to me by Hannah, she smiles and turns to handle the *concierge,* telling him I'll be down in a few.

I rise out of myself, hovering over the Cinderella scene, just as the personal assistant rounds the corner. "Izzie?!" I say, zipping my studded Ariella ankle boots as she walks through the door.

"Kennedy! Or Ms. Lee," she corrects quickly.

"Don't be silly. What are you doing here?"

She was dressed in her basic black, but her look had majorly matured. She donned a tailored charcoal pencil skirt that stopped just below the knee with a white rufflicious blouse that accentuated her petite frame perfectly. Her dainty shoulders were pushed back and her sleekly coiffed head held high. She extended her manicured hand and smiled, designer specs over her eyes. "At your service."

"You're my personal assistant?!"

"You didn't really think I'd pass up an opportunity to work for Mr. Cohen, especially after he explained that I'd be overseeing all your day-to-day."

"But *America's Next*—"

"Well, I just figured if you could walk away from that nuthouse then so could I," she boasts. "Besides, Mr. Cohen is giving me the opportunity of a lifetime. I get to work for you and learn the movie-making ropes at the same time. I mean, you *are* going to be starring in next year's most buzzed about summer blockbuster."

"No pressure, Izzie," I say tensely, as Hannah clears her throat.

"Oops." I turn to Bug. "Izzie, Hannah Love—my bestest friend in the world."

"So nice to meet you." Izzie's handshake is firm, her stance authoritative. Dizzy Izzie was nowhere to be found. I slowly start to exhale.

"Same here," Hannah says, giddy with excitement. She knew I was calming at the thought of being handled in the very best of hands, second to hers. "I'll ask you again, Kennedy Sun Lee, what *are* you going to *do* with that man?"

Credits

The limo swoops through the charter lot and slows to a stop next to a few yards of red carpet. With just my overnight bag and my tote in hand, I climb the stairs of the luxe Falcon jet. Oversized, heather-hued leather recliners, a fully stocked wet bar and a tech-heavy lounge cabin with touch screen sensibility greet me when I step into the galley. A flatscreen TV is looping snippets of Madonna videos as I ease past the cushy banquette. I glance out the window, in love with the bedazzled plane. (In a word: BEEE-YOND!)

"Good afternoon, Ms. Lee," a flight attendant with strawberry-red hair and big doe eyes greets me.

"Hi," I say, composing myself.

"Sit anywhere you'd like. We'll depart in a few minutes, once you're ready."

As soon as I settle into one of the recliners and buckle myself in, Strawberry Shortcake promptly delivers champagne. "After our safety video I'll bring out an assortment of food."

"Thank you."

"No, Ms. Lee, the pleasure is all mine."

I fasten my seat belt and pull out my phone to ring Hannah. The engines rev into a full throttle beneath my bum. If the luggage tweaked her before, this was gonna make her pee her pants.

"And, Bug, there's a double sink in the marble lav," I whisper, not caring that I sound like a prepubescent fourth grader who just got her very first phone line.

"Good afternoon, Ms. Lee," the pilot's calming voice greets me over the sound system. "Looks like we're all set for a smooth ride this afternoon. The skies are clear and we've got a perfect forecast all the way through to the West Coast."

I look around, giddy with excitement, and smile to myself. "So welcome, and please, make yourself at home." I swig back some of the champagne and put my cell away. Izzie had given me a few rag mags to read and had suggested I go to the pages she'd tagged. Casually, I flip through the glossy. I perk up when I see Jesse James splattered across the page being outted à la Lance Bass, à la T. R. Knight, à la Doogie Howser, à la . . . Split pics of him frame the caption "Before Destiny . . . After Surgery!" A prefab photo of Arnold Seltzer in an extraordinarily girly getup donning bifocaled specs and a receding hairline accessorized with an extra seventy-five pounds of pudge outweighs his more recent manly model look. *Hair plugs?* I study the pics closer. *Gastric?* I flip to the caption "... canoodling with ..." JACK THE RAT?! I slam the mag shut. *Way too much!*

"Please take a minute and watch our safety video as we prepare for departure."

I look up and do a double take when Sam's face appears on the screen. He was the kind of man who would host his own safety video, a man living in the details. I love that about him. I stare at the plasma and sip the bubbly as we crawl to the runway, listening to Sam take control. As he's welcoming the passengers (me), running through the layout of the jet, and discussing exit strategies, I drift off and remember his touch.

"Prepare for takeoff, Kennedy Lee—and for the ride of your life," Sam states from the TV.

My neck whips around. *Did anyone else hear that?* I eye the champagne suspiciously. Strawberry Shortcake sits motionless in her seat. After I cough a few times, she turns her head and smiles. *DID YOU HEAR THAT?!*

We race down the runway and are no sooner in the air when I swear I hear Sam say something about how glad he is that I'm here. I cock my head to the side and cautiously push the bubbly away.

"I have wanted you since the day I met you, Gorgeous," Sam confirms my suspicion from the screen. "... Outside the studio in the alleyway." My eyes saucer. I peel them away from the flatscreen just long enough to glance at Strawberry Shortcake. She nods. "... Next to the Dumpsters." He laughs. I reach for the champagne glass and take a giant gulp this time.

"You changed my life that first night at the diner. Five minutes with you and I knew I was in trouble." He stares directly into the camera. "Intense." He smiles. "And our ride through Central Park was just the beginning." His face hardens. "But then I made a huge mistake and I lost you. I can't afford to let that happen again."

My hands start to shake. I know it's not from turbulence; we just jetted into the air.

The PA clicks on again and the pilot orders from the cockpit, "Look outside your window, Gorgeous, just above Manhattan." My heart drops. *IT IS SAM!*

I fumble with the shade and stare out at an aerial banner hovering around the Falcon, somewhere in the vicinity of Central Park. The banner waves in the wind a few thousand feet above where Sam had believed in me. The night he'd asked me to believe back.

WILL YOU MARRY ME, GORGEOUS?

I jerk back around to face the screen but Sam is walking down the aisle toward me. He removes his pilot's hat and gets down on one knee. And that's when I go berserk. I realize I can't feel my fingers even though the rest of my body is orgasmic, awakened into delirium. I feel like I'm jazzed up on epinephrine, razzle-dazzled on ecstasy. My mouth is dry, my eyes are tear-soaked, and as my heart is going gaga, ODing on excitement, I start to feel faint.

"You okay?"

"You were up there . . . the . . . the whole . . . up there the whole time with the pilot?" I choke on my words, pointing to the cockpit. "You—you know how to *fly*?"

"I love you, Kennedy."

Sam and I take turns wiping away my tears. But they never seem to stop.

"Sam."

"Will you marry me, Gorgeous?"

"Are you sure? I mean, really. I come with a lot of baggage and it just won't be easy to love—"

"Kennedy Sun Lee, will you marry me? Will you spend your life with me; let me carry some of those bags."

OHMYGOD!

"I've been on the other side before, and living my life without you just isn't an option."

"But—"

"You're killing me here, Gorgeous."

"I just—"

"Fucking intense!" He puts his finger up to my lips to silence me. "Baby, hear me clearly. I will fucking die if you don't say yes." He grips my hand in his. "Be my wife."

"If you're sure."

"I would risk my life for it."

"Then yes! YES! A million times YES!"

I pull him up from the floor and fold into his arms. He holds me tightly, breathing heavily into my hair. We linger into each other, not needing or wanting to come up for air.

"I love you back, Sam," I whisper.

And I did. I never questioned it, never doubted it, never confused it. And just so I'd always be clear, he pulls out an 11-karat vivid pear-shaped diamond mounted in a platinum band with white heart-shaped diamond shoulders. I gasp . . . and then my face turns blue. Smiling, Sam kisses the ring before sliding it onto my finger.

"I will never stop loving you."

"Me too, Sam. Me too."

"And we can take as long as you want with this, until you're not afraid anymore. Just know that I'm not going anywhere unless you're with me, right here by my side."

He knew me well; the intensity of his love frightened me. No one had ever loved me like that before.

Strawberry Shortcake delivers two full glasses of champagne. "Congratulations," she says, teary eyed.

"So, tell me, Mr. Cohen, where are you taking me?"

He pushes my layered curls behind my ear. "The answer to that question is one of your engagement presents."

"Tell me." I entice him, leaving lovebites on his neck as my tongue trails down to his collarbone. He lifts my head and breathes me in, his kisses send a chill spiraling down my spine. And after an intense mile-high make-out session he finally relents. "Okay, okay, I can't fight it. We're taking a slight detour—to Santa Barbara. We're stopping off for a few days, maybe longer."

"Santa Barbara?"

"To my vineyard. *Our* vineyard now. Horses, gorgeous sunsets, great wine." He whispers in my ear, "I bought you a beautiful Gypsy Vanner mare. I named her after you. Sun."

I get teary eyed all over again and stop just shy of "the Ugly Cry." Barely able to think straight I ask, "But, what about your meetings and preproduc—"

"Everything else has been taken care of. Now, I want to take my fiancée to her winery to celebrate her engagement with her new horse, with her old friends, and with all of her new family."

"You didn't?" I mush my hands over my mouth. The gargantuan ring bangs against my teeth.

"Of course I did. My mother, who I think you know better as Marge, is already there with Winston. She can't wait to see you. And your sister should be landing, oh, right about now." He studies his watch. "Hannah and Max are flying out right behind us with Izzie, and tomorrow you'll meet my sisters, their husbands, and all my beautiful nieces and nephews."

"Sam," I say, amazed. "I can't believe you did that."

"They're gonna love you."

"But how, but when, but—"

"I know how close you all are. Those girls are your life. And now I get to be part of it." Sam intertwines his fingers in mine, kissing each of them with purpose. "There's so much to celebrate, Gorgeous." I rub my free hand along his forearm and fidget with his nicotine patch that's stuck to it.

"Remember when I asked you what you wanted to be when you grew up?"

"Yes," I say, feeling woozy at the thought of my dreams actually having meaning. "A real actress."

He squeezes my hand. "And here you are."

"And here we are."

"Yes. And if you continue to let me be the luckiest man alive, I promise to keep making all your dreams come true."

I place my hand over his heart. "Cuz you're the dreamweaver?"

"That's right, Gorgeous. And it's all for you!"

Acknowledgments

This one is for all my *Delicious* Dolls (*and my dad*).

I'd like to thank my superagent, Stephany Evans, at Fineprint Literary Management, for being the best tour guide through my kickass adventure. Every girl needs a VIP pass through her mind sometimes.

And to my *brilliant* editors, Melody Guy and Porscha Burke . . . Porscha, it was moo-ey rock star taking this trip with you. My characters made me pinkie swear to smooch on you extra hard, Trixie, for your patience, understanding, and badass insight. Thank you for letting/helping me tell their truth. And Dusty, thank you a billion times for believing in my little love stories; you make my heart blush in a *big* way!

I wouldn't be able to honor the little girl inside who dreams up *happily ever afters* if my dad, Benjamin Kendrick, didn't honor her first. Thank you, Poppi, for being the first man to ever love me so hard, and espesh for letting me know that beauty is nice but brains are sooo much better.

Thank you to my mom, Estraleta Kendrick, who helped me cultivate my special gifts and strengths and my step-goddess, Judy Walker-Kendrick, who stepped in to make my picture complete. And may my glam Gramma, Gertrude Jones, rest in peace—after she's done fixin' up some collard greens and hot water bread for the band.

And a special thanks to my wicked worldwide sisters (Tasha, Karetha, Cari Lynn and Erika/Ewok), my chic Chicago squad (Narlan and Alia, Ja Ja, Latoya, Dina, Toi, Joi, Dawn, Dee Dee, Noani, Carmen, Alaina and Arlina, Kristy and Deshawn, Tisha, Jennifer and Charbrielle, and Myata), my MAY-JAH NYC team (Karen, Drenna, Leah, and Shana, Danielle, Erica Superstara Watson, and my Naledi), and, of course, my DST Dolls, espesh OX, and my sands (Channon, Leah, Nadine, Regina, Reshon, Toya, Yvonne and Valeria) . . . I carry you *all* with me every day. Maybe that's why pieces of you sparkle in a few fab characters from time to time. It's been an honor growing into big girls with *each* of you!

And *thank you*, Juanita, for sneaking me in so I could see my scenes. And for all that feeeeyarce hair all up and through!

A sparkly *thank you* to all the African American bookstores who have been a constant support to the authors struggling to get their stories heard. We couldn't breathe without you. You sustain us!

And most important, thank you to all my fans and readers. Please know that I do this for you! It's far too easy to forget that real love, you know that real good *juicy* love, is out there waiting, and we are as deserving as it is ethereal. I read each and every one of your emails and want to humbly say, "You're welcome!" You inspire me.

And, of course, to Cody the Cat! You keep purring, old man, and I'll keep the treats coming!

XOXO

About the Author

ERIKA J. KENDRICK, author of *Confessions of a Rookie Cheerleader*, is a Chicago native (go Bulls!) and was a Luvabull, a Chicago Bulls cheerleader, in a previous life. Erika graduated from Stanford University and has served time working in music and entertainment. She lives in New York City with her pom-poms and her Himalayan, Cody the Cat. And her *appetite* is still insatiable for Chicago's Garrett's popcorn (caramel and cheese mix, of course) . . . and Anderson Cooper! Visit her website at www.erikakendrick.com.